The Rebirth of Innocence

Copyright © 2016 by Robert L. Seago

All rights reserved. This book nor any portion thereof may be reproduced or transmitted in any form or by any means, electronic or mechanical, including photocopying, recording or by any information storage or retrieval system, without the express written permission of the copyright owner/author and publisher, except where permitted by law or except for the use of brief quotations or references in a book review.

Printed in the United States of America
First printing December 2016

This is purely a work of fiction. The names and incidents are the sole products of the author's creation or are used fictitiously, and any resemblance to any person/persons, living or dead is purely coincidental.

OTHER WORKS BY R.L. SEAGO

Tears of the Innocent

"Tears of the innocent kept me on the edge of my seat."

"Loved this book, couldn't put it down, I read it in a weekend, great story"

"R.L. Seago's book Tears of the Innocent is a page turner and keeps your attention."

Perfect description, perfect characters, a killer storyline and one of the best new authors of today… you're going to want to become acquainted with R.L. Seago!

Voices of the Passed

"Great read, well written and the story certainly tugged at my heart."

"This book kept me captivated from beginning to the end. It appeals to the heart and the soul."

"This book was fabulous. From the moment I picked it up I could not put it down. I read it in one afternoon from cover to cover."

"There is a clear line in the sand of life when it comes to a mother's instinct for protecting her child. Very simply defined, that line makes a simple statement- you will not hurt my child. If you do, you will experience a nightmare unlike anything Hollywood could have ever created. Even the calmest, most even-tempered women, when their child is threatened, will storm the gates of hell and face down Satan himself to protect their children."

Author Unknown

"THE BEST OFFENSE IS A GOOD DEFENSE"

Chapter 1

Darius sat in his high back leather chair, staring intently at the blue waters of the Pacific which stretched out before him. The glass in the large picture window was so clean it seemed nearly invisible, and sadly he wished that everything in life was so crystalline and clear. Immersed in watching the waves roll across the immense body of water, he neither heard nor saw Tisha enter the room.

"Sweetheart, Lacey and Ryder are here, and they have the kids and Joker with them. Is everything okay?" she asked, as Darius turned around to look at her.

"Everything's fine honey. They just have some loose ends to wrap up before they head out on vacation." He hated the unpleasant gnawing of guilt in his belly at the lie he was telling her, but the alternative was something he was not even willing to consider. Smiling at his beloved wife, Darius got to his feet and crossed the room, sliding his arm around her narrow waist as they moved downstairs. When he saw the family standing in the large foyer, his heart felt as if it was about to be ripped from his chest.

Ryder stood there, holding Micah's hand, Lacey next to him with the baby in her arms and Joker sitting between them. What truly broke Darius's heart was the look of fear he saw on Ryder's face, something he had never witnessed in all the years he had known the man.

Walking down the wooden staircase, Darius extended his hand to Ryder, who grasped it firmly. Kneeling down, Darius looked at Micah, who appeared as relaxed as if he was heading for a playdate. Next to him Tisha took the diaper bag from Lacey, who in spite of her calm outward demeanor was shaking ever so slightly as she handed over the bag.

"Please guys, come on in and let me get you something to drink," the dark-skinned woman said, noticing the way that Ryder's usually focused eyes kept darting around, as if searching for someone or something.

Darius met his friend's gaze. "Tish, maybe you can get Micah here some juice, and maybe some water for Joker. They look parched," Darius said, smiling at the boy and the dog. Micah looked up at his mom before speaking.

"Can I mom? I am kinda thirsty," he asked, as Lacey reached to touch him gently.

"Of course, sweetie, but stay right with Tisha, okay?" The boy smiled as he and Joker were led towards the kitchen area, while Darius noticed that Lacey still clutched the baby tightly to her chest.

Ryder looked at his friend, paused for a moment then whispered, "We need to talk in private." Darius put his feelings of trepidation aside as he turned and silently headed up the staircase, the couple in tow. When they got to his office he stood as they entered, then closed the double doors behind him. Lacey and Ryder had already taken seats on the leather sofa, and Darius leaned against the edge of his desk, his eyes meeting Lacey's.

Ryder leaned forward on the couch, then looked at his wife and baby before turning his gaze back to Darius. "Listen, what I'm about to tell you is going to sound crazy, worse than what I said on the phone, and if it does then please say something. You know about the incident last summer in Vegas that Lacey and I were involved in."

Darius nodded slowly, recalling the horrendous events that had transpired in their search for Micah. He could see that Ryder wanted to just spew everything forth but was desperately fighting to control the flow of information.

"We thought that Summer, the woman behind everything was dead. I saw Lacey shoot her, but somehow she survived. Last night we got a phone call from her, congratulating us on our new daughter, and her new niece."

At the mention of *her niece,* the black man's heart skipped a beat. "What do you mean, her niece? Are she and Lacey related somehow?" Ryder shook his head as he continued.

"No. That abomination is my sister. We were abandoned as children to foster agencies, and I never had any memories of her, no pictures, nothing." As he talked Lacey reached over to touch his hand, with April still cradled tightly. Ryder continued, his voice shaking.

"We must have screwed up, because she called the other night, and of course poor Micah had to be the one to answer. She told him about some gifts she had left us, and when we got up to April's room there were several horrible surprises waiting. The gloves that Lacey put back on that bitch, after she, you know, a ring for Micah and worst of all a pair of brand-new silk white baby sized gloves in April's crib." Darius sat, stunned by the dreadful revelations.

Ryder had come to Darius several months after returning from the desert fiasco, and over several glasses of 100-year-old Scotch had purged himself of everything, including the gruesome details of what Lacey had done to the blonde woman's hands. As his friend, he needed a sounding block, and as his attorney he needed legal advice. Now that it appeared as if Summer was around again, Ryder knew what had to be done and needed someone to talk it through with, and with Preacher and Cindy away on a two-week cruise Darius had seemed the logical choice.

His hands clasped, Darius spoke slowly and carefully. "Ryder, Lacey, as your friend I have to say this- anything I have, can get or can do is at your disposal. As your attorney, and Ryder you know this, I have to say that the legal system will be of absolutely no help in this matter, so I am going to stay on as your attorney, for both of our own good. Now, let's talk. What exactly is on your mind?"

    Ryder sat for a moment thinking, the air in the tastefully decorated room seeming to grow thick with tension. "Darius, I remember you telling me several times about that cabin you have up north near Tahoe. What I'm, what we are thinking of is getting a new Jeep, untraceable, loading it up with whatever supplies we need and heading for the hills. You know I'm no coward, but we have to get away from here, at least until I can think straight and figure out what needs to be done. If this woman has eyes on us, and I have every reason to believe that she does by her little presents, then I have to take Lacey and the kids somewhere where I can protect them. I can't do that here. There are just too many ways she can track us. I know this sounds paranoid, but if you had ever met this woman you would understand. We have plenty of cash since we've both cleaned out our private accounts except for a token amount. I could use your help though, in getting another four-wheel drive quietly and discreetly. Do you still do charity work with that guy who owns the Jeep dealership here in town?" Ryder paused, his mind going a mile a minute, as Darius went around to the chair behind his desk. Sitting down he opened his Rolodex and looked up a number as he met Ryder's eyes. "Why don't you make a list of all the gear you're going to need and-" Ryder cut him off by opening the folded paper in his hand. Shaking his head Darius smiled at his friend, then spoke into the phone. "Carl, hey this is Darius. Good man, how about you?

How's that new young girlfriend of yours? Yeah, I bet. Listen, I need a favor, but it has to be just between us. No sales slips, no paper, nothing. I need a new Jeep, four-wheel drive, GPS, winch, the whole package, and I need it fast. Now you know me, I don't do anything illegal, it's just for a friend having some personal issues. Don't worry about the cost, I'm taking care of that. Great. How soon can you have her ready to roll? Two hours?" Looking across the desk, Ryder nodded approval. "Great man. Listen, can you have one of your guys bring it by the house and make sure it's gassed up? Thanks Carl, I owe you for this. No, I'll explain some afternoon on the golf course. Thanks again old friend." Hanging up, Darius looked at the couple, and shyly turned his head as he caught sight of Lacey breastfeeding the unusually quiet baby, causing the tired looking woman to smile.

Ryder saw the look on his friend's face, and a look of amusement crossed his tired face, despite the current situation. "I'll tell you what Lacey. Why don't you and the baby stay here, and Darius and I can go pick up the rest of the gear we're going to need?" Ryder said, knowing that Lacey was going to protest. True to her nature she began to speak out, then realized it was a moot point by the look on Ryder's face. The two men would be able to accomplish the task much quicker without her and the baby, and she had no intentions of letting April out of her sight. The two men got to their feet and moved towards the door as Lacey buttoned up her blouse. Standing up, she moved to keep the door shut before they left the room as she spoke up.

"Darius, please don't be angry with me for this, but you cannot tell anyone about this or where we're going, including Tisha. We love you guys dearly, but the fewer people who know, the better our chances, and hell, we haven't even had the chance to tell Preacher. Please don't be-"as she tried to continue she began to cry softly, and the slender man went to her, embracing her. Ryder stood for a moment, then wiped several tears away from her usually clear eyes.

Without a word Ryder opened the door to the room and they made their way downstairs, hearing Micah's voice floating up to them. As they got downstairs the boy came running out, a huge grin on his sweet face.

"Guess what mom? Tish gave me some carrot juice, and it was really good." The couple could see the light orange stain around his mouth and on his teeth, and in spite of everything began to laugh out loud.

Ryder joined in, as a thought entered his mind. "*God, let us laugh now, because we may need it later.*"

Two hours later, as promised, the shiny new blue Jeep Grand Cherokee arrived, as promised, the young driver backing it right into its awaiting place. Darius and Ryder had just returned from their shopping spree and spent the next twenty minutes carefully packing the large cargo area, making use of every inch of space. There were three down sleeping bags, designed for sub-zero temperatures, snow suits for all of them, two cases of MRE's, three sets of snow boots, a large tent, two propane lanterns and even a leather jacket of sorts for Joker. Joker sat, watching, his dark eyes seeming to scan the entire area as the men worked, as if he was on guard duty. When they had the gear all in place, Ryder pulled a small case from the side panel. Opening it he withdrew two phones, one of which he handed to Darius. "These are satellite phones, and don't even ask where I got them. You and I have the only ones, except for the person I got them from. If we get in a bind, I want to have some kind of backup plan, but only as a last resort."

   Darius stood for a moment before looking at Ryder. "What about Preacher? You and I both know when he gets back he's going to see you're gone and is going to come to me looking for answers."

Ryder thought for a moment, then spoke. "Keep in the back of your mind that this woman Summer is insane but being able to get into our house undetected with us there, that adds a whole new level of crazy. It's not just the walls that have eyes and ears, and I don't want you guys in any more danger than you already are. When Preacher comes to you, and yes I know he will, you take him aside and give him the information I've given you, but not where we're going." Darius took the phone and looked it over before sliding it into his pocket, then spoke.

"Okay now, let's talk serious here. The cabin is fully stocked and checked out for damage from the last snowfall, break-ins, etc. I just heard from the property manager last week, and he said everything is fine, but it's still going to be getting cold up there. It's fully stocked, except for perishables like milk and veggies. The woodshed has three cords of wood, so that should do you just fine. The pantry holds enough food to feed an army, the generator is brand new, there's 20 gallons of gas in the shed out back, and there are a pair of 12-gauge shotguns and a Winchester .243 in my gun safe. The ammo I keep in a lock box in the closet, and the safe combination is my birthday. I have a first-rate setup as far as a CB goes, and the tower is on top of the highest mountain out there, so reception should be fine if you need it. There's plenty of fishing gear and some trout filled streams within sight of the house, so you guys should be okay. There's also an alarm system, which you should have no problem operating, and the nearest people are ten miles away, which should make it easy to see if any trespassers get near the house. Do you have any side arms on you?" Darius asked, knowing the answer but leaving nothing to chance. Ryder patted his lower back, then looked down at his right calf as Darius laughed. "That's you, the proverbial Boy Scout- always prepared. Oh, if you get into trouble and need help fast, the sheriff in the town is an old friend and is as reliable as they come. His name is Sam Ramey, but just call him Duke and see what he does."

   Looking at his friend, Ryder tried to fight back the tears and felt as if he was losing the battle. "One last thing. Here are the keys and deed to the house and papers for the old Jeep, and in the glovebox is the paperwork authorizing my attorney Darius Jackson to sell both of them, should the need arise. The house is locked up and shut down, as I called the power and gas companies and told them we would be in Europe for three months." The two men hugged tightly as behind them the door to the house opened and the two women, the baby and the young boy came running out. Lacey hugged Tisha tightly, kissing her cheek, hesitant to break the embrace and the good feelings it gave her. The others began hugging all around, even Joker getting a soft kiss from Tisha, as they loaded up in the new vehicle. With Joker sitting between Micah and the baby in her car seat, and the adults in their respective seats, it appeared as if they were just a normal family heading out on a camping adventure.

   Ryder looked at his friend once more, as the black man gave him a thumbs up. Slowly backing out of the driveway, Ryder and Lacey took one last look back at the couple standing arm in arm.
With a knot in his stomach, Ryder put the Jeep in drive, smiling over his shoulder at the boy. "You ready to learn how to catch a fish and clean it?" he asked, the boy wrinkling his face comically at the thought. Lacey looked at her two babies, and a thought suddenly popped into her mind-
"Bitch, you better stay away from me and my family, because next time I will kill you,

and this time I'll shatter every bone in your fucking evil body."

Ryder turned and looked at his wife, seeing the beautiful smile on her face, and knowing there was something much more sinister going on behind those gorgeous green eyes.

Tisha turned around to go back inside, feeling the resistance from her husband. Looking at her husband, the woman reached down and took his hand in hers. "Baby, why don't we go inside, I'll make us some iced tea, and you can tell me why you look like you just lost your best friend."

Chapter 2

Scab was having the damned hardest time with the fuel line on the old Soft tail and could smell the gasoline that had soaked into his greasy, tobacco-stained fingers. The makeshift line was from an old Japanese street bike that had been abandoned on the property, and since there was no local dealer in the middle of fucking nowhere known as Nogales, Mexico where they now sat, he would have to find a way to make it fit. The diameter of the line was wrong, but then the dirty man had an idea. Going to the battered toolbox he withdrew several drill bits and went back to the Harley. Sitting down on the wooden crate, he took the smallest metal bit and slowly inserted it into the rubber tube, hoping to expand it just enough to fit the American made bike. As he worked the drill bit onto the tip of the fuel line, he slowly manipulated it, then withdrew it and carefully slid it onto the connector on the fuel pump. As he felt it beginning to grip it tightly he was thumped on the back of his head, causing him to jump and accidentally pull the line loose. "God damn it, who in the-" when he looked back, he instantly shut his mouth, cutting off the impending expletive. Behind him stood an extremely large man, but it was not the size of the man that scared him, it was the look in his eyes. "Hey man, what's up?" Scab asked, the tremor in his voice evident even to him. The behemoth behind him stood silent, staring unblinking at the skinny man.

"Get that fucking fuel line fixed yet?" he asked, his gravelly voice sending chills down Scab's narrow spine. Even though they rode together with the Devils Disciples, Scab knew the man's reputation, and had no reason to doubt any of it. Dingo Dave's black eyes bored a hole into the biker's soul, so Scab quickly returned to what he was doing. Grabbing the fuel line, he carefully repositioned it onto the male end extending from the fuel pump. Carefully working it into place, he felt the man behind him watching, and Scab prayed that the jury- rigged fuel line would work. Reconnecting the other end of the line, he slid the clamps on over the hose, then reached for the greasy screwdriver laying under the large man's boot. Raising his toe ever so slightly Dave allowed Scab to pick up the tool. Scab tightened first one and then the other clamp, and with his heart pounding loudly in his frail chest, he stood up and threw his leg over the old bike. Rotating the throttle several times, he looked down and saw no drips or signs of leakage from his makeshift repair job. With his right leg he extended the kick starter, then jumped up and down several times, again praying that the bike would fire up. Suddenly the cleaned-up spark plugs caught, and the engine fired up, revving loudly in the extremely small space he was working in. Scab felt his heartbeat slowing, as the motorcycle warmed up, and he looked up at the stone silent man still staring at him. "Nice job, asshole. Those other dipshits said you'd never get this bike running. I guess those old rice burners are good for something after all." Reaching into his vest pocket he pulled out a plastic baggie containing a small amount of white powder, and Scab smiled for the first time in days. "Now get your ass inside, cause I've got another present for you for getting that bike running." Scab got off the bike, the zip lock bag in his hand.

Inside the rundown old clay house four men sat in wooden chairs, passing around a bottle of Tequila and snorting meth off of a dirty mirror. There were several scantily clad young women laying around, stoned and half asleep. As the two men entered from outside, several of the men started clapping. Scab felt slightly embarrassed, but deep down knew these men were his true brothers and would never let him down. Standing in the middle of the room he wasn't sure what to do, so one of the men named Pete went over to the smallest of the two girls, grabbed her arm and brought her to where Scab stood. "This one's for you brother," he said, pushing the girl into Scab's skinny arms.

Scab looked at the girl, then at his brothers with something akin to love. Taking the girl by the hand he led her into the back of the house and through the curtain dividing the dirt floor rooms, turning and giving his brothers a thumbs up as he went in to claim his reward.

Pete grabbed a chair, took the bottle from the greasy man to his left and took a long pull from it. "She awake yet?" he asked, as an older, grizzled looking man nodded. "Then get her ass in here, cause we need to talk," he growled, leaning down to take a sniff off of the mirror.

Summer lay on the makeshift bed, the throbbing pain in her hands preventing her from anything resembling sleep. She carefully wiggled the fingers of her right hand, trying to get them to loosen up and quit hurting so badly. As the digits slowly moved she laid her head on the dirty pillow, trying to relieve herself of the nauseating sensation caused by the pain. Raising her head slightly she looked at her left hand, seeing the red, thick scars left from that black haired bitch. A slight smile came to her face as she thought about the woman and what she was going to do to her and her entire family. All of course except the boy.

Summer could vaguely remember the skinny man they called Scab lifting her off the floor, the blood still pouring from where she had been shot, her hands and arms on fire. He had put the makeshift dressing on her head, trying to be careful of her arms and hands, especially with the bone fragments sticking out from the shredded skin. When he had slid his arm around her waist and stood her up, they started to leave the room before she quickly realized that she needed several things, so she had stopped him and turned back to the massive oak desk. Stumbling to it, she began opening drawers, then painfully grabbed a set of keys and a metal box from one of the built in drawers. She had been unable to lift the heavy box and told the skinny man to get it. He had acted without question, and she had fainted almost

instantly, the small key ring grasped in her badly fractured hand.
When she awoke several hours later, she was laying in the bed of a pickup truck, the metal box next to her, the dressing on her head soaked through, and had heard two men talking. One of them, the skinny little man who had saved her life came up with a bottle of water, holding it to her lips. Taking a sip, she laid her head back down as he had told her to swallow the two pills he held in his other hand. When she asked him what they were, he had just smiled and told her that they were the only way she would survive the trip they were going to have to make. He had then looked at the container and asked her what was so important about it. She had simply looked at him and told him that if anyone touched or tried to open it she would kill them, then slipped off under the power of the pain killers.

As Summer lay on the bed and thought of the circumstances that had brought her to this hellhole just over the Arizona state line, the man named Pete walked into the room and set down beside her. "Dave wants to talk to you," he told her, as he reached over to caress the woman's exposed bare calf. The blonde woman, knowing where she was and what it was going to take to get out of here, smiled back at him.

"You like that smooth skin, then maybe you'll like this better," she whispered, carefully taking his calloused hand and sliding it further up the leg to the edge of her panties. She wanted to vomit at his touch, but smiled and allowed him to caress her favorite spot anyway. As he continued his molestation of the woman, suddenly in the doorway Dave stood, bottle in hand and anger on his face.

"God damn it, I told you to bring her in the other room, not play backseat finger bang with her." Pete got to his feet quickly and grabbed the woman by her hand, Summer wincing in pain as he dragged her into the other room.

Pete set the woman in a homemade, high back chair that Summer was not sure would support her but was evidently stronger than it looked. Sitting up straight she looked the obvious leader in the face, trying to hide the burning in her hands, and he made no attempt to hide the smirk on his bearded face.

"So, we got your little welcome package delivered, and what gives? Jesus H. lady that was the weirdest fucking shopping list I've ever seen. Them boys in San Diego thought it was a joke, but it's done, and they want their cash." As he spoke to the blond woman, he could hear Scab and the girl in the back room making all kind of bizarre noises. "SHUT THE FUCK UP!," Dave screamed at the copulating couple, throwing the bottle at the wall next to their room, and regretting it instantly, as the precious tequila began to flow down the dusty wall amongst the broken glass.

Summer laughed out loud, despite the agonizing pain she was in, and when the large biker turned around he caught sight of the grin on her face. "I told you they'd get their money, and they will, but it depends on whether you were able to get me the phone I told you I needed," she said, using her softest voice to calm the man's nasty temper. Their eyes locked for a second, and she knew the answer. Trash like this could never turn down a large sum of cash, as Summer thought back to that moment when the skinny man had picked her up. The metal box contained passbooks and nearly 500,000 dollars in cash. It had been her emergency getaway stash, and she knew she would need every bit of it after the desert debacle.

"Yeah, I got your fucking phone. What's so special about this phone anyway? My boy had to go all the way up to Tucson to get it, and in this heat that's a bitch of a ride." Looking over at the men sipping beer, he nodded at one of them, a particularly nasty looking man. His hair was matted and greasy, and Summer swore she could smell him all the way across the room. The man got to his feet, his oil-stained jeans seeming to almost leak grease. He walked up to Dave and handed him the small package he had retrieved from his vest, then looked at Summer.

"I think maybe me and you should talk about some things," he told her suggestively, moving towards her. Summer got to her feet instantly, as if daring him to touch her.

"Touch me with that greasy hand of yours, and I swear to God it'll be the last time you touch anything," she said softly, the menace in her eyes giving him pause for thought. Before they could have anymore interactions, Dave grabbed the biker and pushed him away, as Summer sat back down, her head swimming in the desert heat and pain.

"All right, enough of this bullshit. It's been four long ass months, and I'm tired of playing nursemaid. Now, here's the special phone you said you needed, so get busy and get that fucking money moved before I lose my patience." Tearing open the package, he handed the phone to Summer, who took it carefully from him. Moving towards the back room, Pete stopped her with a hand on her arm.

"Where the hell do you think you're going?" he asked her, as she stopped.

"I'm going to retrieve one of my books with the number I need in it," she said quietly, without turning her head. Dave took his hand away as Summer went into the next room. Retrieving the keys from the pocket of the cotton dress she wore, she sat down and unlocked the metal box, sifted through the contents, and pulled out a small red notebook. Her fingers aching, she looked over the names and numbers, then spied the one she needed. Using her still bruised index finger she gently turned the phone on, waited for a second then pressed a series of numbers.

Chapter 3

Looking in the rearview mirror, Ryder saw Micah playing with April, pretending to get her nose, a game which thankfully, seemed to be keeping them both occupied and amused. Turning his attention back to the road in front of him, he saw a threesome of motorcycles coming in their direction, weaving in and out of traffic, and his gut instinctively tightened. Lacey saw his hands grip the wheel a little harder and reached over to touch him. "Honey, not every motorcycle belongs to them," she whispered softly, as the trio blared past them, the powerful engines rattling the windows in the Jeep slightly. Ryder looked in his side view, hoping to catch a glimpse of their colors, or the rockers on their vests which would identify them to a specific club. They were too far past him, so he focused once more on the road ahead. Lacey had her phone in hand, tracing the best route to Tahoe. "If we go out towards Palmdale, we can get 395 North, but it's almost 10 hours. If we head north on the 5 we can cut an hour off that. What do you think?" she asked, seeing the look on Ryders face. It was the same look he had had back in the desert, and while it gave her a great deal of comfort, it also scared her a little.

"Well, if we go out 395 there's almost nothing between Palmdale and Tahoe, and at first glance it seems like a good idea by making it a lot easier to see anybody following us. The 5 seems like a better idea because it is more heavily travelled, so if we had to get away we would have more options." As he spoke Ryder took several deep breaths before continuing. "I say we head over and hook up with I-5. I think it'll give us better cover, just in case." Lacey reached over and laid her hand on his.
"I love you, you know," she whispered, as Ryder turned to look at her.
"I love you too Lacey, and those kids are something else," he told her, letting her smile ease some of the stress in his heart. He wanted more than anything to end this situation, but he also knew, from experience, that to attack an enemy without knowing their strengths and weaknesses was foolhardy. He wished he could just lock his family up in a safe somewhere and face this bitch and her people one on one.

"Do you really think she's going to be able to track us?" Lacey asked, noticing that Micah and the baby had quieted down. "I mean, she doesn't have supernatural powers or anything. She's just flesh and blood. I proved that." As she talked to her husband, he expertly maneuvered the Jeep into the left lane, seeing the sign for I-5 North toward Sacramento. The traffic was fairly heavy, despite the late morning hour, and he breathed a little easier as they began their trek north.

"Supernatural, no. Instinct, yes. I think that psycho is going to be able to keep an eye on us, and if she has linked up with those bastards on motorcycles, it will be a lot easier for her." Lacey looked at him, a funny look on her face.

"What makes you think she's in with them? After all, they were the ones sent to kill her at that ranch. Why would she have anything to do with them?" Ryder squeezed his wife's hand gently before answering.

"Sweetheart, think about it. Who do you think she hates more, us or them? You shot her and mutilated her hands, which I applaud you for, and that, my love puts us as number one on her hit list. I have no doubt that, while they might make strange bedfellows, the end line for biker trash like that is money, and that is what she has more of than anything. Now, I need to talk to you seriously. I know you have your pistol, and your license, and that's great. Keep it at the ready at all times. Be alert, and I mean really hyper alert to everything around you. Let's try something. Look around at the cars in front of you, beside you, behind you, everywhere. Really look around. Good. Now shut your eyes for me. Now tell me what the license is of the blue BMW ahead and on your right. What decals does the Ford truck have to my left? Is it a man or woman driving the BMW? What state plates?" As Ryder quizzed her, Lacey opened her eyes and looked straight at Ryder and tried to recall what she had seen.

"Blue BMW, plate is California, 35V something, Ford truck has an NRA decal, a US flag and a "My Son is a US Marine" decal. Can't tell you the driver though, of the BMW.' As she finished, Ryder was impressed with her powers of observation and recall.

"Excellent. Now try this. Close your eyes again and tell me what the kids are dressed in, what color shirt you're wearing and whether I shaved this morning." Lacey closed her eyes, then began to speak.
"April is in, umm, a yellow shirt and pants. Micah has on jeans and a Patriots t-shirt with sneakers. You didn't shave today, because there are no whiskers in my sink and I'm wearing a blue button up blouse and jeans." Opening her eyes, she looked over her shoulder, where her daughter was

still asleep in her pink elephant shirt and pants and Micah sat in jeans and his Tom Brady jersey. Lacey then looked back up front at Ryder driving, his face, clean-shaven, then down at her brown pullover and jeans." What the-" As Ryder tried not to laugh he looked over at his wife.

"You see, you nailed the detail stuff in front of you, the cars, licenses, etc. You noticed the decals and the plates, but when it came to those right in your space, well I'm sorry to say but you muffed it sweetheart." Lacey looked at him, a curious shadow on her face.

"Why did that happen?" she asked, as Ryder explained.

"The mind has a way of paying attention to everything around us in our environment, but not necessarily what's right next to us. It figures you already know the immediate stuff, so it focuses on the external stimuli around you, taking it all in. That's why they have such good success with crime victims being hypnotized, they can recall things they saw but the conscious has forgotten." Lacey sat, amazed at her husbands' insight into the human mind and psyche.

"Where did you learn all of this?" she asked him, impressed and a little taken aback. Ryder looked at her, then turned his attention back to the rearview mirror.

"Damn it," he whispered, "There's a Highway patrolman behind us with his lights on." Lacey started to turn to look, and Ryder stopped her with his hand. "Don't look back, and in fact, why don't you pick up April and feed her." Meeting his gaze, Lacey saw something in his eyes, and turned around to get her daughter as Ryder slowly pulled to the right, giving her extra time. Lacey lifted the infant from her seat and laid her across her lap and chest, the movement waking the baby from her slumber, while Micah and Joker continued dozing. Ryder pulled over and stopped, as the car behind him, lights flashing, did the same.

"Lacey, don't say anything, just look slightly embarrassed at his being here with your breast exposed. I'm just a little concerned that, out of all this traffic, we were the ones he pulled over." Lacey caught the meaning of his words, as her daughter latched on, and Ryder rolled down his window to the approaching officer.

"Good morning sir, may I see your license, insurance and registration please?" Ryder already had the documents out and handed them through the open window to the dark-skinned Hispanic man.

"Can I ask what the problem is, officer?" he inquired, as the man took off his glasses to meet Ryder's stare.

"Yes sir, we had a report of a stolen 2016 Jeep Grand Cherokee out of Tustin yesterday," he answered, as April began to fuss and Lacey adjusted her position, her eyes momentarily catching the policeman's. "How old is your little one?" he asked, a slight smile crossing his weathered face.

"She's about five months old now," Lacey answered, turning her eyes back down in a gesture of modesty. The officer stood back up straight.

"I'll be right back," he told Ryder, returning to his vehicle. Keeping her eyes straight ahead Lacey asked softy, "Are you okay?" Ryder nodded slightly, then saw the officer returning at a steady pace to the Jeep.

"Here are your documents," he said to Ryder, who took them and replaced them in the glove box.

"Everything checked out fine, I take it," Ryder said, meeting the policeman's direct gaze.

"Yes sir, everything checked out just fine. Where you folks headed? Looks like you're loaded for a long road trip," he said, his voice slow and steady. As he talked, Lacey, her head turned slightly, spotted the distinctive tattoo on the man's muscular, tanned forearm.

"Oh, were you a Marine sir?" she asked, her voice soft and gentle to avoid waking Micah, and noticing the small tic on the side of Ryder's neck.

"Yes ma'am, I was, and still am at heart. Why do you ask?"

"Well, my younger brother was a Marine, and he died several years ago in Afghanistan. I just like to say thank you to a veteran when I see one." As she spoke, April began fussing again, and the officer resumed his stance.

"Thank you. Okay, well you folks drive safely now, and enjoy wherever it is your heading to." Ryder watched as he walked back to his cruiser, got in and pulled back into traffic, waving as he did.

Ryder sat for a moment, impressed with his wife's alert eyes and tactics.
"That was great," he said, "the way you spotted that tattoo, and used April to keep him off guard." Lacey, a slight flush on her cheeks, finished feeding the baby and turned around to replace her in her carrier. "And that part about your brother being killed-that was brilliant." Resuming her position up front she reached for Ryder's hand.

"I always was a fast learner, especially with a teacher as good as you. It just seemed natural, the lying part, which I guess I shouldn't feel good about, and yet it seems okay." Ryder squeezed her hand, then turned his head back to the left to merge back onto the freeway. Getting back into the flow of traffic Ryder spotted a sign for several gas stations and some fast-food restaurants, as from behind him he heard the sounds of stretching and awakening from Micah and Joker both. Lacey looked back at the boy, who was rubbing his eyes and looking around.

"Boy, how far did we go? How long was I asleep?" he asked, siting forward to talk to his parents.

"Oh, we've been on the road for about an hour and a half, and I'm glad you woke up because we need to stop for gas and to grab something to eat. You hungry?" he asked the boy, already knowing the answer. At 11, the boy was like a bottomless pit, and both Lacey and Ryder took his healthy appetite as a positive sign of his continuing recovery.

"Oh, can we have Burger King? I love their Whoppers, and besides that, I really need to pee," he asked, as Lacey and Ryder tried hard not to laugh.

"Okay buddy, Whoppers it is." Pulling into the half full lot, Ryder surveyed the surrounding areas, and couldn't find anything out of place. Parking the Jeep in front of the business he got out, as Lacey did the same, opening the back doors to retrieve the children. April was half asleep from her feeding, but Micah was wide awake and darted toward the door to the business. Ryder quickly went and took him by the hand, leading him back to the vehicle. "Listen son, you can't just take off like that. You have to wait for your mom and I, okay?" he asked sternly, not wanting to alarm the young boy but also acutely aware of the potential dangers.

"I'm sorry," Micah replied, waiting with Ryder as his mom and baby sister came up, Joker staying behind. Ryder held the door for them, then entered the relatively clean fast-food spot.

Looking at Lacey, Ryder spoke, softly, but loud enough for her to hear clearly. "I'll make a pit stop with Micah while you go in and take care of business, then meet back out here. Right here, okay?" Lacey nodded in agreement, as the two guys went into the men's room, and she entered the ladies.

Ryder stood washing his hands, as Micah came up next to him. Imitating the larger man, Micah squirted some soap into his hands, rubbed it then added some water. Out of the corner of his eye Ryder watched the young boy and felt a love so deep it scared him. How any father could do what Michael had done to his own son was, even to Ryder, unimaginable. Shaking his hands dry he pulled down several paper towels, then several more for Micah. Drying their hands together, they *swished* the crumpled paper into the garbage can. "Hey, nice shot," Ryder told him, as the boy held up his knuckles in the modern version of the high five. Lightly tapping the boy's knuckles with his, the two of them exited the bathroom, and saw no sign of Lacey or the baby. His heart skipping a beat, Ryder took a deep breath. "*Maybe it's just taking her a little longer,*" he thought to himself, as the door suddenly came open. An elderly lady came out, her right hand clutching a cane as she walked slowly. Micah stepped aside, as Ryder lightly touched the woman's arm. "Ma'am did you happen to see a woman and a baby in there?" he asked, trying to keep his voice calm.

"No, just me in there," she answered, a gentle smile on her face. "Are you okay?" she asked, the mother in her coming to the surface.

Ryder swallowed before answering. "Yes, I'm sure she's just out in the car. Thank you though." Turning away, the two males began to walk towards the exit, when it came open and Lacey walked through, the baby in one arm and the diaper bag in the other. Ryder exhaled deeply as she caught his eye.

"Let's get a table and order," he said to the group, Lacey catching the tone in his voice. They walked over to a table away from the door, Lacey noticing that Ryder took the bench facing both side doors, with Micah next to him. "Okay buddy, let's get some Whoppers."

The duo returned several minutes later with a tray holding four burgers, two orders of fries and three drinks. Ryder set the tray down as Micah retook his seat.

"I goofed, didn't I?" Lacey asked quietly, as they each took a hamburger from the tray, leaving one, minus onions, for their furry companion. Ryder met her gaze, and despite his earlier fear was unable to be angry at her.

"It's okay, just remember what we talked about, being always aware, noticing, and most of all don't disappear like that." Unwrapping the burgers, the family began to eat, Micah, as always, tearing his sandwich in half, and plopping some fries on his wrapper as he took a drink of his soda. They sat for about 15 minutes, just a normal family having an early lunch, Micah making his parents laugh with his imitation of a walrus, using two French fries as tusks. Even April, now awake, seemed to find her big brother funny, giggling and smacking the tray top with her hands. As they finished their lunch Ryder looked at the group. "Anyone need to use the bathroom? We have a long trip ahead of us and it might be hard to stop." Lacey and Micah both shook their head, then Micah picked up the tray and took it to the receptacle to dump the garbage. Ryder noticed that Lacey kept her eyes peeled the entire time on her son, which pleased him immensely. Gathering their belongings, the family exited the building and walked back to the Jeep, Ryder helping Micah in as Lacey strapped the baby into her seat. Walking around the back, he opened the hatchback and unwrapped the last burger, which Joker wolfed down in two bites, while Ryder rubbed the dogs head and neck .As he closed the back door, Ryder spotted a man and woman sitting in a blue Ford truck at the gas pump, the man seeming to be staring in Ryder's direction, then climbing out and sauntering in the direction of the mini-mart. Discreetly getting into the Jeep

Ryder started the engine as Lacey fastened her seatbelt.

"What's up?" she asked, seeing the all too familiar look on his face.

"I'm going to pull up to the pump over there on the left behind that blue Ford truck and fill up. Grab that map out of the glovebox, and when I get out you look at it and shake your head. I'll head toward the store, and you get out and go ask the woman for directions to Bakersfield. I'm going to slow down her man while you distract her." This was all said and explained while he kept his gaze straight ahead, and Lacey agreed with a slow nod of her head. She was terrified at being separated, even for a moment or two, but accepted his plan without argument. Ryder backed up and flipped around to the forward pump. Shutting off the engine he casually climbed out, popping the inside lever for the gas cap as he realized the man had not yet returned. Walking up to Lacey's window he spoke softly but firmly. "I'm going into the store, and I need you to pay with cash for the gas out here." He handed Lacey two twenty dollar bills and opened her door, realizing that his time was drawing short to delay the man's return. Lacey got out, looking at her babies in the back, and an anger came over her at being

forced to go on the run with her children. Slipping the bills into the ATM, she watched Ryder causally walk across the lot toward the store, then enter the business. The smell of gas fumes made her want to choke, but she kept her game face on, watching the woman in the truck, then the door to the store. As the pump kept going, she decided the time was right to make her move. Leaving the nozzle in place, she reached through her open window and picked up the map, then walked around to the lady in the Ford.
"Excuse me, but can you show me the fastest way to Bakersfield? My sister was in an accident last night, and I'm trying to get to her." The woman smelled of sweat and cigarettes, but Lacey maintained her anxious face as she spoke.
"Well, once you get up over the Grapevine and drop down, there's going to be a highway cutting off to the east. I forget the number, but it'll say Bakersfield." As the woman talked, Lacey saw Ryder exit the store, spotting her at the Ford. With his eyes he told her to get back in the Jeep, and Lacey thanked the malodorous woman for her help and went back to the Jeep. Getting in, she saw Ryder replace the nozzle in the pump and replacing the cap, silently berating herself for having forgotten

the gas. As Ryder opened the door and got in, Lacey kept her eyes locked on him. "I know I screwed up, but it seemed like the right thing to talk to the woman as a distraction." Ryder met her eyes, a stern look on his stubbled face.
"You know what-you were right. You went with your gut, and that was good. Of course, her man is out cold on a toilet seat, so let's get out of here before he wakes up," Ryder said, trying to sound stern, but his love for the green-eyed woman and those two beautiful children in back forcing him to play it easy.

"Next stop, Lake Tahoe." Ryder kept his eyes straight ahead, merged onto the freeway, and silence filled the Jeep for the next 10 miles, before Ryder spoke.

The injured man opened his eyes, his head feeling as if he had been run over by a truck, his right eye swollen shut. He had seen the brown-haired man enter the washroom, and before he could react the man had cold cocked him and shoved him into one of the stalls. His hands had quickly and efficiently been zip-tied behind his back, a huge wad of toilet paper shoved into his mouth. Trying to spit out the gooey material, he stumbled out of the stall door, scaring the elderly cowboy standing and urinating.

"Boy, looks like you bit off more than you could chew," the weathered old ranch hand said, pulling a large knife from his belt and slicing through the plastic ties. Without a word of thanks, the scruffy man pulled the gummy paper from his mouth and ran out the door, seeing the blue Jeep gone. Running to his pickup he climbed in, then realized the keys were still in his pocket. "Give me your cell phone, bitch," he growled, his arms and wrists burning due to the injury. Dialing with his left hand he waited, then heard the voice on the other end. "Yeah, it's me. We saw him up here on the Grapevine, but the bastard got away. No, he got the drop on me. Hey, fuck you man-" the line went dead, and he tossed the phone into the cab. Taking his wife's set of keys from her purse he turned on the ignition and squealed away from the store. "Call your sister in Tempe and tell her we're coming for a long visit," he told the woman, who looked at him, saw the fear in his eyes and did just that.

Chapter 4

Preacher lifted the hatchback of the shuttle van, retrieving the three bags and two garment bags from where they lay. Picking them all up, he stepped back as Cindy came around from tipping the driver and lowered the lid of the vehicle. "Is that everything?" she asked, as Preacher nodded and began the final leg of this incredible trip they had undertaken.

If anyone, at any time had told Preacher that he would spend two weeks on a cruise ship, and would have the time of his life, he would have called them crazy. The first day out of Miami they had hit some rough seas, but with Cindy's help and some hot tea, they got through. The next day they had begun to venture out, and Preacher had discovered his new passion. The sunsets were amazing, and he and Cindy had spent each evening on the bridge, watching the bright orange ball drop behind the ocean. They had enjoyed several excursions into the coastal Caribbean towns, and had spent one lovely afternoon sipping virgin Pina Coladas on the beach as the waves crashed in. The captain, a delightful man with a similar countenance to Preachers, had invited them to dine at his table the last

evening out, and the feast and company had been first-rate.
The couple had been a little saddened when they pulled back into port and promised each other that each year on their anniversary this was their vacation.

The flight home had been uneventful, and when they got back to Santa Barbara it was almost 9:30. They had taken their bags into the house, as Cindy noticed that the newspapers and mail had piled up while they were gone. Mrs. McKay, the elderly widow next door had promised she would pick up the items while they were gone, and the unattended piles concerned Cindy.

"I'm going next door to see Vera and make sure everything's okay," Cindy told him, as Preacher nodded. Setting the three cases and other bags in their bedroom he went out into the kitchen area to check messages. Sitting on one of the oak bar stools he saw the light flashing multiple times. Hitting the button, he picked up the pen and pad of paper next to the phone, writing down several messages for Cindy, deleting several telemarketing calls, and several from Sy, the young man who had run the beach shop while Preacher was gone. Picking up the phone he dialed the man's home number.

"Hey Sy, what's up? Yeah we just got back and are tired, but damn, that was nice. How was business? Really? Three times? Well, I always told you if I ever sold it would be offered to you first buddy. No worries, I'm too young to retire yet anyway. I'll swing by your place in the morning and get the keys. All right brother, see you tomorrow." Hanging up the phone Preacher heard Cindy coming back inside, her voice and face appearing anxious.

"Preacher, I just talked to Vera's daughter Rhonda next door. I guess Vera had a heart attack two days ago, and that's why the stuff is piled up. She's at Valley Ridge, and her daughter told me that she's going to need bypass surgery, so Vera has agreed to sell her place and move in with her family." As she relayed to him the goings on, he felt himself saying a silent prayer for the elderly lady. She was a very sweet woman, always with a smile and a green thumb that Preacher truly admired.

"What about her dogs?" Preacher asked, retrieving a bottle of water for his wife. "Well, Rhonda told me they were being boarded right now, but she also said she'll have to find homes for them. Her youngest daughter is allergic and can't have them in the house." As she filled Preacher in she could already see the wheels spinning in his head, and she walked up and kissed him softly. "You really are a true humanitarian. I'll go let the daughter know so she can tell Vera. She's been very worried about her girls, and this will take a huge load off of her mind." Preacher could picture the two Corgi's in the yard with Vera, helping her dig up the dirt to put in new flowers each spring, and the thought of those two dogs staying with he and Cindy warmed his heart.

Suddenly he realized there were no calls from Ryder, not even a *welcome home* call. This was highly unusual, and for some reason he felt the need to call his friend.

Dialing the phone, he opened a water for himself and waited. After thirty seconds and no answer or machine, Preacher hung up, then dialed another number. For Ryder, being out of communication was unacceptable, and he always had his cell with him. He was about to hang up when a man answered.

"Hey Preacher, just get back?" Darius asked, as Preacher put the phone on speaker. The man's voice was always cheerful, even at the worst of times, a feat which Preacher admired.

""Yeah, we got back about a half hour ago. Long damn flight, but man, what a beautiful way to spend two weeks. Just got the bags inside, and Cindy's next door taking care of some things. Listen, I just tried to call Ryder, but his phone just rings and goes to voice mail. Any idea what gives?" There was a silent pause for a moment, a pause which any other time would not have alarmed the large man, but he also knew Darius, and the pause spoke volumes.

On the other end of the line the attorney's mind was racing. He wanted to let Preacher know what had taken place, but he also knew it had to be done discreetly and without Cindy's knowledge. "Yeah, I know what gives. Listen, I need you to meet me in about a half an hour so we can talk." Looking at his watch he heard Tisha coming up the stairs.

Preacher was more than a little alarmed at the cryptic comments but was smart enough to know not to ask many questions until he met Darius face to face. "Okay, half an hour- where do you want to meet? Yeah, I remember that spot. I'll see you there." As he hung up the phone he heard Cindy coming back and went to retrieve the baggage and take it upstairs. Easily lifting the three cases he moved toward the stairs and began the climb, when he was suddenly pinched from behind. Cindy laughed out loud at her husband's feeble attempt to get away, and when they entered the bedroom she went up behind and wrapped her arms around him.

"So, want to wait to put this stuff away?" she whispered to him seductively, her hands caressing his stomach through the shirt, then moving lower. Preacher slowly turned around and wrapped his large arms around her, loving the smell of her hair, and had to fight to resist the urge.

"Sweetheart, I can't right now. Darius called and needed to talk about something important. I have to meet him in about thirty minutes, and I never want to have to hurry with you." Smiling at his new bride he could literally feel her resistance to his wanting to leave.

"Now, what could be so important as to leave me high and not so dry?" she asked, her lower lip pouting in a very sexy way that made his heart pound. Preacher exhaled slowly.

"It has something to do with Ryder," he told her, her eyes instantly catching the meaning. "I tried to call him, but his phone just goes to mail, and when I called Darius he was very reticent to tell me anything." Setting the baggage on the bed he reached in and grabbed his leather jacket, then gave his wife a soft kiss. Taking her hand, he led

51

them downstairs and into the garage. Opening the large door, he fired up the Harley, then hugged Cindy tightly before kissing her. "I'll be back in a bit, and we can pick up where we left off," he told her, his mind telling him *Darius this better be good.*

Darius backed out of the driveway, looked to his right down Canyon Drive and saw it was clear. Putting the Lexus into gear, he headed south towards the 101, then picked it up and headed towards Leo's Place. When Preacher had called him, he had at first not wanted to say anything, but could hear Ryder's words. He wanted to meet his friend somewhere where they could talk in private, and Leo's was just the place. Darius knew the owner from many years back and knew he could talk freely with Preacher in the back room. He had wanted to drive by Ryder and Lacey's place to scout it out, but realized that could be a bad idea, given the current situation. He reached down and clicked PLAY on the CD player, as the soothing strains of Tony Bennett filled the car. Spotting the sign for his exit coming up, he looked out at the Pacific to his right, loving the color of the water. Suddenly a loud sound came from his left side, and he turned to see three motorcycles next to him, the driver on the

lead bike giving him the finger. Darius kept his attention focused straight ahead, not wanting to cause any disturbances. The trio pulled ahead, and as they did Darius saw them taking the same exit he needed. "Shit," he whispered, as the crooner's voice filled the car. The bikes stopped at the stop sign, then turned right, and to Darius's dismay pulled into the very parking lot where he was headed. Driving past, he watched as they went into the tiny bar, and when they did he pulled over, dialing Preacher's number. "Hey Preach, not sure where you are, but I just saw three of our friends pull into the same place we were going to meet," then began to laugh at the man's response. "Okay old buddy, I'll meet you inside, but if there's trouble I'm getting behind you. My bar fighting days are done."
Turning around, he went into the business, pulled in and turned off the car. Several minutes later he saw, in his rearview mirror, Preacher and his bike pulling in and parking.
"What, you needed to wait for me?" Preacher asked, climbing off of the motorcycle and hugging his longtime friend.
"Needed, no. Thought it was a good idea, yeah." Entering the bar, the two men saw Leo tending bar, a smile filling his face when he saw the pair. Tossing the rag on

the counter, he walked out from behind, shaking Darius's hand up and down, then Preachers.

"Can we use your back room?" Darius asked, keeping his voice down in the half full establishment.

"Sure," Leo told him, turning and leading the way, as the three bikers shouted out for a round of beers.

Entering the room was like getting into Fort Knox, and now Preacher realized why Darius had wanted to meet here. The alarm system was disengaged, and Leo led the way through and into the anteroom. Preacher could tell the walls were thicker than usual but was having a hard time deciding why when Leo turned to them.

"This may not look like a lot, but these walls are eight inches thick, and as soundproof as any recording studio in Hollywood. Beneath you are two rooms, fully stocked and able to withstand an atomic blast." He looked around the room proudly, a smile on his face, and Darius was loathe to ruin his moment.

He had helped Leo when he had decided to purchase the property and had watched as the man turned the very profitable bar and restaurant into a local hot spot. "Leo, thanks for letting us use this room. I know it sounds weird, but this was the only place I

felt comfortable talking to my friend here." Leo stuck out his hand to shake Darius's, then Preacher's.
"No sweat Darius. You know mi casa is su casa." Stepping into the foyer of the room Leo left without another word, and the two men left took seats.
"So, what does all this cloak and dagger mean?" Preacher asked, meeting Darius's eyes. He could see something brewing behind the dark eyes, praying it was better than he expected.
Darius sat, confident that he and Preacher could talk in private. "Okay, all cards on the table. Ryder stopped by two days ago with Lacey and the kids and told me a tale. You remember all the melee in the desert last summer? Well, it looks like the woman behind it, that Summer lady, wasn't killed after all. Ryder and Lacey were left a couple of sick little gifts several nights ago in the baby's room, and he and Lacey decided that the best way, the only way to protect themselves and the family was to hit the road. I arranged a brand-new Jeep for them, to avoid being traced, we loaded it up with gear and they left quietly." Preacher sat in his chair, his massive hands together and fought to remain calm.

"So, where were they heading?" he asked softly, his gut in knots at the thought of his friends in trouble.

Darius inhaled deeply. "I told him that I would keep that to myself. He made me promise that much. He told me to let you know that this woman is nuts, insane, and that if she could get into his house without him knowing, well that adds a whole new level of crazy to her resume'. I've never seen him scared, but I tell you this- he looked as afraid as any man I've ever known. He has supplies, guns, everything he needs, but again- he made me promise. He left me a satellite phone, in case he gets into trouble, but I have the only one." Darius felt like shit not giving Preacher what he wanted, but he understood Ryder's reasoning also.

Preacher sat, not moving. "So, where is he going?" he repeated quietly, letting Darius see the degree of seriousness in his eyes. He wanted to break something, hit the wall, anything, but he remained calm despite his burning fury. He wanted to know where Ryder was going, but he also knew that Darius would never betray the trust given to him, and while he understood it, he would never accept it.

Darius sat, feeling the large man's anger and glad it was not directed at him. "Listen," he said, trying to defuse Preacher, "You know Ryder can take care of himself, and so can Lacey. He knows what he's doing, and if he needs anything he will let us know. Now, the best thing we can do for them is to be here, in case he does call me." Preacher sat, unmoving and staring at his friend.

"So, how was the cruise?" Darius asked, his voice calm in the quiet room, as Preacher stared at him, his eyes dark and brooding.

"So, you aren't going to tell me where he is, are you?" the large man asked, as Darius took a seat across from him.

"Sure doesn't look like it, does it big man?"

Chapter 5

Summer leaned back against the wall as she heard the phone ringing in Nassau, the Bahamas so many miles to the southeast of the dirty, dusty shithole where she currently found herself.

"Hello," came the Caribbean lilted voice, and a rare, warm smile crossed her pained face.

"Hello Jean-Pierre, this is your old friend Summer." She could almost see the smile on his handsome face, and that too made her happy. The smooth voiced man had been the key player in Summer's money transferring plan and had always come through without question. As president of the largest bank in the entire Bahamian network, he had been influential in establishing her as a major player in the money laundering schemes. By Summer's calculation she had nearly nine hundred million dollars residing in his bank, and to her way of thinking that made her a preferred customer.

"Well hello Ms. Summer. I heard things went a little crazy up your way a while back. I hope you are doing better now," he asked, the sing-song tone in his voice soothing her frazzled nerves.

"Well Jean-Pierre that is where you come in. I need a couple of very large favors from you, the kind that only you can supply. First I need you to wire 500,000 dollars to this account number immediately. Second, I need you to arrange for a large, family sized, brand new RV, top of the line, to be delivered to a location in Tucson, Arizona in three days. I need a top-of-the-line laptop computer, with connections, and these specifications. I need it to have at least 2 terabytes of memory, an Intel 8 processor, and no less than 64 gigabytes of memory. It has to be extremely fast and able to multitask for me." On the other end, the black skinned man sat making notes on a manila pad, as he thought about who he could get to put this computer together, and fast. While he continued his note taking, he had reached down and texted his brother, who, short of Einstein, was the smartest man he had ever met.

"Okay me lady, I have just the guy to put this together for you, as well as the RV, but it gonna cost a pretty penny or two." Before he could continue, Summer's voice came through, crystal clear and as serious as a heart attack.

"Listen Jean-Pierre, I didn't expect it to be free, but don't try to screw me around either. I'm in a tremendous amount of pain here, so let me know when you have it arranged. Oh, and by the way, I'm going to need a driver for the RV also. The guys I'm with don't exactly look like the RV type, and I can barely dress myself, let alone handle a full-sized rig." As she spoke to the man so many miles away, she almost felt bad for snapping at him. He had always been straight up with her, charging her only a 3% transaction fee up to the first five hundred million, then 2% after that. He had made probably in the neighborhood of seventy-five million dollars off of her in their time together, and for a man living on a Bahamian island with almost no overhead, that was a lot of money.

"Hey, no worries me friend, you know that Jean-Pierre no get big eyed to you," he said, his voice soft and soothing. Summer took a deep breath before she continued.

"I know you would never big eye me, old friend, it's just this pain in my arms and hands from that black haired bitch. When I catch her, she's going to regret ever meeting me. I plan on giving her a cut-hip when I catch her, and this time she won't walk away. So, call me on this number once everything is set, and again thank you my friend." The dark-skinned man could barely keep his laughter contained at her use of the Bahamian slang she was using. In the

islands a cut-hip meant to give someone a severe beating, and even through the distance he felt bad for the woman who had hurt his favorite customer.
"Yaa, I will give you call in a day or so, and you go and try to rest while ole J.P. takes care of things down here in the islands." Summer disconnected the phone and set it on the makeshift night table, then jumped when it suddenly rang. "Hello," she said, bumping her left thumb painfully against the wooden table, bringing a tear to her eyes.
"What do you mean they lost them? Fuck, they're travelling with a baby and a small boy, so please explain to me HOW THE FUCK THEY LOST THEM?" At the sound of her raised voice, the large biker walked back into her room. Ignoring him, Summer listened to the man on the other end. "Fine, get ahold of your guys and tell them no more screw-ups. I want these people found, and fast, but they are not to be touched. I get it. You lost some men in the desert last year and you want payback, but this is bigger than your club. The man is my brother, the woman is the bitch that shot me and destroyed my hands and is the mom to my niece. The boy is mine also, so get this straight. I will pay you two million dollars to locate these people but keep your hands to yourselves. You know how serious I can be,

so let your brothers know who they're dealing with. We're headed towards you in a couple days, and I'll let you know exactly when. What? Vince Bandini is stirring up trouble for you locally? Well, as far as I'm concerned Mr. Vince Bandini is all yours. No, I don't want anything to do with him, so you guys have some fun. I understand he has a beautiful young niece living in Vegas, and you know what they say- What happens in Vegas, stays in Vegas." Summer began to laugh, softly at first, then louder, and the eerie sound sent a winter chill down the biker's spine as he turned and walked out of the room. Gaining control of herself, Summer spoke quietly into the phone. "Call me when you locate them. Yes Jake, the money's being wired as we speak." Setting the phone down again, Summer leaned her head back against the dirt wall, allowing her that rare moment of peace, and as her eyes closed, she saw only one image-Lacey.

She could still see the bitch standing there in front of her, that pistol in her hand, Sierra that traitorous bitch right beside her. When the black-haired lady had started cutting on her hands, Summer had taken herself to that special place in her mind where there was no pain and no distractions. This destination never failed to take her pain away, and when she was in the void, as she called it, she could see everything as clear as day as she thought about her beloved Giorgio.

Summer thought back to that horrible morning three years past, when Giorgio had begun wheezing worse than ever. She had held him, murmuring soft, loving sounds to her distraught son, his head cradled in her lap, her silk covered hands gently caressing his hair as he struggled for each breath. Fahim had brought the Escalade around front, and she had quickly opened the door and climbed inside, as her faithful friend tenderly handed her son to her. They had been about ten minutes from town when Summer had realized that the wheezing had stopped. Panicked, she began to scream at the driver to pull over. Stopping the huge vehicle, the large man had jumped from the front, opened the back door and grabbed the small boy, whose face was already turning blue. With Summer screaming in the background, Fahim had laid the boy down on the road and leaned over him, his massive frame covering almost of the small boy's frail frame. He began to breathe into the boy's mouth, desperate to make him start breathing again. While he performed his version of CPR, Summer had been calling 911 in an attempt to save her son. As she had hung up the phone she looked at her man servant, his eyes dark with sorrow. When Summer realized that her precious Giorgio was gone, she let out a shriek to pierce the skies, a sound so mournful it scared the large man. Six minutes later, when the life support crew pulled up, they found an extremely distraught woman sobbing and rocking her son, his brown hair nuzzled gently by the breeze. The crew had approached the scene very carefully, due to the size of the man standing beside her, as well as the look on his face.

After they had taken the boy to the nearest hospital to be pronounced, Summer had composed herself, doing what she needed to have her son's remains taken care of. She had set about making arrangements to have his body transported back to Greece, when in the back of her mind she knew he would always stay with his mother.

She had arranged to have his body taken to a local funeral home run by a man well known to her. When she arrived and he saw who his latest client was, his heart began pounding in his chest. He had welcomed the large man and the blonde lady into his inner office, where the woman sat and the man stood silent next to the door. He had offered his sincere condolences to the distraught woman, the man's own child, having passed unexpectedly at the age of nine. Summer had listened to the man's words before she had told him exactly what she wanted from him. The director, a local preacher and a closet pedophile who had been serviced numerous times by one of Summer's younger girls, knew that she was aware of his dark secret, and would do whatever the woman wanted, without fail.

   Two days later a black Chevy van showed up at the Ranch, carrying the embalmed body of the young boy to his permanent resting place.

Summer's memoires were broken by the sound of the satellite phone ringing. Picking it up, she listened for a moment before speaking. "Perfect. Now we know where, we just have to figure out the best plan of attack. I'll be in touch."

Chapter 6

Ryder looked over at his dozing wife, then back over his shoulder at the sleeping twosome in back. April's head was tilted slightly to the left, in the direction of her big brother. Micah's head was leaning to the right, as if protecting his baby sister even in sleep, while he murmured in his sleep. Ryder was glad they were resting now, because when they arrived at their destination they would need all the energy they could muster. In the back of the rig, he could hear the soft snoring of Joker, who was sleeping off his Whopper induced lethargy.

Spotting the road sign, he saw that they were about 120 miles from the I-50 cutoff which would take them into Nevada and Cedar Pass, the small mountain town of about 450 people which was the closest place to the cabin. The cabin, as he put it, was about ten miles up the pass from the small town, and the last two miles in would have to be taken slowly and in four-wheel drive. Ryder already had a partial game plan in place, which would include trekking back down to relock the gate and remove whatever tracks the Jeep left, which hopefully would be minimal and covered over by the nightly dusting of leaves and snow. The home was at about 9,000 feet in elevation, and he sincerely hoped they could get in and get settled before anyone found them. If they could just get the supplies unloaded and get situated, it would be much easier to prepare for what he knew inevitably was coming.

Looking around at the afternoon traffic, he saw nothing that concerned him, which of course was precisely what he was worried about. Traffic was going at a steady pace, and as he continued his surveillance he heard Lacey moving next to him.

"Where are we?" she asked, stretching her back and neck as she moved in the seat.

"Well, we just passed Santa Nella, and since you don't like pea soup I saw no need to wake you up," knowing of his wife's aversion to creamy soups. Lacey yawned, then reached over and laid her hand on Ryder's forearm.

"So, let's talk. How far is this town we're looking for, this Cedars Pass?" Ryder thought for a minute before answering.

"Well, it's about two hours north-northeast of Sacramento, in the mountains near Tahoe. I googled it while you were sleeping, and the town is about 9,000 feet in elevation, and the cabin itself is about ten miles outside of town. Not to worry, we have the perfect gear for the weather, and plenty of food, ammunition and supplies in the cabin. I'm almost glad it's getting this time in the year, because if it was summer or spring we would be out of luck." As he talked, Lace was thinking, her mind going a mile a minute at the current situation.

"Do you really think we'll be safe there, you know, not only from her, but the bikers as well?" Ryder, his best poker face in place, gently squeezed his wife's hand.

"Once we get to the cabin we'll be just fine. It's secluded and with the high balconies it's easy to spot anyone coming towards it, which is exactly what we need. I know they'll come for us at some point, and my hope is that it will be sooner than later. When they find out we've split Santa Barbara that should frustrate them to the point where they will screw up, and either the authorities down there can deal with them, or if they get this far I will. Make no mistake about it, I plan on having some nice little surprises waiting for them, and I will kill any one of them that try to get to you or the kids."

About that time Ryder saw Lacey's eyes shift to the left, indicating that Micah was stirring. "Hey sleepyhead, how you doing back there?" Ryder asked, as the boy leaned forward and placed his head between the two seats.

"I'm good. Where are we?" the boy asked, as they passed by a series of mini marts along the highway.

"Well, we're about two hours from Sacramento, the state capital, and about two hours past that is the cabin." As Ryder was talking, the boy laid his head against the leather seat, as Lacey leaned over to kiss his cheek.

"Can we stop somewhere, cause I really need to pee?" Micah asked, the semi-tense look on his face confirming the boy's words.

"Well, we need to stop for gas, so what say we make it an early dinner break as well? How does pizza sound to everyone?" Ryder had spotted a sign about 15 minutes earlier for a Shakey's Pizza and had recalled the flavorful pizza from his time in San Diego.

"Sounds good to us," Lacey said, as April began to fuss in the back and Joker began to stir. The long trip had to have been very hard on the dog, who was usually very active, but Ryder noticed, he had settled in quite comfortably between all of the gear in back without a single whimper or whine. As Lacey reached back to take the baby from Micah, the smell hit all of them at the same time. Micah began to gag, exaggerating it to a near comical level, causing the couple in front to break out in laughter. Even Joker seemed to take offense, as he scrambled towards the partially open window in back on Micah's side. Ryder spied the sign for the pizza parlor, and quickly made a bee line for the parking lot. Pulling into an empty slot he shut off the engine, as Lacey exited the Jeep, April in tow. When Micah opened his door he and Joker both jumped out, as Ryder went around the back of the rig, calling for Joker. The dog came trotting around, Micah on his heels as Ryder opened the lift back. Rummaging through the sided pocket he found what he was looking for. Unfolding the green harness cover, he held it out for the dog, who slipped his chest comfortably into the garment.

"What's that?" Micah asked him, as Lacey looked over Ryder's shoulder.

"This is a therapy dog vest, and while I don't use it often, it does have its advantages in certain occasions." Lacey understood what he was saying but could see Micah was confused.

"So, it's kind of like lying?" he asked, as Ryder fastened the vest on the sitting dog.

"Well, you know what, it's kind of like telling something to someone that may not be quite true, but you do it because it's in their best interest. Joker is kind of my therapy dog, helping me through some hard times, the same as you, wouldn't you say?" Micah stood for moment, processing the words.

"Yeah, and he has been really helpful to me too," he answered, making Ryder smile. "You see, if I don't put this on him he can't go inside with us, and we need him as much as he needs us, right?" Micah nodded in confirmation, as they walked toward the front of the business. Opening the door, an elderly couple were coming out, and asked if they could pet the beautiful dog. Ryder had nodded, stopping as the man and woman petted the smooth coat. When they had finished and thanked the family, Ryder led them to a table just inside, helped Micah get his seat while Lacey headed towards the lady's room to change her daughter. When they returned, she set the carrier for April on the end, then took her own seat next to Ryder with an unobstructed view of the entrance and the Jeep. As Ryder looked around, a freckle faced young woman approached, the braces on her teeth shining in the well-lit business. "Hi folks, I'm Tracy and I'll be taking your order. Can I start you with some drinks, maybe some ice water or soda?" The young girl's grin was infectious as Lacey and Micah both gave her huge smiles, even Joker seeming to look up at the girl with a canine version of humor.

"You know, I think we'll have a milk for Micah, two iced teas and three waters. Oh, and can I get a small container of water for my therapy dog?" Ryder met the girls gaze directly, and she winked as she turned away. Less than a minute later she returned, carefully balancing a tray with all of the requested items. Setting it down on the table she expertly handed the glasses to each of the family, then picked up the half full paper bowl and knelt down next to Joker. As she set it down and gently rubbed the dogs head, a chubby man with a sour look on his face came striding up, his breathing labored due to the extra weight around his belly.

"Tracy, what are you doing? Get back in there, wash your hands and pick up that order in the window." As she stood up and began to do as told, the obese man smacked her on the backside with a haughty laugh. Ryder looked at Lacey before getting to his feet, but before he could say anything Micah was standing on the wooden bench.

"Hey, you didn't have any right to hit her," he said, his small fists clenched at his side. The manager, seemingly amused by the small boy's reaction, shooed him away and turned around to walk back to the kitchen. "Hey, I'm talking to you," Micah said, his voice becoming more forceful. Other patrons were beginning to look around at the pint-sized David. The manager stopped at the sound of the boy's voice, while Ryder and Lacey sat quiet, watching their son's unusual reaction.

"Son, sit down in that chair right now," the man said, his eyes glaring at Micah, who seemed unfazed. Seeing that the boy had no intentions of doing as told, the manager walked back to the table where Micah stood, still on his perch, when suddenly Joker stood up, a silent guardian to his young charge.

"First off, don't call me son, because I'm not your son. Second, who do you think you are, hitting her like that? Want me to hit you?" he asked, his face growing redder by the moment. Ryder, seeing that the young boy was indeed getting angrier, got to his feet and stepped in front of the man.

"Listen, you better control your boy there before he gets hurt. I don't know what kind of place you think I run here, but we don't put up with dirty animals and mouthy little bastards like that." At the use of the horrible word, Lacey had gotten to her feet, when out of nowhere a muscular man in a khaki shirt and pants stepped in between all of them.

"All right folks, let's settle down and act like adults. If I ever hear you use that language towards any child again, I'll come by after duty and we'll talk out back. Now why don't you take these nice peoples order, get it to go and ring it up as a charitable donation?" The deputy was nose to nose with the manager, who quickly backed down and retreated, with the young waitress returning to take their order. After they had ordered their pizza and salad, the deputy sat down with them, extending his hand. "I'm Mike. Mike Litrell, deputy for El Dorado County." Ryder looked at him, skeptical but yet wanting someone to trust. The deputy closely resembled the late actor James Garner, but with a much heavier build. "I'm Jake. Jake Ryan, this is my wife Elisabeth, our son Tyler and our baby Crystal." Shaking the man's hand, Ryder hated lying and could see the look on Micah's face.

"Well listen, I know a weary traveler, or in your case travelers, when I see them. As my way of apologizing for the rudeness of our local manager, let me offer this- my wife and I run a nice little place down the road about forty miles. It's called The Gables, and we offer the same creature comforts as the big chains without the price tag. I'll call my wife Sheila and let her know you'll be there in, what about an hour? That sound good to you, Tyler?"

Micah was helping his mom with his baby sister and failed to acknowledge the name. The large deputy met Ryders gaze, then rubbed his hands together.

"Okay, well I'll call my missus and tell her to watch for you. It's down on the left-hand side, and you can't miss it. The sign was her idea, just wanted that out there," causing Lacey to laugh out loud. As the deputy walked away, the young waitress returned to their table, a large pizza box and paper sack in hand.

Ryder went to remove his wallet to pay, but the girl laid her hand on his.

"No charge, my manager is paying for this one," she told him, keeping her voice down. "You have a beautiful little girl, and your boy is something else," she continued, as Ryder thanked her. "I told my manager that the next time he touches me, I'm going to break his fingers and sue him for assault." Ryder could tell that the girl was dead serious and handed her a ten-dollar bill for a tip. Gathering up his family, they exited the restaurant and quickly made their way back to the Jeep. Helping Micah in, then Joker, he buckled the boy up then went around to

help Lacey, who was struggling with the seatbelt.
Opening the passenger door, Ryder helped Lacey inside, then completed fastening the baby in securely. Striding around to the driver's side, Ryder climbed in and started the engine, letting it sit for a moment. "Everybody ready?" he asked, putting the Jeep in reverse, looking at Lacey with a *what the hell was that* look on his face as he backed up, then returned to the interstate and headed for their last stop of the night.

Mike Litrell sat in his cruiser, watching the Jeep start down the road. *Who are you really, Jake Ryan?"*

Forty minutes later the road weary family saw the fluorescent sign for THE GABLES, and Ryder entered the half full lot, parking the Jeep towards the back of the property. Getting out, he assisted Micah and Joker, then helped Lacey with the baby. Entering the almost surgically clean office, they were greeted by a woman who looked as if she had been typecast in the role of a welcoming matron in a Disney film. She was average height and weight, medium build, but her face and eyes reflected peace and calm, and maybe a home cooked meal.

"I'll just bet you are Mr. and Mrs. Ryan," the woman said, her smile easing the tension Ryder could feel in his shoulders.

"Well yes, your husband said you had a nice place, and he was spot on." Taking out his wallet he pulled out a driver's license he laid it on the counter, along with three twenty-dollar bills. The woman looked down at the license on the counter, then slid a registration book to him. Ryder quickly filled out the information, then slid it back to the woman, who seemed to be ignoring the cash.

The lady looked down at the money on the unusually clean countertop. "Why don't you pick that up and put it back in your wallet," she said quietly, as the baby began to fuss. Turning around, she picked up a set of room keys and handed them to Ryder. "I put you in number 14, towards the back of the complex so it will be quieter from the interstate noise and all." Ryder picked up the bills and slipped them into his front pocket before speaking.

"Well, thank you very much for everything. I'm not sure why you and your husband are doing this but thank you anyway." Extending his hand to the lady, he shook hers gently before picking up the bags. Before she let go of his hand, the lady looked at Ryder, meeting his gaze directly.

"I have no idea what you're running from, but I can see you're the man to handle it. We serve a continental breakfast starting at 6:00 a.m., so be sure to stop by on your way out." As the family turned to leave the comfort of the office, Micah stopped and looked back at the woman.

"Thank you for everything," he said, his voice sounding more mature than his young face. The woman behind the desk blew him a kiss as they proceeded out the door. Watching them leave, the lady wiped a spot on the countertop, then tore the registration slip in half and ran it through her shredder.

Ryder kept a vigilant eye as they walked toward the room, on the lookout for anything out of the ordinary. There were four other vehicles in the lot besides their blue Jeep, and he scanned the license plates for anything unusual. Two of the cars, a Kia Optima and a red Toyota Rav4, must have been travelling together, as they were both sporting Oklahoma plates. The silver Durango truck looked as if it had been run through a mud bog, with the entire body coated in mud. The Harley Road King looked well used, and the sight of it made Ryder miss his friend Preacher more than he had realized. His momentary melancholia was broken by the sound of Joker whining next to his leg, staring at the motorcycle. "I know boy, I wish he was here too." Unlocking the door, the small group entered the room, as the smell of clean hit their noses.

Once they had entered the room, Lacey saw the exhaustion on her son's face, and realized she too was drained from the long day. Ryder had placed the bags on the floor before turning on the bathroom lights and looking inside. While he was checking things out, Lacey had undressed April, then laid her on the first of two queen sized beds. Micah had kicked off his shoes and removed his jacket, while Joker took up position in front of the door. "Okay everybody, let's grab a bite and get ready to call it a night." Ryder shut the bathroom door and checked the locks on the front door, happy to see that they were indeed sturdy and well secured. Micah was already laying on the far bed next to the baby, eating a slice of pizza as April dozed, with Joker laying in front of the door, as always on guard. Lacey was sitting on the edge of the second bed, and patted the spot next to her, the dinner already forgotten.

"So, this is nice," she said, a sly smile on her face as Ryder took his place. Exhaling deeply, he looked at the two children on the other bed, and a sad smile crossed his face. Lacey reached down and took his hand and started to speak, but Ryder stopped her with a finger to his lips. Silently they got to their feet and went around the bed and into the larger than expected bathroom. Closing the door softly, but keeping it open just a crack to hear the kids, he leaned against the sink, while Lacey sat on the edge of the bathtub.

"Okay mister, where did that credit card and license come from with the elusive Jack Ryan's name on it?" Ryder let his eyes meet hers and saw the exhaustion in those beautiful green eyes.

"That, my love, is called always being prepared. I actually have a variety of alter egos that I go by. I have credit cards, drivers' licenses and even social security cards in a variety of names, and I guarantee they will stand up to scrutiny, even up to and including the credit reporting agencies." Lacey let a small laugh escape her as she stood up to hug her man.

"Well, well, will the mysteries with you never cease?" she asked, sliding her arms around Ryder's neck. Pressing into him, Lacey felt powerless to stop herself as she began to kiss the side of his neck and jawline, along the same path as the scar.

Ryder closed his eyes for a moment enjoying the waves of pleasure coursing through his exhausted body. He could smell the perfume Lacey always wore, and as she continued her tracing along his neck, he let his hands slide down and begin to caress her buttocks through the jeans. Pulling her to him, he could feel her responding, when suddenly April began to cry. Ryder held tightly to his wife for a moment, letting the intense feelings begin to subside. Kissing her mouth gently, he whispered, "We can pick this up tomorrow at the cabin." Lacey, her passion being squelched for the moment, used her tongue to lightly tease her husband, then turned and opened the door to attend to her baby girl.

Chapter 7

Preacher laid on the floor, the carpet soft against his face, watching the two dogs slowly sniff around the living area, using their canine senses to acclimate to their new home. Bella, the slightly larger of the two, was a little more aggressive in her searches, while Sophie, the younger, seemed to approach each area as if expecting something bad to happen. Her nose began to twitch as she neared Preacher's massive leg, and he stayed still to avoid scaring the Corgi. Cindy stood in the doorway to the kitchen, watching the two dogs interact with her newlywed husband, and a warm smile crossed her face. How someone so large could be so gentle and compassionate to two creatures he had just met was amazing.

    Softly, to avoid spooking the dogs, Cindy whispered, "Keep still, because Bella's coming up behind you." Preacher maintained his position as the two dogs began to explore the massive form laying on the rug. Sophie began to sniff his shoe, while Bella poked her nose into Preacher's beard and began to ruffle the white mane, causing Preacher to laugh, startling the pair of explorers. Reaching down, he gently stroked the soft coat of the smaller dog, his fingers tenderly massaging Sophie's head, while Bella came around front and renewed her exploration of the beard. As Cindy watched, the phone rang, and reluctantly she went into the kitchen to answer it.

"Hello?" Hello?" Assuming it was a wrong number, she started to hang up, when suddenly she heard a man's voice.

"Yes, can I speak with Preacher please?" the man asked, as Cindy tried to recognize the voice.

"Sure, hold on. Can I tell him who this is?"

"Yes, my name is Officer Stan Williams with the Santa Barbara Police Department." Cindy's stomach dropped as she hollered for Preacher, who had both dogs in his ham sized hands, as if juggling them. Getting to his feet he quickly went into the kitchen area, handing off his two new friends to his wife.

"Hello, this is Preacher, can I help you? Yes, I own the Manatees Cove down on the beach. What can I do for you?"

The man on the other end of the line spoke, a tone of authority in his voice. "Mr. Preacher, we were alerted to a break-in at your business about thirty minutes ago, and we need you to come down and give us a hand to see what may be missing." Preacher felt the old anger stirring inside him but forced it down to keep a level head before responding.

"Sure, I'll be down in about ten minutes. Thank you for the call." Hanging up the phone he set it back on its base as Cindy stopped him on his way out.

"What happened?" Preacher paused for a moment as he slipped on his leather jacket.

"Oh hell, somebody broke into the shop, and the PD needs me to come down and figure out what's missing." Cindy looked dismayed at the news, and Preacher reached over to pull her and the two dogs close. "It'll be fine, I just sent in the insurance payment, so that won't be a problem. I'll be back in a bit." Kissing his wife, then rubbing the two dog's heads, he took his keys from the wall hanger and went into the garage, opening the large door as he warmed up the Harley. Straddling the motorcycle, he saw Cindy standing in the doorway.

The woman stood watching as her man took off into the night, then closed the garage door and went back into the house. "Come on girls, let's go outside," she hollered, the two dogs running into the kitchen. Opening the French doors, Cindy let the puppies into the back yard, then took a seat in one of the chairs, when suddenly they came running back full steam, bumping into the small table next to Cindy. She decided to let them play for a few minutes and leaned back in her chair.

The night air was cool as Preacher accelerated down the highway toward the beach, while inside he was seething with anger at the thought of someone breaking into and violating his sacred shop. Preacher approached the turnoff that would take him to his shop, and when he exited the highway immediately spied his business, but no sign of any police cars. Quickly pulling up behind the shop, he pulled out his cell phone and dialed 911. "Yes, I was called earlier by one of your officers about a break-in at my place of business. Yes ma'am, it's the Manatees Cove down on Ocean Front Boulevard. No, I got the call about fifteen minutes ago. Are you sure? All right then, I guess maybe it was a prank. No that's fine, I'll just go and check it myself, and if anything is out of place I'll call back. Thank you so much." Hanging up the phone, Preacher dismounted from his bike and approached the back door of the shop, keeping his eyes peeled for anything amiss.

The back door seemed secure, and stepping up onto the back porch area he disarmed the alarm's system, then unlocked the back door and slowly opened, his eyes peeled in the semi-darkness.

The two pups were wearing out, as apparent by the way they had both flopped down next to Cindy on the patio. Reaching down, she rubbed each dog's fur, loving the feel of the soft fur. Stroking the coats, a feeling of melancholy washed over her, as she thought back to that time so many years earlier, when a young teenage girl had done what she thought best and given up a new-born baby for adoption. Chelsea had been a beautiful, dark-haired girl, and when Cindy had found out she was pregnant at first she had been thrilled. As the pregnancy evolved though, she had begun to accept that, at nineteen she was not going to be able to care for her unborn child the way it deserved, and she and her mother had approached a local child service agency about placing her for adoption. They had been very helpful in locating a loving, stable family who was financially and emotionally able to support and love her daughter. That July morning when her water had broken, Cindy's mom had called the caseworker at the agency and informed her of the impending birth. Cindy's mom had driven her daughter to the local hospital, and six hours later a beautiful little girl came into the world. The adoptive parents, with their five-year-old son by their side, had stood, staring in amazement at their new daughter and sister. They had agreed to let Cindy hold the baby after the birth, and they had also agreed on the name Chelsea. Cindy's mother had sat beside the bed, her daughter holding the newborn, and they both began to cry. When the nurse had arrived several minutes later, Cindy had slowly held the baby up, kissing her forehead as she whispered a soft goodbye, and her mother wiped away a tear from her own cheek.

Cindy's daydreaming was broken by the high-pitched yelp of one of the dogs, as Sophie began digging at her hindquarters. Picking up the Corgi, Cindy gently searched the area, finding a small burr under the thick coat. Carefully she removed it, while Sophie chewed at the irritated area. "Okay you two, time to call it a night," she said, setting Sophie down next to her sister.

Getting to her feet Cindy realized that it had been nearly half an hour since Preacher had left the house, and as she opened the French doors to allow herself and her companions in, she reached for her cell phone. Dialing his number, she watched the pair heading for their water bowls, then heard her husband as his voice mail kicked in.

Preacher walked through the shop, looking for any signs of a break-in or vandalism. He opened the front door and walked the perimeter of the business, stopping to pick up several pieces of trash that the ocean breeze had blown in. As he deposited them in the city supplied receptacle, a disturbing thought hit him, and he ran back into the shop, quickly locking the front door and engaging the alarm system as he exited out the back. Taking his cell phone from his belt he quickly dialed his home number as he climbed aboard the Harley, waiting like a silent, faithful steed.

Cindy had put the two pups into their large, wire framed crate for the night, allowing them to lick her fingers as if saying good night to the woman. Placing the sheet over the enclosure, she retrieved her cell phone and went back out to the patio, took a seat and dialed Preachers number again. As she did, she saw that the message awaiting light was flashing on the phone. Quickly she pressed 7 to listen to the message, then heard her husband's voice. As she listened to the message, her heart began to beat rapid fire, and her chest began to feel tight. Cradling the phone between her shoulder and her ear, she half walked, half ran down the hallway into the master bedroom, where she took the Beretta 9mm pistol from her nightstand. When the message was over, she slipped the phone into her front pocket and went back into the front room area, when suddenly a loud pounding shook the front door. Chambering a round, Cindy clicked off the safety as the loud noise persisted and the dogs began to bark. With the gun in her right hand, she reached across her body and pulled the cell phone out of her pocket, quietly dialing 911 as she heard a man's voice on the front stoop.

"There are two men trying to break into my house," she whispered, when, without warning, several shots rang out into the door frame, the front bay window shattered, and a jelly jar container landed on the carpet, igniting a blaze of fire as it rolled against the sofa. Dropping the phone, Cindy ran into the kitchen and took the ever-present fire extinguisher from its nook by the sink, then went back to try and douse the flames before the fire spread. Pulling the pin, she began to sweep the nozzle across the base of the flames, when suddenly several more shots rang out, and she felt an instant burning sensation in her side. Looking down she saw the rapidly spreading stain across her shirt and began to feel lightheaded. As she heard the sound of a motorcycle engine in the dark, she fought to keep spraying the foam onto the fire, then felt her knees buckling, while in the background the puppies were barking fiercely. As she dropped she saw a large man burst through the front door, a gun in hand. Before she could say anything darkness enveloped her, and her head hit the floor.

The paramedics gently loaded the gurney into the ambulance, and Preacher fought to keep his composure. Cindy's face was ghostly white as they prepared to depart, and despite wanting to ride with her, the police had insisted he stay with them to explain what had taken place.

"Mr. Murrell, we need to find out what the hell happened here. You say you got a call from someone claiming to be a police officer, telling you your business had been burglarized. When you get there you find nothing out of place, but when you arrive back home you see two men on motorcycles in front of your house, shooting at it. Now, we have one dead piece of biker trash, a second on the run and your wife wounded. Why in the hell would two pieces of Disciple's garbage choose to shoot your wife? I know you have a license for that piece you carry, but I still need to see it, and we'll need to take the gun, at least for now." The middle-aged policeman, who knew Preacher from the shop and his charity works, had just summarized the events, but he could also see there was more to the story than met the eyes. He could tell there was something else untold behind Preachers eyes, and he was bound to find out what it was. For now though, he decided to let the man go check on his wife.

"Listen, I'm going to call you in the morning, and we are going to get to the bottom of this, regardless of whether you want to or not. I know there is something you aren't telling me, but for now go check on Cindy. I can take care of the pups for you, so don't worry about them."

"Thanks Brian, I appreciate it. Call me tomorrow on my cell." Handing the man his permit to carry a concealed weapon, he then pulled the gun from his waistband and removed the clip, then ejected a single shell before turning it over. Leaving the officer to his duty, Preacher went back into the house, the smell of smoke and the red stain on the carpet both causing his eyes to water. Preacher went to where the dogs sat, watching the unfolding events in their new home. Reaching into the cage, he touched the two dogs, trying to soothe them from the noise and activity. Bella and Sophie both sat still, as if knowing this was not the time for fun and games. Preacher caressed both dogs for a moment, then went out into the garage and started the Mustang. Going back inside, he stopped by the bedroom, taking a .40 caliber Smith and Wesson from his closet, loaded a clip and slid it into his ankle holster. Leaving the bedroom, saw the policeman counting bullet holes in the window and door. "Be sure and lock up as best you can when you guys are done. I'll be back later." Turning around he went back into the garage and climbed into Cindy's car, put the car into gear, then backed carefully out of the garage.

When he arrived at St. Mary's fifteen minutes later, he spotted an empty parking space, and expertly maneuvered the sports car into the place. Climbing out, he went into the large lobby, spotting a woman at a desk. "Yes, they brought my wife in about a half an hour ago after being shot, and I need to know where she is." He could feel himself wanting to lose control and fought down the urge. The doe eyed woman behind the desk appeared sympathetic as she spoke.

"What's your wife's name sir?" she asked, her voice soft and flowing, and Preacher felt his emotions slowing down.

"Cindy Murrell," he told her, leaning against the counter for support, both mental and physical. The woman's fingers flew across the keyboard, then she looked up. "Mr. Murrell, your wife is in the emergency room right now, so let me get someone to show you where that is." Dialing a number, the woman reached up and patted the large man's slightly shaking hand. "She'll be fine," the woman told him, as Preacher met her gaze.

Before he could respond, a young man in burgundy scrubs appeared, a soft smile on his face. "Are you Mr. Murrell?" he asked, a slight Filipino accent to his voice. Preacher nodded, and the young man took his elbow and slowly led him across the lobby and towards his injured wife.

Using his badge, the young assistant led Preacher through the double doors, and into a room where a nurse looked up, her eyes meeting Preachers.

"Mr. Murrell, my name is Tami, and I'm the triage nurse. Your wife is back in the trauma room with our doctor and the surgeon being evaluated. All we know for sure is that she has a bullet wound to her right side, and it appears as if the bullet nicked her kidney, causing some internal bleeding. I saw her less than five minutes ago, and she was conscious, in pain of course but conscious. We're giving her what we can for pain, but also have to be able to get information from her. Now, does your wife have any allergies to any medications? Does she take any medication? Does she have any more medical problems? As she asked the questions, she tried to get them out before the man fell apart.

Preacher leaned on his folded hands before answering. "No, no allergies, she only takes Norvasc for her blood pressure, which is well controlled. No other major issues-can I go see her now, please?" He hated to ask, feeling as if he was begging, but he desperately wanted to see his wife.

As the nurse escorted Preacher down the hallway, he could feel his heart pounding in his chest. As they neared the emergency room, he was acutely aware of the urgent pace kept by the staff. "Over here Mr. Murrell," the nurse said, taking him by the elbow. Leading him into the bay, he saw the physicians standing next to his wife as she lay on the gurney. Preacher quickly walked to her side and took the offered chair from the nurse. Gently picking up her left hand, he raised it and placed a soft kiss on it. "Oh my God honey, I'm so sorry this happened," he said softly, as tears begin to fill his eyes. Looking at his wife, he smiled at her as her hand softly stroked his.

Chapter 8

Summer watched as the RV was loaded with supplies for the eight-hour trip. The scorching Arizona sun was beating down upon her, but the thought that she was back on the right track put a smile on her face.

The quartet had arrived early that morning at the predestined location after the long, dusty drive from Nogales, and true to his word Jean- Pierre had delivered admirably. The 36-foot vehicle looked brand-new, had all current tags and plates, and best of all, all the latest high-tech gadgets installed. There was room for six or seven people, even though only four plus the driver were making the trip to California. The prearranged driver, a quiet, non-descript young white man in his late 20s seemed perfect for the role of driver. Summer, Scab, Dingo Dave and one other named T-Bone were making the trip, and Summer had been more than pleased to discover a hollowed-out section in the floor of the RV where two or three people could easily hide. The blonde woman walked around the vehicle, then returned to the door where the three bikers waited. "Okay guys, let's load up and get headed out. I want to be in San Diego by tonight." The young driver climbed in around the waiting people, set down in the cab and started the powerful Titan engine. Summer carefully climbed in, trying to avoid bumping her hands and settled in beside the driver in the large captain's chair. The other three entered and took up seats in the main area, as Dingo Dave stretched his long legs out on the leather sofa, and Scab and T-Bone took up residence on the other. Summer looked at the young driver and was more than pleased with Jean-Pierre's choice. The tanned, blonde haired young man could easily blend in anywhere, and as Summer stared at him, he turned his head to look back at his companion. Smiling at the attractive woman, he spoke for only the second time today. "Hi, I'm Gary," he said, extending his hand to shake Summer's, then realized she was not returning he gesture.

"I'm sorry, I don't shake hands. My hands were badly injured a while back, and still cause me a great deal of pain." The young man looked genuinely sad at the information, then returned his attention to the highway. Once they were headed west on I-8 which would take them straight into San Diego, he set the cruise control, then looked back at Summer.

"So how do you know these guys in back? You don't look anything like them, and if you don't mind me saying so, I don't get it? A beautiful woman like you travelling with three dirty bikers seems like an odd pairing." As he spoke he was smacked from behind, his head jolted forward, as Dingo Dave looked at the driver.

"Who the fuck you calling a dirty biker, you scrawny beach bum?" he growled, as Summer shot the biker a hard look. Dave slowly retreated, but not before he gave the drivers head another smack. Gary shook his head, then returned his attention to the road and decided it might be wiser just to drive for the next eight hours in silence, but damn, that blonde next to him was sweet. Summer looked at the young man and gave him her best smile before she spoke.

"I know it seems strange, the four of us travelling together, but trust me when I say they are actually very useful in my current situation. I'm meeting up with their boss in San Diego, and they are helping me find someone who I desperately need to find." The young man had his gaze fixed on the road ahead, the back of his head still smarting.

"Well, as long as I get paid, then I guess I shouldn't care why or who you travel with. Now, it should be about eight hours to the

California border, and this little baby here will keep the Highway patrol off our butts." Patting the radar detector mounted on the dash he continued. "Now, why don't you go join your travelling buddies, and let me concentrate on the road." Summer was a little taken aback at being dismissed so rudely, a feat which in previous days would have resulted in the immediate and very painful termination of the young man. However, in her current predicament, she had to be flexible and willing to let things slide. Standing up, she stepped back into the main living area, where T-Bone was sound asleep stretched across the full length of the sofa, snoring loudly. Scab, the crusty little creature who had been her knight in shining armor back at The Ranch, was playing a hand of solitaire, while Dave was in the only restroom. Summer pulled up a seat on the smaller of the two sofas and carefully retrieved a laptop from a drawer under the bench. Placing it on the small Formica countertop, she opened it and gingerly entered her password. When the screen popped up, she placed the headphones onto her head, adjusted the mouthpiece and began to speak.

Jean-Pierre had been overly thoughtful when he made the arrangements for Summer, making sure that every detail was considered. He had even sent the latest version of a hands-free dictation program, knowing how much her hands pained her. When Summer had opened the package, she had been impressed at the man's thoughtfulness, then had laughed out loud when she realized that 75 million dollars did indeed buy a lot of consideration. The hands-free set was extremely useful and helpful, and Summer saw several emails from San Diego. "Open emails," she whispered, as the computer obliged. Using her index finger, she gently scrolled down, reading the first one. It was from Jake, the club president in San Diego, telling her that they had a lead on the man and woman she was after. It also stated that he wanted to up the price of their deal to five million dollars. Summer shook her head, anticipating that this was bound to happen when you dealt with greedy scumbags like the Disciples. "I'm fine with the amount, but I need to make sure that everything is ready when we get there. I don't want to waste any more time, so the five million is contingent on you being ready. If not, then the whole deal is done, and I'll find some other biker trash to help me out." As she dictated, she felt like she was finally going to fulfill her destiny, which had been so rudely shattered by the bitch and her husband. The black hatred she felt towards them had no comparison, but the boy, now that was something different. She could still feel him when she went deep into her meditation, and she also knew that he could feel Summer as well. When she was done with Lacey and the bastard, the boy would be hers, as would the little girl child, her sweet, innocent niece.

Returning to her emails, she read several others, and smiled when she saw the information that had been provided to her. Looking at the screen, Summer closed her eyes for a moment and accepted how good it was to be her. She now knew the location of the bitch, and the source of the information was even more happiness inducing. Using a mapping program, she checked the mileage between San Diego and the last place Lacey would ever know, seeing that the I-395 route would bring them right up the southeast section of the small town to where the cabin was. She figured it would take about ten hours to get from San Diego to the mountain cabin, and she wanted to make sure no one got there before she did. She wanted the first (and last) face the black-haired cunt ever saw to be hers, smiling as she took her children. The drive would give her plenty of time to plan everything to the last detail, and Summer quickly dictated another email to Jake, with a detailed list of what she wanted upon their arrival in town. She would need several of his men on bikes, plus two in the SUV, but the current driver would be left out and sent back to Tucson. Summer was exhausted with the day's events, so she signed out of the computer, carefully placed it back underneath and got to her feet. "Scab my sweet, I'm going to take a nap. Would you please make sure no one disturbs me?" The dirty man looked at her with something like love on his face, collected his cards and stood up.

"I'll make sure you're left to rest," he told her, almost bowing in deference to the woman. Summer made a mental note to tell Jake that Scab was to be left unharmed, indefinitely, no exceptions. Summer smiled at him and blew him a kiss as she disappeared through the curtains and carefully laid down on the queen-sized bed. After spending so much time in Nogales, the RV and especially the soft bed were like four-star accommodations, and she let her head gently touch the pillow, her mind going back to the days following The Ranch.

They had been taken back to the barn where the bikers had stored their gear and had made a phone call back to the club house. After they had explained what had happened, and told them they needed a ride home, the club had made arrangements with one of their members named Swamp Beast. He was a former Army Blackhawk pilot, and he had been dispatched to a small airstrip to pick up the remaining members, the doctor and the woman. When he had arrived, they realized he had only room for four passengers, and loaded Summer, Dr. Rudan, Scab and Pete, leaving the others to load up the bikes in the pickups and make their way back. Summer had passed out during the bumpy takeoff, the elderly doctor holding her in his arms as they climbed to a safe altitude. The flight had taken nearly two hours to Nogales, where Swamp Beast had been instructed to take them. Dave, the club vice-president had immediately taken off to meet them in the dusty Mexican town. When the plane had finally landed, Summer had been in excruciating pain, the bone ends bumping together painfully on the dirt landing strip. Members from the Tucson chapter had met them at the airfield, and quickly and quietly loaded them into a waiting van and took them to the series of dirt buildings where, Summer had been treated like royalty. The old doctor had made sure she was handled gently, and then he began trying to repair the shattered bones. Having only local anesthesia and alcohol to numb the pain, he carefully re-attached the nearly severed thumb, set the radius and ulna in both forearms as best he could, and placed a number of stitches in the gunshot wound to her scalp. One of the bikers from Tucson was a former Army medic and had access to a variety of pain medications to assist Dr. Rudan. When she awoke, Summer was in more pain than she thought humanly possible, and only the heavily muscled men were able to keep her restrained. Dr. Rudan had given her small dosage of Fentanyl, then forced several Percocet down her throat, followed by a sip of dirty water, and within minutes the narcotics had taken effect. The men had cleared out of the room, satisfied to occupy their time with the local girls who were at their disposal.

Summer's eyes had opened that evening, just as the sun was setting over the Mexican desert, and when she saw her bandaged arms and hand, she felt the pain leaving her body. In its place was an emotional thirst, a quench a desire for revenge against the bitch that had torn her precious hands apart. Looking down, Summer focused on the left thumb, heavily wrapped in thick dressing, and closed her eyes as she tried to move the damaged digit. Slowly the dressing began to move, painfully but moving, and a smile crossed her face. "Bitch," she thought to herself, "I'm coming for you, and I will take everything you cherish, just like you did to me."

Chapter 9

Ryder kept his eyes focused on the dirt road, watching for anything out of the ordinary. The trip to Cedars Pass from Sacramento had been uneventful, the family even enjoying an early morning continental breakfast with the deputy and his wife before leaving. The pastries had been fresh baked, the juice ice cold and the coffee fresh and hot, and for the first time since taking off on the run, Ryder had allowed himself to relax. Micah had indulged in a bowl of Cheerios with the deputy, matching him spoon for spoon with the tasty cereal. April had taken her bottle, then dozed off, and Lacey had even let her guard down, letting the elderly woman hold and rock the sleeping infant. Joker had excused himself to go outside, and when he came back inside the woman had a warm piece of toast with peanut butter waiting for him, which he graciously accepted.

When they were finished Ryder had excused himself to use the restroom, while Mrs. Litrell and her husband freshened up the area for the other guests. When Ryder returned, he and Micah had taken their bags out to the Jeep, loaded them in and rearranged them to make room for Joker. The German shepherd jumped into his place, his eyes seeming to scan the local area for problems, Lacey and April came outside, the deputy in tow, settled April into her car seat, then Micah. Lacey got in and fastened her seatbelt, then saw the officer on the other side talking to Ryder. Ryder shook the man's hand before getting into the rig, then closed the door. Lacey and Micah waved to the man, who almost seemed sad to see the family leaving. "What were you two talking about?" she asked, as Ryder pulled out onto the side road and headed for I-50 East.

"He was just wishing us well and told me if we needed anything to call this number." Handing Lacey a manila card, Ryder carefully merged onto the interstate, praying that they were still on the right course.

They entered Cedar Pass about an hour and a half later, the sides of the road showing signs of an early snow fall. The town was small, but very neat and tidy, and Ryder hoped that maybe it would stay calm, if and when the storm hit. They had stopped at a small hardware store, and Ryder looked at Lacey. "I'm just going to run in for a couple of items, and I want you to stay here with the kids." Lacey started to argue, then saw the look on her husband's face and knew it was futile.

"What do you need from a hardware store?" she asked, as April began to stir in the back, while Micah read one of his books.

"You wouldn't like it if I told you," he replied, an uneasy on his handsome face. Opening the door, he climbed out before she could ask any more questions. She was comforted by the weight of the pistol in her purse, and she held it tightly to her belly as she waited for Ryder to return. Opening her door, Lacey got out and opened the passenger door behind hers, wanting to check April for a change. Micah closed his book loudly, catching Lacey off guard, and making the boy laugh.

"Mom, what does na eíste prosektikoí o gios mou mean?" he asked her, as Lacey looked directly at him.

"What does what mean?" she asked him, the foreign words sounding very odd coming from a young boy.

"I heard them in a dream last night, and I just wondered what they meant," he repeated, as Lacey finished with her daughter.

"Well, right off the top of my head I don't know but maybe we can look them up later." As she climbed back into her seat,

Lacey saw Ryder coming out of the store, a medium sized cardboard box in his arms. He stopped by the side of the Jeep and removed some rope from the box, then slid it onto the roof, tying one end to the corner of the rack, then moving around the vehicle and tying it in all four spots. Dusting off his hands he got into the Jeep, as Lacey stared at him.

"So, want to tell me what's in the box?" she asked, seeing the slight movement of his eyes towards the back seat. Catching his signal, Lacey buckled up as Ryder did as well, as he looked around the area, saw nothing to raise any alarms, then pulled out onto the nearly empty street and headed for the cabin and safety.

Twenty minutes later Ryder spotted the small side road that Darius had told him would lead them to the cabin. He spotted the orange marking on the base of the large pine tree, which if the usual amount of snow been present would have been rendered invisible. Slowing the Jeep, he made a right turn, thankful they had four-wheel drive. The rig handled the extremely bumpy road with ease, as Micah stared out the side window and Joker did the same from the rear window. The road was lined with massive oaks and pine trees, manzanita and scrub brush, but there were also a variety of colorful native flowers still in bloom. "Oh mom, look at those orange ones over there," Micah hollered excitedly, as Lacey spied the source of his enthusiasm.

"Those are California poppies," she told him, as he looked at her strangely.

"How can they be California poppies if we aren't in California anymore?" Lacey and Ryder both held back their laughter at his innocence despite everything.

Fifteen minutes later Ryder spotted a large metal gate and stopped the vehicle. Taking a small can from the jockey box of the Jeep, he exited the car, pulled a single key out of his pants pocket and approached the barrier. Removing the cap from the can, he sprayed the deicer on the lock, grateful that Darius had added the small container to their shopping list. Inserting the key, it easily popped open, and he pulled the gate open easily. Lacey had already gone around and gotten behind the wheel, pulling the vehicle through the opening. Ryder pulled the barrier closed and relocked it, then went back to reclaim his driver's position. Ten minutes later the large cabin came into view, and Lacey whistled under her breath at the gorgeous structure. Micah sat, wide eyed as well.

Driving around the back of the home to the oversized three car garage, Ryder pulled the Jeep inside the middle bay, using the remote that Darius had also blessed him with. The family quickly got out and began looking around the area, as April began to fuss again. "Okay folks, first things first. We need to unload the Jeep into the house and bring in some wood, so let's chop chop." The unusual term seemed to tickle Micah, who began to make chopping motions with his hands.

Ryder opened the back hatch of the Jeep, and Joker immediately jumped down and headed for the nearby forested area. Several minutes later he reappeared, a much more relaxed look on his canine face. Ryder handed Micah a bag to take inside, then a slightly heavier one to Lacey, then lifted the last two out and set them on the ground. Waiting for his wife and son to enter the house, he quickly took the larger of the two bags into the garage, setting it on a work bench in the neatly organized room. Walking back to the Jeep, he picked up the last bag and went into the house, amazed at how beautiful the location was. He had entered on the main floor, walking through the large, expensively decorated kitchen and into the dining area. He could hear Lacey and Micah upstairs, and the sound of their voices made him happy despite the fact that he was about to burst their bubbles. Making his way up the ornately carved staircase, he found Lacey changing April's diaper in one of the master suites, while Micah explored the second floor. When Lacey was done, Ryder had her take a seat on the four-poster bed, then hollered for Micah. The boy came out of one of the two large bathrooms, a grin on his face. "Man, this bathtub is huge. It's so big I bet Joker and I could swim laps in it."

"Micah, come here for a moment please," Ryder said, getting his mindset back on why they were here. Micah entered the room and jumped up on the bed, as Joker came trotting down the hall. "I'm glad you're all excited about how beautiful this place is, but we need to remember why we're here. First off, I think we will be better suited if we take up rooms on the first floor. It's easier in and out, in case we have to, you know, make a quick exit." He was trying his best to not scare Micah, but at the same time he wanted to make sure he realized how serious this situation was. "Second, no one, and I mean one goes outside alone, and that means you too buddy." Staring at his partner, he saw a look in the dog's eyes that, despite common thinking, showed complete understanding of the words being spoken. Their eyes locked, and he saw nothing but courage and love in the brown eyes of his canine sidekick. "Third, and this is the most important, when I say something it needs to be done immediately and without question. I don't mean to sound like a drill sergeant, but it has to be this way."

Lacey could see the intensity in her husband's eyes, and instantly recalled the same look back in the Vegas desert. She understood the necessity and would do whatever her husband said. Unless, of course, he told her not to kill that blonde bitch that was hunting them. In that case, she would be forced to disobey his orders.

Micah sat listening to Ryder speaking and found himself growing more excited. He may not have been full grown yet, but just let anyone try and hurt his mom or little sister and watch out. As he had these thoughts he caught Joker staring at him, his head slightly cocked to the right. "Micah, do you understand what I'm saying?" Ryder asked, as he caught the dog's gaze locked on the boy.

"Sure, yeah," the boy responded, standing up extending his hand to Ryder.

Shaking the boy's hand, Ryder said "Okay, let's get our gear stored downstairs, then Micah, you and Joker can help me gather some firewood." The three of them gathered their bags, Ryder carrying his daughter in one arm, Joker right at his side as they descended the stairs. "Micah, why don't you take the one over here, below the stairs, and your mom and I can bunk in the one right over here." As he spoke, April began to fuss, and Ryder walked into the large bedroom and laid her down on the goose down comforter, as Lacey came in. Ryder looked to make sure Micah could not hear, then unzipped one of the bags. "I don't want you anywhere in this house without a gun handy. I'll put one in the kitchen in the breadbox near the sink, out of Micah's reach, and another one in the end table closest to the bay window. Keep yours with you all the time, no matter what. I'm going to take Micah out tomorrow and show him how to use one also, and no arguments." Lacey could see the old Ryder speaking, the one who had done unspeakable things in unnamed countries and was grateful that he was theirs.

"Okay, fair enough, but you be careful with him out there, you get me?" Ryder smiled at her and winked, then turned his attention to his fussing daughter. Picking her up, he sniffed, not detecting a need for another change. Gently he rocked her for a few minutes, as Lacey unpacked the few things they would need. When she was done, Ryder walked out of his room and over to where Micah was, noticing proudly that the boy had not unpacked anything but his toothbrush and a set of pajamas. "All settled in?" Ryder asked, as Micha turned, a little surprised at Ryders sudden appearance.

"Sure am. I figured since we don't want to get caught with our guard down, I better leave most everything packed." Ryder gently cupped the boy's face, turning it up to his.

"Great job. What say tomorrow you and I go out behind the barn, and I'll teach you to use a pistol?" The boy could barely contain his excitement, and Ryder felt his love for the boy grow a little more. "Okay, let's finish up here, then maybe you and your mom can make some dinner for us while Joker and I check out the property?"

Lacey stood at the stove, cooking a pot of chili and hot dogs for their first night in the cabin. She had allowed Micah to carefully slice up the hot dogs into bite size chunks, then add them to the pot while she tended to April in her carrier. While they cooked dinner, Ryder and Joker had gone out the front of the house, the man wanting to get a feel for the layout. Standing on the front deck he saw that there were a number of windows in the front of the house, mostly on the first floor, but some on the second, and realized they could be potential security breaches. Walking the perimeter of the large cabin with the dog at his side, he felt an increased sense of comfort by his presence. They then returned to the Jeep and Ryder removed the cardboard box from the top. Carrying it into the garage, he set it on one of the large workbenches and carefully withdrew several of the items, laying them out. There were two dozen flares of the roadside hazard type, a dozen metal spikes such as would be used to set up a tent, a spool of heavy-duty baling wire and a larger spool of razor wire. Going over in his mind his survey of the house, he removed a notepad and a black marker from the backpack next to him as Joker laid down, facing the double doors, then Ryder began sketching the house and surrounding areas.

When Micah came up behind him he jumped, not realizing he had been at work for nearly an hour and was a little angry at the boy being out there by himself, Joker looking sheepish at having dozed off also.

"Micah, we need to talk." As Ryder spoke, he wanted to make sure his fear did come not out as anger at the young boy yet wanted him to understand the seriousness of the situation.

Micah looked up at him, and Ryder picked him up and set him on the work bench, eye to eye. "Okay, here's the rules. One, remember we never leave the house by ourselves. Two, we never leave April by herself, not even for a moment. Three, you never, and I mean never touch any of the guns in the house." Pausing for a moment, Ryder looked the boy square in the face. Micah cocked his head slightly to the right before speaking.

"I understand the rules, and I won't break any of them. However, you came out here by yourself, and Mom asked me to come out and get you. Isn't that breaking the rules?" The boyish face was dead serious, and Ryder had no choice but to nod his head.

"You know what. You're absolutely right. I broke the rules, and so did your mom. What do you think our punishment should be?

Doing the dishes? Changing April's dirty diapers? Picking up after Joker poops?" The boy smiled, a sight that warmed Ryder's heart, and he picked up the boy in his arms. As they headed towards the house, they could smell the chili cooking, and Ryder let the boy down, as they raced for the house. Joker stood in the large doorway of the shop, his eyes locked on the retreating man and boy. Suddenly his nose caught the scent of the food, and he padded in the direction of the house, a low growl emanating from his throat.

Sitting at the large wooden bench that served as a dinner table, the family enjoyed each other's company, even Joker laying by Lacey's feet as she fed her daughter. Before the food was dished out, Ryder looked at his family, a serious look on his face. "Guys, I want to talk about something before we eat. I know we don't usually say grace before we eat, but with the current set of events, I was thinking maybe we could say a blessing. It sure can't hurt to have someone on our side, and I think maybe having God looking out for us might be just the edge we need." Lacey looked at her husband, as a smile crossed her lovely, but tired face.

"You know what, I think you're right. Maybe now is the time to ask for some blessings, and to show how grateful we are for all that we have been given, and for what we've been through. I think it's a great idea honey." Reaching over, she took Micah's left hand in her right hand, her left in Ryder's, their arms touching April's carrier. Ryder even moved his foot to the left to let it rest against his furry partner and friend.

Bowing their heads, Ryder began to speak, feeling bad for how long it had been since he had prayed. "Dear Lord, we thank You for the food before us, for each other and we ask that You protect each of us as we endure these coming trials. We know that You watch over us each day, but I just ask, please, that You keep us all safe, especially our precious children. They are truly gifts from You, and we thank You for them. Amen." Finishing the prayer, Ryder gently squeezed the two hands he was holding, as Joker moved against his leg. Micah picked up his spoon and took a bite of the aromatic dinner, then looked at Ryder.

"Listen, I agree with your rules, but please tell me I don't have to go to the bathroom with one of you." Lacey looked at her son, then her husband, and they both broke out in a loud, almost raucous laughter that she hoped would see them through the coming days and weeks.

Chapter 10

"Honey, would you like cheddar or Monterey Jack on your sandwich?" Preacher stood at the granite countertop, ready to slice serval thick pieces of cheese for the grilled cheese, the perfect accoutrement to the slowly simmering chicken noodle soup on the stove. Not hearing anything from his wife in the bedroom, he turned off the stove and laid the knife down, walking out of the large kitchen and down the long hallway. Nearing the partially open doors to the master suite, his ears were filled with the soft sound of her snoring, and he quietly closed the doors as he noticed the two pups curled up on the king-sized bed with their new mother.

Since being discharged from the hospital, Cindy had been making great strides in her recovery from being shot, something Preacher wished had happened to him. In his gut he realized how close he had come to losing the one person, besides Ryder, who meant the most to him, and to nearly lose her to those fucking greasy bikers, well that was where the line in the sand was drawn. Physically, Cindy was doing great, the bullet having missed any major targets and the nick on the kidney not requiring surgical intervention. He had to admit the scar was indeed a little sexy, but he pushed that thought down as he plotted his payback against the Disciples. Quietly he walked back into the kitchen, where he replaced the bread in the bag and back into the refrigerator. Making sure the stove was off, he opened the door into the garage and went into the massive space, where the pair of Harleys sat on their pads. Going to his work bench, he picked up a large roofing hammer and tossed it back in forth in his oversized hands. The handle felt smooth and sleek in his grip, and he smiled as he thought about the biker trash and how best to handle them. As he stood lost in thoughts, his phone rang, and he answered it quickly to avoid disturbing his sleeping wife.

"Hello," he said, his voice gruff and raspy.

"Hey there big man, how are you, and more important, how's Cindy doing?" Preacher could not have been happier at the caller, unless maybe it was his missing friend.

"I'm great, Terra. How's by you?" Listening to the woman's voice across the miles, Preacher could not help but smile. Terra was one more reason that the Disciples had to be eliminated, once and for all, and by God he would make it happen. "Cindy's doing great, honey," he told her, as he took a seat on one of the stools he kept in the garage, after pulling a root beer from the cooler he kept stocked.

"I'm damn glad to hear that. You really scared me with that call," Terra said from the other end. Pausing for a moment, Terra continued with her next question. "Listen, I was wondering if you could spare a room for an old friend for a week or so while they prep my new condo. I'm taking a job with a new company, but my new place won't be ready for several weeks." Preacher was shocked by the request but answered instantly. "Well, hell yes. We always have a room for you. When are you getting out here?"

"Well, my plane landed about 15 minutes ago, so a soon as I can grab a cab, if that's okay."

" A cab, hell. I'll be out to the airport in about twenty minutes, so be looking."

"Preacher, are you sure? I know Cindy's recuperating, plus you have the two dogs, so if"- Preacher stopped her with a single word-family.
"I'll be out in about 20 minutes, and what a pleasant surprise it will be for Cindy to see you. See you in a few." Hanging up the phone, Preacher polished off the soda,

tossed the bottle into the recycle bin, then went back inside where could hear one of the girls gently scratching at the bedroom door. Making his way down the carpeted hallway, he opened the door, wanting to let Cindy keep sleeping. As Bella slipped out the door and toward the back area via the newly installed doggy door, Preacher felt eyes on him.

"Who were you talking to?" came the drowsy voice of his wife.

"That was Terra. She just got back out here, and took a new job with a drug company, but her condo won't be ready for a week or two, so she asked if she could stay here, and I told her absolutely not." He could hear Cindy trying not to laugh due to the pain, and as he entered the room he spotted Sophie cuddled up against Cindy.

Looking up at her husband, Cindy asked, "Can I go with you when you pick her up?" Preacher stared at his wife and was almost overcome with emotion when he realized how quickly she could have been ripped from his life. As he looked at her, his eyes shining, Cindy gently slid the half-asleep dog across the bed, then tossed back the covers, wincing slightly as she did.

"What makes you think you're going with me?" Preacher asked, as he assisted his wife out of bed, being gentle to avoid hurting her. As Cindy got to her feet, suddenly Bella came running back into the room and leapt up onto the bed, using the small steps that Preacher had fashioned to help the stumpy legged dogs up onto the bed.

"Well, I'm up, so I guess you can't stop me, can you?" she said, as Preacher handed her a pair of jeans and a button up blouse. Helping her into the clothes, Preacher took her black boots from the closet and handed them to her, as she carefully sat down on the edge of the bed. "You go make sure the guest room is ready while I put these on," she instructed him, raising one leg up and sliding the boot onto her foot. Preacher turned and walked out, then back down the hallway to where the guest room was. Opening the door, he saw the linens were fresh, then he went in to check the guest bath. Spying the cotton towels hanging on the hooks, he made sure there was adequate toilet paper, then took a small bottle of Febreze from under the sink and squirted a small amount into the air of the room, a delicate rose scent filling the air. Satisfied with his handiwork, he went back into the hallway, where Cindy was slowly making her way in his direction. Her color was better than it had been, and she was moving well on her own, but he still worried.

"Guest room ready for inspection ma'am," he said, snapping a halfhearted salute as she passed by, the dogs in tow. Cindy stuck her head in the room and gave it a once over before looking at her husband. Before she could ask, Preacher held up three fingers. Cindy smiled at him, the love evident on her face despite her pain. "Okay girls, let's load up," Preacher told the dogs, who immediately ran to where the large crate sat on a thick wool blanket. Entering the cage, Preacher retrieved two small dog treats from the jar on the counter, giving one to each dog.

"We'll be back in a little while," Cindy told the two pups, who had already curled up next to each other. Frequently they took the girls with them on their outings, but tonight with Terra it made more sense to leave them at home, and it seemed to be just fine with the dogs. Holding open the front door for his wife, Preacher helped her out, then closed and locked the door, using his cell phone to engage the newly installed alarm system. Walking down the sidewalk, he took Cindy's arm, and guided her to the Dodge truck. Unlocking the door, he helped her onto the metal step, then assisted her with her seatbelt. Closing the door, he went around and climbed in, starting the truck's powerful diesel engine. Looking over his shoulder, he saw the road was clear. Backing out of the drive, he headed towards the airport, anxious to see his old friend, as Cindy's hand squeezed his on the steering wheel.

Pulling into the airport, there was minimal traffic, and Preacher attributed that to the late evening. Pulling up to the yellow marked area of the curb, he jumped out of the truck, as a young woman with two pieces of luggage came running out of the terminal doors. Preacher half ran, half walked towards her, picking her up in his arms and sweeping her off her feet.

"God girl, you look great," he exclaimed, as she planted a soft kiss on his furry cheek. Setting her down, Preacher picked up the two bags and turned back towards the truck, where Cindy sat smiling at the pair. Terra went up and climbed onto the metal step, throwing her arms around Cindy's neck and kissing her as well. Cindy returned the gesture as Preacher opened the rear door for their guest. Setting the two bags inside, he helped the slender woman into the truck, shut the door and went back to his side. As he got in, Terra suddenly slid her arms around the couple's necks, as Cindy reached up to squeeze her arm. Preacher carefully navigated his way out of the airport, then back onto the freeway.

"So, how are you feeling?" Terra asked Cindy, who turned slightly to speak to her.

"Well, my side still hurts a bit, but the big guy here has fallen right into the role of caretaker. I'm afraid I may be getting spoiled, but damned if I want it to stop." Terra laughed and sat back in the seat, as Cindy continued.

"So, Preacher tells me you have a new job for some big drug company. That sounds exciting." Terra began to fill her friends in on the new job, talking a mile a minute, something which before she had been assaulted and left for dead would never have happened. She went on to tell them that she had, during her recovery, begun to study meditation and spiritual awareness, and had discovered that she, despite her previous life, was truly a people person. She had begun to, as she put it, find out who the real Terra was and let her shine. As fast as it had started, her rapid-fire update stopped, and she looked at Preacher in his mirror.

"So, what's the update on Ryder and Lacey? Any clues yet as to where they might be?" Preacher met her gaze, giving her a look that said *we'll talk about it later.*

When they pulled up into the driveway, Preacher turned off the truck and jumped out, going around to help Cindy down. Despite her claims of feeling better, her face revealed the truth about how tired she actually was. Preacher took Cindy's elbow as Terra slid out of the truck and pulled her two bags out. Following the couple up the walkway, she felt a sense of relief about being here, back with people she trusted and loved. As Preacher helped Cindy into the house, she went into the living room and took a seat in one of the recliner chairs, exhaling deeply. Preacher took the luggage from Terra and went down the hallway, opening one of the bedroom doors and setting the bags inside, then returned to the living room, where Terra had already gotten three bottles of root beer from the kitchen. Cindy looked at Preacher, then asked, "Can I get a pain pill? My side is hurting really bad." Getting to his feet, the man went into the back of the house, returning a moment later with a small beige pill. Cindy reached out and took it from her husband, then swallowed it with a drink of her soda. "I'm sorry Terra, I'm just really tired, so please excuse me." Terra got to her feet and hugged Cindy, her arms gentle around the woman's body.

"Believe me, I get it. It took me almost six months before I got my steam back, so no worries." Terra released her friend, as Preacher guided her to their bedroom. "I'll be right back," he whispered to Terra, as he opened the bedroom door and led Cindy to the bed. Several minutes later, having helped her undress and get into bed, he went back out to the front room where his guest was on the floor playing with the two pups. They seemed enthralled with their new playmate and romped and jumped over the young woman as she laughed at their antics.

"Okay girls, time for bed," Preacher said, not feeling the least bit foolish at treating them like children. Terra was impressed by the way they responded to his voice, watching as they ran to where their crate stood open. Preacher took two dog treats from a jar, got down on his hands and knees and gave each dog a treat as they went inside, kissing their soft heads. Standing up, he draped the maroon sheet over their bed, helping to keep them quiet and sleep, then returned to the living room where Terra sat waiting for her host.

Preacher took a seat in his favorite recliner, then looked at Terra. "So, you asked me earlier about Ryder and Lacey. I don't want to worry Cindy any more than she already is, and no, I don't know where they are. That, my dear friend is where you come in. I need you to do some digging for me and find out the location of a cabin that Darius owns." Terra sat, staring at Preacher. The severity of the situation with Ryder had to be deadly serious for Preacher to expend so many words in one mouthful.

Getting to her feet, Terra walked quickly down the hall to her room, returning with a laptop computer in her hands. Sitting down on the chair next to Preacher, she laid the computer on the ottoman and opened it up. "Okay, what exactly are we looking for?" Ten minutes later the pair knew not only the location of his cabin but could tell you how much the property taxes were, how many square feet it was, a number of color photos and how much he had paid for it, as well as its current value. Preacher was amazed at how quickly the information had been gathered, but still had some reservations as to why the lawyer had been so resistant to revealing Ryder's location to him.

"Okay, so now figure out for me how long it would take to get there from here by truck," he said, as his mind went into overtime. He knew time was growing short for his friend, and by God he was going to do everything he could to help him, even if he had to hogtie the attorney and drag him along for the ride.

"Okay, it's about eight hours from here, and I'm printing up the directions right now," Terra told him, while Preacher got to his feet. Picking up his cell phone from the oak table, he dialed a number, then put it on speaker phone.

"Hey Darius, it's me. Listen, I think we need a little road trip, and I have just the place for us to go. Pack a bag, and I'll swing by about six tomorrow morning to get you. No, this is a trip we have to make buddy, so be ready when I get there, and don't make me come knocking." Terra could hear the man on the other end trying to get a word in edgewise, but having no luck, and despite the situation it made her smile.

"So, when do we leave?" she asked him, closing the computer. Preacher sat for a moment after he hung up the phone.

"WE aren't going anywhere, my friend. I need you to stay here and keep an eye on Cindy. Something tells me I need to get to Ryder, and fast, and I always go with what my gut tells me. I'm sorry if you think I'm sticking you with babysitting duty for Cindy, but I have to do this. Ryder is in real danger, I can feel it, and I need to get to where he is." Terra sat, listening to the man, and could understand the loyalty to Ryder. She herself would walk through the fires of hell for him and his family, and keeping an eye on Cindy would be just fine. Preacher got to his feet and without a word walked into the kitchen and out into the garage. Terra could hear him rummaging around in the space, then reenter the house, a large duffel style bag in his hand.

"I need to pack, and let Cindy know, which is not going to go well, but she'll have to understand. I'm leaving early, so I'll try to be quiet when I head out. I'll take the pups out too, so you won't need to worry about that. Just take care of all three of my girls while I'm gone." Getting to her feet, Terra could feel the long days travel settling into her body, and decided a good night's rest was just what she needed. Going into her room, she retrieved the printouts of the directions to the cabin. Stepping out into the hall, she handed the papers to Preacher, then threw her arms around his neck.

"Bring our boy and his family back in one piece," she whispered, "And give him this from me." Kissing his cheek, Terra turned and went into her room so the large man would not see her tearing up.

Early the next morning Preacher walked as softly down the hall as he could, duffel bag in hand. Cindy had not been happy at his plans but understood the connection and his burning need to help. She had kissed him softy, whispering *I love you* to him as he picked up the bag. Stopping by the laundry room, he let the girls out, as Sophie stretched her legs, and Bella rolled over for her morning tummy rub. Preacher obliged, then let both dogs out through the French doors, watching as they took care of business. Returning to the house, both dogs slurped noisily from their silver water bowls, then Preacher said, "Load up." Getting back into their crate, he closed the door and leaned down. "I'll see you in a couple of days." Checking his ankle holster, he picked up the bag from the counter and headed towards the front door. Opening it, he looked back at his home, with a melancholy feeling in his gut. Shutting the door, he locked it and set the alarm, made sure it was locked again and walked to his waiting truck. Climbing in, he let the engine warm up and shut his eyes in a moment of silent prayer.

"Lord, please keep us all safe, and let me find my friend in time. Ryder, I'm coming buddy."

Chapter 11

Crossing into California, Summer felt like she was returning to the scene of a crime, and a delicious, almost erotic feeling of revenge filled her. It had been a long trip, and not without several minor hiccups. Two hours earlier Dingo Dave had gotten a call from another club member in San Diego, informing him that Jake, the president of the Disciples had been killed in a freak accident in the downtown area. He had been heading back from picking up a load of meth, and as he crossed an intersection a city bus whose brakes had failed broadsided him, killing him instantly. The two brothers with him had been quick to remove the evidence from their fallen leader, casting severe glances at onlookers to keep their mouths shut. Dingo had been informed that, as of right now he was the new president of the California chapter of the Devils Disciples. Since getting the call he had been quiet, but Summer could see the wheels spinning behind his dark eyes. The second glitch had come about twenty minutes before they hit the California border, when out of nowhere an Arizona state trooper had pulled the rig over for a faulty turn signal. The minute they had seen the lights come on behind them, Dave and

Scab had taken shelter in the hidden compartment beneath the queen-sized bed. Summer had opened the door for the police officer, who asked to see the driver's license, registration and insurance, showing her best smile as Gary, the young driver produced the requested documents.
"What's the problem, officer?" Summer asked her voice soft and flowing despite her anxious desire to get to California.

"Oh, I just noticed that when you made that lane change back there your left turn signal was burnt out." The young man stood at the doorway to the RV, his eyes looking for anything out of the ordinary. The gorgeous blonde woman talking to him, however, was making it extremely difficult to concentrate on the task at hand. Shifting his feet, the police officer looked at the papers, then turned around and walked back to his car. Summer watched, a desire to kill the officer burning in her gut. She could feel herself drawing nearer to her quarry, and any delay was unacceptable. She gently rubbed her fingers together, in an effort to lower her thermostat as the officer returned.

"Ma'am, it looks like everything is in order, so here are your papers, and you folks have a nice day." Tipping his hat to Summer, he went back and got into his car, closing the door as he watched the RV pull away. Wiping his forehead, he set his hat on the passenger seat, then turned on the air conditioning in the sedan. "*Damn,*" he thought to himself, "*I sure wouldn't mind a little play time with fine that piece of ass.*" Looking over his shoulder, he saw it was clear, flipped around and headed east on the highway.

Through the back window, Summer watched the police car heading in the other direction and allowed herself to calm down. She was so glad that the encounter had not taken any longer, as she was afraid that she would have done something which could have way-laid her plans for the immediate future. In the back room she could hear the two men extricating themselves from their hiding place. Jesus' man, couldn't you wait to do that until we got out of that fucking closet? Your breath is bad enough, but damn, that fart about made me puke." Scab was laughing as they came back into the main cabin, the three of them stretching to ease their muscles.

"Well, sit back and enjoy the rest of the ride folks, because we should be seeing San Diego in about forty minutes." Gary looked back over his shoulder as he relayed the good news, anxious to be rid of these people. Jean-Pierre had paid him handsomely for this task, but not even the hefty pay was worth dealing with this kind of trash for too long. The woman, despite her beautiful face and smoking hot body, made him very nervous. There was something about her, an underlying presence of something really bad, and he had decided when they hit San Diego he was dumping them all off, selling the RV and catching the first flight back to the Caymans and that dark haired, big breasted girl he had met three days earlier.

Summer sat in the front of the RV, her eyes closed as they sped towards the next stop, and as she let her mind free itself, she could almost feel the boy. During the time she had spent with him at The Ranch, she had begun to plant certain key words in his mind, during their conversations, a technique she had been studying since that period of her life in Greece. She had begun to learn them in order to give her a leg up on that abusive bastard of a husband, but when Giorgio died and she found that sweet Micah, she understood that she had actually been developing her skills to use on him, which of course now, due to circumstances, would be of the utmost advantage to her. Using the Greek she had learned, she had been able to plant certain key words, subliminally, to later make the young boy do her bidding. To feel guilty about this was not within her scope, and as she let her mind float she thought- *den empistévontai kanénan, allá eména,* sending him the silent message- *don't trust anyone but me.*

Gary looked at the woman sitting next to him, her eyes closed, and let his eyes fall upon those silky gloves she always wore. Jean-Pierre had sent several pairs with him on his journey to the U.S. for the woman, and he had been more than curious about why she wore them. As he stared at her hands, then her tanned legs extending from under her sundress, he began to feel an urge to caress the smooth skin. As he slowly let his right hand leave the wheel and begin its trek, suddenly a dirty, scarred arm came shooting into the cab, grabbing his wrist tightly.

"Don't even fucking think about it pretty boy, or I'll turn your shit out." Scab came forward into the cab, his grip still firm on the now startled young man.

"I wasn't going to do anything," he said, his voice shaking as he looked straight ahead.

Scab placed himself between the two occupants, his body odor filling the small space.

"I suggest you keep your eyes peeled straight ahead until we hit San Diego, or I swear I'll turn the whole club loose on your sweet little ass." Scab let his eyes do the rest of the talking, as Gary kept his eyes on the road.

"*No more jobs like this, no way,*" he thought to himself, as he spied a road sign showing San Diego 11 miles. Scab spotted the sign also, and gently touched the woman in the captain's chair. Slowly her eyes opened, and she saw the disheveled man to her left.

"We're almost there," he said quietly, as Summer stretched her legs and back. Looking at Scab, she gave him a smile that could melt the polar ice caps.

"Thank you, my sweet," she whispered, then motioned for him into the back of the rig. As he did, Summer joined him and the other two, who were working on what appeared to be their second or third can of beer. "Dave, I need to talk to you. Now that you're in charge, I need to make sure our deal is still in place. Jake and I agreed on five million dollars, but only if everything was ready when we got to San Diego. I need you to make sure that everything is indeed in place." Dave looked at her, a look on his face of both pain and pleasure. He and Jake had done several long stretches together, one at Chino and another at Pelican Bay, and the two men had been thick as thieves. Now that he was the new president, he needed to make sure he honored his dead brother's legacy by making the Disciples even stronger and more powerful.

Reaching up, he wiped his hands across his mouth, removing an invisible object before speaking. "Yeah, our deal still stands. Five million bucks buys a lot of loyalty." As he spoke, he pulled his cell phone from his vest pocket and dialed. "Hey, it's me. Yeah, we're almost there, maybe another 10 minutes or so. I need to make sure you guys are handling everything like Jake would have wanted. Excellent. Now, what about the other items Jake was working on? Everything a go? No, I want to send Scab, Mutt and Jeff, Mongo, myself, Rat, Shaggy and Spiderman on this job. No, don't fucking argue with me. I'm going on this run because it's personal for me, and I need you to hang tight and keep things running. Yeah, we'll have Jake's party tonight at the clubhouse. All right brother, we'll see you in a few." Laying down the phone, Dave folded his hands on the table and smiled at Summer, a look she found disheartening at best.

"So, is everything set? I had it worked out with Jake to get refueled and load up as soon as we got to San Diego, so we can get back on the road towards Tahoe." Dave just looked at her and shook his head.

"Sorry, but tonight is the sendoff for our brother Jake, so no travelling tonight. First thing in the morning, no sweat, but not tonight." Summer began to speak, and Dave, without warning slammed his fists down on the Formica table, rattling it and startling Summer. "I FUCKING TOLD YOU NOT TONIGHT! TONIGHT IS ABOUT MY BROTHER, SO SHUT THE FUCK UP!" Summer sat, staring at the man screaming at her. She focused on keeping her composure, then exhaled deeply before speaking.

"Listen, I appreciate your loyalty to your brothers, but what if I bump it up to ten million dollars? Would that help get us on the road tonight?" Her heart was pounding in her chest, her hands and arms throbbing, but she kept her poker face in place.

Dave looked across the table at the blonde woman, his face blank. He was trying to think what Jake would do in this spot. Loyalty is one thing, but *ten fucking million dollars* would make the club the most powerful group on the West coast, and maybe in the U.S. With that kind of cash, they could expand the club, and he wanted to be sure he did the right thing.

"How bout this, sweetheart? We hit the clubhouse, get this bitch ready to move, have a few drinks in Jake's honor, then move out at midnight? How's that sound?"

Summer, her heart rate now slowing down, smiled at him. "Not one minute past midnight." Jake threw back the rest of his beer, then nodded as Scab came back from the cab.

"We're there."

Ten minutes later the RV was parked behind an abandoned warehouse in National City. When the passengers exited the RV, there were a large number of bikers present, the women hanging back until told otherwise. Dingo Dave was greeted with a warm reception by his brothers, hugging and high fiving many of them on his way inside. Scab came along behind, with Summer in tow, as most of the men, and some of the women eyeballed the gorgeous blonde.

Summer sat in what appeared to be, by minimal standards at least, the office of the president. Her hands and arms were throbbing, but she sat in the wooden chair straight faced and quiet. Behind the makeshift desk, Dingo Dave sat staring at her as he was serviced under the desk by one of the hootchies the gang kept for just such occasions. Summer was used to shocking the people around her, or at least she had been before that bitch Lacey had showed up. She was not impressed by the show, but to keep the peace she sat, while the ragged looking young girl finished her task, as indicated by the tensing of Dave's face and the animal grunts he made. The girl crawled out from behind the desk, wiped her mouth on the dirty Harley Davidson tank-top she wore and left without a sound. Dave leaned back, smiling at his guest. I hope that didn't bother you none," he said, a stupid grin crossing his face, as Summer shook her head.

"No, not at all. I'm just surprised it took so long, since it's been a while since we left Nogales." She hoped she wasn't overplaying her hand, but before she could decide if she had or not, there came a loud rapping on the wooden door.

"WHAT?" the man yelled, as the door squeaked open and two burly men entered, sweat on their faces.

The larger of the two wiped the perspiration from his forehead before he spoke. "We're just about set," he told Dave, ignoring the woman, at least for the moment.

Chapter 12

As a blonde-haired woman sat negotiating a deal to track down and kill an innocent woman, 200 miles away in a Las Vegas office, a stocky man sat at his desk in his three-piece silk suit, staring at a photograph of his son and wife. Vincent Bandini was many, many things, most of which would not gain him entrance into heaven. The one thing he was, however, was unforgiving, and when the call had come in five minutes earlier from his source, for the first time in many months he had reason to rejoice. Ever since the day he had received the sick little gift from that bitch Summer, his world had consisted of only one thing- payback. In his line of work, it was wise to never let your emotions get involved, but when the bitch killed his son and mutilated him, well that rule went into a box and got put away.

    As he held the picture, his heart was glad that his beloved wife Maria had not been alive to see their only son brutally murdered. She had been a truly gentle, loving soul, and that would have crushed her heart and spirit, despite her deep faith. Vincent looked at the image of his boy, his beloved son, and the anger he felt welling up again felt good, like seeing a long lost, cherished old friend. Vince could not recall the last time, prior to Joey's murder, that he had truly felt excited about something. Gently kissing the photo of his family, he laid it on the desk, picked up the cell phone laying to his right and dialed a number. "Tony, yeah, it's me. Get Leo and Pete and get over here right away. No, I'll tell you when you get here. Now fucking MOVE!" It felt good to yell at someone, anyone, for any reason, and he felt his old self coming to the surface. Dialing another number he waited, then spoke. "Hey, it's Vince. Yeah, it's been a while, and I need a job done, the type that's right up your alley. No, nothing like that, you perverted fuck. It's her. Summer. Yeah, you heard me right, I said Summer. I just found out the bitch that killed my boy is back, and now she becomes the hunted instead of the hunter. No, I don't want her dead. I want you and your boys to go pick her up and bring her beautiful, blonde ass back here. I have a very special surprise waiting for her. Well, maybe when I'm done I'll let you guys have a crack at her, but not until then. This bitch killed my son, cut off his dick and mailed it to me with a fucking red bow tied around it. Quit laughing you sick prick, that was my boy she killed. No, I'll call you in about an hour and give you the details but start getting ready. She's on her way to a little place called Cedars Pass, west of Tahoe in the mountains, and I need you and the boys to be ready when I call. I'll give you everything you need, so don't worry." Vince hung up the phone without any further words and laid it on his desk. Outside he could see dark clouds on the horizon, framed perfectly by the massive picture window, and a sad smile crossed his weathered face at the irony.

"Summer, wherever you are, whoever you're with, you better pray to whatever deity you worship, because when I get hold of you, oh baby, you are going to ever regret hearing the name Vincent Antonio Bandini.

His dark eyes locked on the coming storm, Vince stood silent as the three summoned men quietly entered the room, as quiet as church mice. Vince smiled, a cold, calculating look, then turned around to see the trio. "Pack your shit men and kiss your girlfriend's goodbye, because we're going on a road trip." Vince began to laugh at his own wit, a cold, fear inspiring sound, and none of the three men had the guts or were stupid enough to say anything about it or ask any questions.

In a rundown apartment near the Haight Ashbury section of San Francisco, three scruffy men sat on a pair of battered, beer-stained sofas, passing a small, dirty mirror between them and snorting a fine white powder. The largest of the men, 6'2" and almost 300 pounds of tattooed fury, got to his feet and went into the back of the house, as the other two occupants finished off the meth. Before they could reload the mirror, the large man returned, zipping his stained jeans and stopping the other two from resuming their activity. "Listen up dipshits, that was my guy in Vegas, and he has a job for us." Mikey stood, staring at his two cohorts, as they leaned back on the couch.

"Well shit, let's get our gear and get ready to ride," Cowboy said, the unusual drawl in his voice sounding out of character for an outlaw biker/bounty hunter.

The trio had been riding together for as long as they could remember, and their fierce loyalty to one another would never be broken. They had done many, many jobs over the years, including several for Vince Bandini, and none of them had any hesitation to do whatever they were paid to do. Three years earlier they had been contracted to take out an attorney who had shortchanged a fellow outlaw biker, sending the man away for life, and when they had firebombed the lawyers house that December night, the fact that his wife and two children were home had never fazed any of them. Afterwards, they had gone to a local strip club, had some drinks, picked up a young woman and took her back to their place for an all-night gangbang.

Cowboy pulled three cans of beer from the small ice chest setting on the dirty floor, tossing one to each man. "Here's to the three fucking musketeers," he yelled, laughing at his own joke, as they all took long pulls from the cans. "So, who's the wop in Vegas want us to do now?" As he sat back down, Mikey drained the last of the beer, then looked at his two friends, a peculiar look on his face.

"Remember the bitch that cut off Vince's son's dick and mailed it to him last year? She's headed this way, and he wants her, and bad." At the mention of Summer, the other two men stopped drinking. Her reputation in Vegas had been legendary, and the stunt with Vince's son, well that had made it all the way to California. The men had all been impressed with her bravado and creativity, and when it seemed she was dead they had been somewhat disappointed. The feud with Vince had been a great meal ticket for them, but now that she was back, they had to admit, at least to themselves, they were a little apprehensive about dealing directly with the blonde psycho, but nothing that a few more lines of crank wouldn't cure.

Cowboy walked across the room and into the back bedroom, opened the closet door and looked inside. Reaching in, he removed two AK-47 assault rifles, a Mac 10 submachine gun, tossing them on the bed behind him. Stepping in a bit, he withdrew three silver .357 pistols, shining and clean in the light. "Hey shit bags, get in here," he hollered at the two other men, who came into the room and smiled. They loved using the big toys, and this sounded like a job tailor made for them. Mikey picked up the Mac 10, running his hands over it as if caressing a newborn baby. While he fondled the weapon, Cowboy pulled out a large metal ammo box and laid it on the bed, causing a depression with its weight. Opening the box, he withdrew three loaded clips for each rifle, then two boxes each of ammo for the pistols. Each man took his own weapon and carefully wiped it down, removing any dust or particles from its storage. The room was deadly silent as they prepared for their job, each man getting himself to that place where he needed to be. This was a regular ritual with them, especially when they used guns, and the solemnity of the ceremony they were undertaking had an almost religious feel to it. One by one they reached their point and left the room without a word being spoken. Terry was the first to leave, cradling his guns carefully in his tattooed arms. He took a seat in the torn recliner, letting his eyes stare out at the dirty street. His mind went to the little redhead at the massage parlor just across the street, and he made a note to pay her a visit when they got back.

Mikey entered the room, the pistol in his waistband, the Mac 10 semi-auto slung over his shoulder. He sat down on the sofa, the springs squeaking under his weight, and looked at Terry. "You're thinking about that little ginger down the street, aren't you?" Terry just looked at him, silent and focused.

"Well fuck faces, let's get this party started," came the voice from the bedroom, as Cowboy came back in. Terry picked up a small bag of white powder on the table, rolled it up and slipped it into his vest pocket. Each man standing up, they came together, arms linked, as Cowboy spoke. "No one will ever love you like a brother, nor protect you, nor die for you. These are the words passed to us by Kong, may Satan bless his black soul. He spoke them in love, and they are the words that keep us together." Three heads bowed for a moment as they remembered their fallen leader, then all three looked up and headed to the scarred front door. Leaving the apartment, they went downstairs to where their steeds awaited them. Climbing aboard, they fired up the engines and sped off towards destiny.

Chapter 13

Micah stood, his hands still as he held the pistol and his breath. With his left eye squeezed shut, he sighted in on his target, then stopped as something moved just to his left in the brush. Before Ryder could say or do anything, the boy had adjusted his sights and let loose a single shot, sending the unsuspecting rabbit tumbling into the high weeds. Lacey stood, stunned at her sons' actions, as April began to cry at the sound of the gunshot breaking the still morning air. Ryder immediately snatched the gun from the boy's hands, placing the safety on and ejecting the clip as a single empty shell spun off into the dirt, and Joker sat watching, his dark eyes on the boy.

"What the hell are you doing?" Ryder shouted, his angry, shocked voice echoing loudly in the air. Micah stood, looking at where the rabbit lay, a soft smile on his face as Ryder grabbed his arm. "I'm talking to you-what the hell are you doing?" Lacey took three steps in Ryder's direction, placing her hand on his arm to get his attention. Ryder kept his focus on the boy, as Lacey tugged at his arm.

"Ryder, what are YOU doing?" she asked, as stunned by his swearing at her son as he was at the senseless killing. Micah, the smile still on his face, looked at the man standing next to him.

"There are only two types of people in this world- sheep and wolves. If you aren't a wolf, a hunter, then you are their prey, the sheep. Now, let go of my arm." Ryder and Lacey were both in shock, not only at his cruel actions, but even more by the unusual words he spoke. Lacey saw the color drain slightly from her husband's face, as April continued to fuss.

The preceding two days had been uneventful, if preparing to fight for your life could be termed uneventful. They had weapons all around the house, Lacey and Ryder had not spent so much as five minutes alone since they had left Santa Barbara, and last night Micah had awakened from a terrible nightmare, screaming the phrase "Eímai o lýkos , eíste ta próvata," something neither of them had understood. Lacey had finally managed to calm him enough to get back to sleep, with an occasional mumble under his breath. She had sat next to her son, stroking his hair as she gently eased him back into slumber. Ryder had stood in the doorway watching, his daughter in his arms, his heart breaking for the boy and whatever was causing his disturbances. In his hand he also held his cell phone, recording the words coming from the boy. Since arriving at the cabin, Micah had, on more than one occasion, said or done things that were completely out of line for him, such as swearing when he had accidentally nicked himself while cutting up potatoes, using a word that Ryder himself tried to avoid at all costs. He and Lacey had gone back to bed, laying April between them and talking in whispers. They both just chalked the unusual behavior to the events of the past year, and now being on the run from his tormentor. Once the baby had gone back to sleep, the couple held hands and talked quietly, Ryder hearing the underlying note of stress in his wife's voice and reassuring her that everything was going to be okay.

Taking Micah back to the house, Lacey kept shooting daggers at Ryder, angrier with him than she could ever recall. When they got back, Ryder had sent Micah straight to his room, the boy slamming the heavy wooden door behind him. Ryder joined Lacey in the kitchen, where she had laid the baby on a blanket on the floor and was changing her diaper. Ryder stood, silent, as she finished, then picked April up and set her in her rocking seat, cooing at her, as Lacey washed her hands.

"What the hell was that all about? I know he didn't have any right to kill that rabbit, but to grab him and curse at him. Really? What were you thinking?" Lacey's face was flushed beet red, and Ryder knew he needed to proceed slowly and carefully.

"Listen, I'm sorry I cussed at him and grabbed him like I did, but that look on his face when he pulled that trigger was scary. I've seen that look before on men, men who truly enjoy killing, and I don't want to see him like that. And what was that speech about wolfs and sheep?" A strange look suddenly crossed Ryder's face, and he grabbed his cell phone off of the counter. Entering some letters and numbers, he listened to a recording, then waited while it responded, then looked at the display, a stunned look on his face. "Guess what that phrase was he kept repeating over and over again the other night when he woke up screaming- I am the wolf, you are the sheep. Sound familiar? Oh, and the best part is, guess what language it is?" Lacey stood, her mind spinning wildly, as April chewed on her chubby fingers, Joker sitting right next to the table where the baby was.

"Oh my God, somehow she's poisoned his mind, even after all this-." As she tried to speak, Ryder could see the tears welling up behind those beautiful green eyes, and the anger he felt at this situation filled his soul like grain filling a silo. Lacey began to shake, her hand and torso visibly quivering, as Ryder went to her, his arms wide open, and was dumbstruck when she shoved him backwards, away from her.

April sat, watching her parents, and Joker, sensing the tension in the room, moved closer to the baby, settling in against the wood cabinets. Ryder watched as his wife, the woman he loved and the mother of his daughter, seemed to morph into someone else. There was an anger on her face, a viciousness in her appearance that scared him, for one of the very few times in his life. Lacey leaned against the marble countertop, gripping the edge so tightly that her hands were bright red. Ryder slowly approached her, letting his right hand touch her shoulder, feeling the tautness of the muscle's underneath. Moving slightly closer, he slid his hand down to hers, wanting to ease her grip just a bit before she hurt herself. As he pressed into her, she turned and looked at her husband, a very familiar look on her face, one that Ryder hoped he would never see again.

"That bitch better hope she doesn't get within a hundred miles of me, because I swear what I did last time will pale in comparison." There was a tone to her voice that seemed like an abomination for someone so beautiful and delicate. Lacey allowed Ryder to embrace her, sliding her arms around his neck, gently at first, then tighter, as he pulled her to him. Lost in one another, they were startled out of their moment of peace by Micah's voice, soft and quiet, coming from the doorway.

"I'm sorry. I didn't mean to shoot that poor rabbit. It just kind of happened, and I'm really sorry." Lacey saw his eyes shining in the light of the kitchen, and went to him, grabbing him and picking him up in an embrace. Ryder stood, looking at the boy, and saw just that- a young boy who had been through more emotional trauma than most people would ever know. Micah met his gaze, and a sad smile crossed his face. Ryder went to where the mother and son were engaged, put his hands on Micah's head and leaned in. Hugging him tightly, Micah returned the embrace, his face tight against Ryder's neck. Lacey watched her two men, and began to cry, more out of anger than sadness, then went to where her daughter sat, watching the scene playing out.

Picking her up, the family walked into the large family room and took seats on the sofa, while Joker took up his ever-present position near April.

They sat on the couch, silent and touching one another, letting the quiet of the mountains calm their rattled nerves. Joker laid down at Ryder's feet, his nose occasionally twitching as his eyes drifted shut. While the family sat on the couch, Micah leaned in against his mother, his head resting on her shoulder. April lay sleeping in Ryder's arms, her soft breathing soothing his mental state. Lacey's eyes were shut, as she too napped, a rarity over the past few days. Ryder's ears kept a close notice of any unusual sounds outside of the seemingly secure home.

Joker, his eyes closed, was chasing the elusive rabbit that often haunted his dreams. He could see it in the murky vision of his dreams, but every time he seemed on the verge of catching it, it slipped away. His paws twitched as he slept, as if in hot pursuit, but this time, just as he closed in on his prey, suddenly a low growl came from the dark. Stopping, he turned his head and looked through the mist, as two shapes came into view. It was a large wolf, its hackles raised and teeth bared, the yellow eyes glowing and staring at Joker. The German shepherd stood his ground, showing his teeth in response. The smaller wolf standing next to the larger one moved slightly closer, daring the dog to make a move. Joker stood, his haunches taut, his muscles rigid as the stare down continued. Suddenly a strangely familiar smell hit Joker's nose, and without any warning he propelled himself at the two animals- then opened his eyes, his heart racing, confused for the moment as to where he was. When he saw his man and the baby, he let himself calm down, taking notice that each of his people were asleep on the sofa. A little ashamed at leaving his people unguarded, Joker quickly went into the large food room, took several long drinks of his water, then went back into the room where they were sleeping. Sitting down next to the sofa between the baby and her brother, Joker kept his eyes and ears peeled for any signs of trouble, especially the she-wolf that he had dreamed about.

"*No,*" he thought, "*I won't let you hurt my people. You may be the wolf, but I am the sheep dog.*"

Micah let his eyes slowly open, surprised that he had fallen asleep. He was a big boy now, a young man, and he had no need for naps. Next to him on the couch, his mom was asleep, her hair drifting down over her forehead, and he gently reached over to brush it back. As he did, he felt someone watching him, and he turned around to find his little sister staring at him from where she lay in her dad's arms. Scooting over, he tenderly kissed his baby sister on the cheek, making her giggle and begin to squirm around. As she did, Ryder began to stir, and Joker looked up at his man and the baby.

"Well, I guess we were all pretty tired," Ryder said, getting to his feet and stretching. Propping up his daughter with several pillows, he looked at Micah. "Keep an eye on April for me if you would," he said, heading towards the bathroom. Micah watched him go, then turned to April and began a game of Got Your Nose. For some reason this game always made the baby laugh, which in turn brought out the giggles in her brother. As they amused themselves, Lacey's eyes popped open, and when she didn't see Ryder she jumped to her feet.

"Where's your dad?" she asked Micah, her voice louder than she intended. Micah turned and looked at her, a strange look on his face.

"He's in the bathroom, and don't call him my dad." The unusually rude comment was like a slap in the face to his mother, and as she started to chastise the boy, Ryder returned, drying his hands on a cream-colored towel. Sensing the returning tension in the room, Ryder stopped drying his hands and tossed the towel aside.

"What's going on here?" he asked, his eyes going back and forth between Lacey and Micah. When neither one answered, Ryder felt as if he was losing control of the present situation, something he refused to relinquish. "I'm going to ask the question again," he said, using his voice to elicit a response. Lacey stood, her hands slightly trembling, as Micah took a seat next to his sister on the couch. Ryder noticed also, almost imperceptibly, that when the boy sat the dog had adjusted also, moving closer to the baby, as if protecting her. "*What the hell is going on here*?" he wondered to himself, as Lacey spoke, her voice revealing her nervous state.

"Nothing's going on here, we were just playing a game and got carried away," she replied, Ryder noticing that she was avoiding making eye contact with both him and her son. Micah sat, staring at the people standing in front of him, and that same look crossed his face, the one he had had when he shot the rabbit that morning. His eyes locked on his mother, he slowly reached over and took his sisters hand in his, bringing it to his lips to kiss it. This made the little girl laugh, so he repeated the act again, never letting his eyes leave his mother's. Lacey was unable to look away, but when Ryder touched her arm she seemed to garner the strength to break the boy's gaze. Ryder took several steps towards the couch to get his daughter, but when he did Micah seemed to tense up, his grip on the baby's arm tightening just enough to make her squeal.

"Let go of her arm-NOW!" Ryder said, his voice rising to convince the boy to do as he asked. Instead, Micah just looked at him, his dark eyes seeming to shine.

"Make me," he whispered, as Ryder reached over to break his grip. As he did, Joker got to all fours and began to growl, a low, menacing sound, and this seemed to break the boys hold on his sister. Ryder took the baby and handed her over to her mother, then looked back at Micah, who had shrunk back into the cushions of the couch, now his eyes seeming to be only scared, all traces of defiance gone. In its place sat a young, confused boy, who looked around the room as if he had just awakened. Joker, now less defensive than before, bumped the boy with his nose, making Micah laugh. The air in the room seemed calmer, less tense than before, and as Lacey held her daughter, her mind began to run wild with thoughts as to what was happening to her family, and most importantly her son.

Chapter 14

The early morning traffic out of Santa Barbara was lighter than expected, and Preacher was as happy as he could be, given the circumstances. Darius had only spoken a few words since getting into the truck, feigning being tired as a reason for his lack of chatter. Preacher had not been concerned, seeing as how they had eight to nine hours of travel time to spend together, and by God In heaven above, he was going to get some answers. He let Darius sleep for the first couple of hours, until they got out of the valley and headed towards I-5 north. When he merged onto the freeway and began the ascent up the Grapevine, he reached over and gently shook the man, who grumbled under his breath at being disturbed. Preacher just smiled at his travelling companion, then shook him again.

"Come on big boy, time to wake up. The sun's overhead and we need to burn daylight." Darius sat up, stretching his neck and back and yawning, then looked around at the traffic of the morning commute.

"Where are we?" he asked, reaching for the thermos of coffee that Preacher had brought with them. Pouring himself a cup,

Darius looked at the driver again. "Where are we?" he repeated, as Preacher turned to meet his gaze. "We're on I-5 headed north, then we make an easterly turn and head for Cedars Pass." As he answered, Preacher could swear he saw the color drain from the black man's face, and he knew his gut had been right.

"Cedars Pass? What the hell are we going up there for?" Darius asked, sipping the delicious coffee and trying to keep his hands from shaking. Preacher kept his eyes straight ahead, his best poker face in place.

"Oh, I thought maybe we could do some fishing and relaxing in that beautiful cabin of yours," he said, keeping his voice light. Darius took another sip of the coffee, then offered some to Preacher, who declined.

"Hell Preach, we can go fishing in Santa Barbara, and not have to make this long ass drive," he countered, finishing the coffee and replacing the cap, then leaning back in his seat.

"True, but those streams up there are chock full of those beautiful rainbow and brook trout, like the ones I've seen in your pictures, and I thought hell yes, I want some of those for my freezer." Darius, an experienced and cunning litigator, knew how to play the game, and decided to let it play out.

"Sure Preach, those trout are amazing, but we could have gotten them in Mammoth just as well," he said, turning his head and adjusting in his seat. Preacher looked at him, a sad look on his face, then spoke.

"Okay, here's the 64,000-dollar question Darius, and I want an honest answer. Why wouldn't you just tell me that Ryder's hiding up there?" Preacher felt himself getting angry at the refusal of the man to own up, but at the same time he appreciated his holding fast to his word to Ryder.

"Look, Ryder made me promise not to say anything to anyone about where they were going or what they were doing. You know how he is. When you make him a promise, you keep it. Now, please explain to me why the hell you're kidnapping me and taking me where he doesn't want us." Darius could see the big man thinking and decided to change tactics and the subject. "By the way, I heard about your visitors last week. How is Cindy doing? I hope the gunshot wasn't too bad." Preacher kept his eyes straight ahead, focusing on the highway, and refusing to play along. He knew Darius was up to something, and he was damn sure going to find out what before they hit Cedars Pass.

"No, Cindy's okay. The bullet just barely nicked her kidney, but the surgeon said she should heal fine. She has a fair amount of pain with it, but I think a little of it's so I'll keep waiting on her hand and foot, which of course, I would anyway. I'm not really supposed to be leaving Santa Barbara, what with me killing that sack of garbage that shot her, but I know some folks in the PD, and they'll let me slide. Now, how long has Ryder been up at the cabin?" Preacher was trying to distract his travelling partner, and tried to pose the question innocently.

Darius stared into Preacher's eyes, not falling for the ruse. "Listen, if you want to keep talking about Ryder, that's fine, but you'll do it alone. I'm not saying another word about it." Preacher could see they were at an impasse, and decided to let up, at least for the moment.

"Okay, well we have about six hours to Cedars Pass, so how about some music?" Darius reached down and turned on the radio, looking for a satellite station that might play some classical music, something both men enjoyed. Darius shifted in his seat, then located a suitable station.

Three and a half hours later Preacher spotted a sign for I-50 East and exhaled deeply. "Time for a pit stop and refuel," he said to Darius, who had been texting Tisha back home.

Terra sat at her computer, the two pups laying at her feet, as Cindy pulled her legs up onto the cream-colored sofa and stretched out. "Can I get you anything?" Terra asked, as Cindy shook her head.

"No honey, I'm good, just had to get out of bed for a bit. What are you up to there, looking so intense?" Terra looked up at her hostess and winked, as Bella curled up against the woman's foot and began softly snoring while her sister lay chewing on a rawhide toy.

"Just checking on something. I suppose I should tell you. Before Preacher left, he asked me if I knew how to plant a GPS tracking device in a phone, which of course is exactly what I do. I put one in his phone so I can track him every step of the way while they try to find Ryder. I can tell you exactly where they are, how much gas they have in the truck, even when they stop for fuel and food. Pretty cool, huh?"

Cindy had to admit that she was indeed impressed. She could handle her cell phone, texting was a breeze and her laptop, well they were best friends, but things like GPS were not her bag. "I also installed an app on his phone that, when activated, acts as a listening device. I can hear anything that he says or does, and either he or I can activate it." Cindy sat, staring at the dark-haired woman.

"You know, you could have been a model with your looks, but that brain, now that's a thing of real beauty." Terra blushed slightly at the compliment, as Sophie stood up, giving Terra her the *I need to pee look*. Getting to her feet, Terra went and opened the back door to let the dogs out, as Cindy came in right behind her, heading for the icebox.

"Can I get you anything?" she asked, as Terra smiled.

"Always the gracious hostess, aren't you?" she asked, smiling as she shook her head. Cindy pulled a bottle of diet root beer from the refrigerator and removed the cap, then leaned against the marble counter.

"I don't suppose I could talk you into a short walk around the block, could I?" Cindy asked, her voice soft and low, as the barking dogs came running back in. Terra shut the French doors, reached down to pet the friendly pups and looked up at Cindy.

"I think maybe a short walk might do you some good, especially some fresh air." Without giving her a chance to change her mind, Cindy walked down the hallway towards her room, the dogs in tow. Opening the door, she went in and sat down on the small settee looking out over the backyard, reached down and carefully pulled her shoes out from beneath. Cautiously she slipped her feet into the Sketchers, wiggling her toes at how good they felt. Preacher had been wonderful during her recovery but had been very hesitant to let his wife outside, fearing she was pushing too hard. Getting to her feet, she saw Terra in the hallway, her slender legs in the black tights she was wearing, and Cindy felt a moment of jealousy at the young woman's slim shape and tiny little bottom, then realized that her size was exactly what had brought her and Preacher together. Walking back into the living room, she saw the pups already leashed and ready to go. Cindy loved taking the girls with her when she walked but was secretly glad that Terra had them on the single extended leash that she could handle.

"Ready?" Cindy asked, as Terra opened the door for her hostess, the two pups leading the way. Stepping out into the cool air, Cindy felt a sense of renewed freedom, as she stepped over the thresh hold and onto the sidewalk. Terra came out behind her, closed and locked the door, then set the security system. Stepping down to where Cindy was, she placed her hand gently on the waiting arm, as the quartet proceeded to head left towards the water.

As they walked, the two women talked about everything- Preacher, Ryder, Terra's experience last year and subsequent recovery, as well as Cindy's. As Cindy listened, she detected not so much as a single note of self- pity at what had happened to the young woman, not one note of *poor me* or one desire to shake her fist at the heavens and *say why me? It's not fair.* Instead, what she got from Terra was a sense of strength, of refusal to allow anything to break her, a true warrior's spirit. Cindy recalled, as they walked past Shane Walton's house, how she had stood her ground when her ex had cheated on her, and how good it felt to take everything from him and felt a kinship with Terra she had never before experienced. Terra saw the look on her friend's face, and it too made her very happy.

"Oh, wait a minute. I need to stop here and get my breath," Cindy said as she leaned against the brick planter box in front of the tidy, stucco house. The two Corgi's stopped and sat quietly, as Terra leaned on the brick also. The lawn was well manicured, the flowers freshly trimmed, and as she rested, Terra stretched her hamstrings by bending at the waist.

"Hey, who's"- Terra started to ask-"Cindy, is that you?" The man's voice came booming from the open garage, and Cindy stood up as it did.

"Shane? What are you up too? My Gosh, how long has it been?" As Cindy spoke, the man came striding down the smooth as silk driveway, a rag in one hand and a wrench in the other. As he approached, Terra noticed how tall he was, maybe 6'2" or 6"3", well built and, well hell, admit it, a damn fine-looking man. She was not one for girly shows of affection or overly demonstrative acts, but when she spotted the handsome man, she had to admit she definitely liked what she saw.

Cindy stood up as the man approached, gently embracing him in a warm, friendly hug, and he returned the greeting, as the black and white cat behind him jumped onto the brick box, greeting the two canine visitors and awaiting its receipt of love from the woman also. "God, you look wonderful," Cindy told the man, who wiped his hands on the rag and laid the wrench down next to the cat.

"Boy, I was sure sorry about what happened. I've been meaning to come by, but I didn't want to disturb you while you were recuperating. I saw Preach down at the shop, and he kept me posted on your condition." As the pair spoke, Terra was petting the unusually friendly cat, who seemed smitten with the dark-haired woman, as well as the two dogs.

"Oh God, I'm so sorry. Terra, this is Shane Walton, a good friend and neighbor. Shane, this is Terra Tomasino, a friend and houseguest. You remember Ryder Raynes, Preacher's friend? Terra and he used to run the P.I. agency up until last year. Oh, and these are our two new housemates, Bella and Sophie." As Cindy made the introductions, Shane knelt down to pet the dogs, then extended his hand to Terra, who took it in both of hers, the connection almost palpable.

"It's very nice to meet you Terra," he said, his brown eyes locked on hers. Terra, reluctant to release the man's hand, smiled back at him.

"It's a pleasure to meet you as well," she replied, her voice soft, enjoying the feel of his hand. They stood for an instant, the moment broken by the meowing of the cat, who began to rub against the man's leg.

"Oh, by the way, this is Midnight, my roommate and most trusted confidant." Terra and Cindy both laughed at the man's words, knowing how true they were. Cindy had met Shane right after moving into the neighborhood, even before she met Preacher, and they had developed an almost immediate friendship. He had just gone through a nasty break up with his long-time girlfriend, and when Cindy saw the way he and Terra had just looked at each other, she began to have definite ideas. "Would you all like to come in? I have a fresh batch of sun tea that just came in, and a fresh bowl of water." Cindy looked at Terra for a moment, then nodded.

"Sure, that would be great." Taking Terra by the hand, the foursome went up the driveway with Shane, the cat right behind and staying close to Terra.

Shane returned to the living room, a pitcher and three glasses on a serving tray. Setting it down on the metal framed coffee table, he expertly filled the three glasses and set the pitcher down, then handed each woman a glass before picking his up. "Here's to new friends and old friends," he toasted, raising his glass to theirs. Terra and Cindy raised theirs as well, then took a sip of the delicious tea. "So, where's Preacher?" Shane asked, as the ladies sat back on the leather sofa they were sharing.

"Well, he and a friend are off on a fishing trip," she answered, as the cat jumped up between the two women, and immediately took up a place on Terra's lap.

"Midnight, get down from there," Shane scolded the cat, as Terra stroked the soft fur.

"No, really it's fine. I like cats. They're independent, clean and easy to take care of, kind of like me.' As she spoke, the cat began to rub against her hand, his purring audible to everyone in the room.

"Looks like you have a new friend," he said quietly to Terra, who gave him her best smile while continuing to pet the creature resting in her lap. Bella and Sophie watched the interaction from their spot on the floor, their mouths wet with water from Shane.

"Well, I can always use another good friend," she answered, her dark eyes connecting with his, while Cindy looked on.

When the two women and the dogs got back to the house, Terra let the girls outside, while Cindy took a pain pill to ease the discomfort. Cindy had been so glad that Shane had been home when they walked by, and the almost visible connection between he and Terra made her heart feel light. She loved seeing people meet others who could possibly make their lives richer, and she could tell that the two new friends had a definite interest in each other.
Her daydreaming was broken by the return

of the two dogs into the family room where she sat, her shoes off, her feet and legs up as Terra joined her. "Thank you for the walk," she said to her guest, who leaned forward in the chair she was sitting on.

"That was really clever, the whole walk thing. What an amazing coincidence that you got tired right in front of Shane's house, don't you think?" Cindy, a sheepish *what, me* look on her face. Before Cindy could respond, Terra reached over and touched the other woman's hand gently. "Thank you," she said quietly as, as Cindy saw the look on her face.

"Wow. You two really hit it off, didn't you?" she asked, a light blush coming over Terra's face.

Terra, hesitant to say anything too soon, just smiled at her friend. She knew, however, that when she turned in for the night her new friend down the street and his great smile would be at the forefront of her dreams.

"What say we give your husband a quick call?" Terra asked, moving over next to Cindy and the girls, and picking up her cell phone.

Chapter 15

Summer was furious, angrier than she could recall being since the Ranch. She had made the deal with Dingo Dave to leave at the stroke of midnight to head north, and the lousy bastard had been almost two hours late getting back from the sendoff for Jake. When he got back to the clubhouse, he smelled of alcohol, gasoline and sweat, and the very fact that he was still breathing was a testament to Summer's restraint and dire need for his services.

"Listen damn it, we need to move. I told you I wanted to leave at midnight, and when we agreed on ten million you said we would. Now, let's cut this shit out and get on the road." The disheveled, stoned biker looked at the woman chastising him, and if not for the massive amount of money she was paying him, he would have slit her throat, then fucked her. But business first.

"Sorry baby. Some of the boys from the Oregon and Idaho chapters showed up, and we just lost our fucking minds. There was so much blow and pussy going around you wouldn't believe it, but then hey, you don't want to hear that. Tell you what. Give me two minutes to grab my shit, the boys are out back and ready to go, and Scab has the rig all loaded up, so we can be on our merry way." Summer forced herself to stay calm, and smiled at the man, who had turned and gone into a back room. Summer picked up a small bag on the table next to her, then headed for the door and stepped into the night air. Tilting her head back, she inhaled of the salty sea air, and felt her mind relaxing, as she prepared for the long drive. In the driver's seat, Scab had the window down, smoking a cigarette and when he saw Summer, a smile crossed his ragged face as he tossed the butt out the window and onto the ground.

Summer looked at her protector, and walked up to the driver's door, placing her hands on the window ledge. "Scab, my love, how long do you think it will take us to get up to where we're heading?" Scab turned his head and let his greasy fingers touch the dash mounted GPS.

Fiddling with the buttons, he peered at the screen before answering. "It looks like it should take about eight hours, give or take," he told Summer, who looked dismayed at the information.

"Can you find a faster route, or some way to make it a quicker trip? I really need to get up there, and Dave already has us two hours behind." Before Scab could answer, Summer's arm was grabbed from behind, the woman crying out in pain as Dave spun her to him.

"Listen to me, and fucking listen good. You may be the money behind this little excursion, but these are my brothers, and my responsibility. If you want anything changed, or done differently, you talk to me, and no one else. These guys only answer to me, and that includes your little pussy whipped nugget here." Scab seemed unfazed by the derogatory comments by his brother, but Summer was not.

"Fine. Let's get this show on the road now. You've cost me two hours, which I could hardly afford, but I can't change that fact. Now, you listen to me. I need to be in Cedars Pass, at that cabin in eight hours and not one minute more. You do whatever you have to too make this happen, because if it doesn't, and I miss that black haired bitch who butchered me, getting your money will be the least of your worries." Her blue eyes glaring at Dave, Summer prayed she hadn't overplayed her hand, then was stunned when the Australian man began to laugh.

"Damn sweetheart, you've got a mean streak in you, and I like that. No worries, you want to be there in eight hours, you'll have it." Summer stared at him, their eyes locked in a battle of wills.

"Fine. Now, let's get moving." As Summer walked around the Jeep, Dave went to the front parking lot area, where six men sat, their engines revving loudly in the early morning air. Dave went up and spoke to the largest of the men, sitting in front, slapped him on the shoulder and stood back as the bikes roared off. The Jeep came up beside Dave, who watched his brothers leaving with something akin to sadness, as he wanted to take his bike, but knew he needed to be in the rig and following them to run the show. Opening the back door, Dave climbed in and sprawled across the spacious back seat. Propping himself up against the rear driver's window, he thumped the back of Scab's seat. "Hey dipshit, wake me up when the sun starts to come up." Scab looked back over his shoulder at his president and nodded. Dave leaned back, closed his eyes, farted loudly then drifted off to sleep, as Summer sat, quiet and unmoving in the front seat.

"Scab, why do you let them call you names like that? I thought you guys were supposed to be all about respect, but I don't see any of that towards you." As she asked him the question, Summer shifted in her seat to look at the grizzled little man sitting next to her, the one who had saved her life, despite having been sent to kill her.

Scratching his unshaven cheek, Scab kept his eyes on the road as he entered the freeway, then started to speak.

"You know, the only ones who ever showed me anything but hate was these guys. I used to get the shit beat out of me on a regular basis, by the kids at school, my mom's boyfriends, my mom, and anybody else who wanted a shot. The first time I fought back I hurt the kid bad when I cracked him with a brick. They sent me to juvie, and that was where the real fun started. After three months there I got out, and when I did I swore I'd never go back. I was beaten and raped on a regular basis in that place, and when I got old enough I kept mainly to myself. I worked construction jobs, roofing, anything where I wouldn't have to deal with people except roughnecks like me. When I was 24 I got into a fight when one of my co-workers tried to take my sandwich. I hit him with my roofing hammer and split his skull. I got five years for that, but when I got locked up, that was where I met Jake. We were cellmates at High Desert prison, and he took me under his wing. He always said I had potential, but just to have somebody protect me and watch over me felt wonderful. When he was released I was pretty leery of what might happen, but he told me he had left word that I was to be left alone, and when I got sprung to call him and he would hook me up. I had always been really good with motors and stuff like that, and when I was paroled I had some money saved. I bought an old used Harley and fixed it up, scrounging for parts and doing odd jobs around Susanville. About October it started getting really cold, so I called Jake up, and when I told him I had a bike he told me to get my ass down to San Diego, where he was riding with the Devils Disciples." Pausing for a moment, Scab turned his eyes towards Summer, his heart beating fast at the sight of the beautiful woman. Turning his attention back to the road, he felt Summer watching him. "When I got to San Diego and met up with Jake, he introduced me to the other guys in the club, and I never felt more welcome than I did right then. I had to start as a prospect with the club, which basically meant I had to do whatever they told me to, but I didn't mind. They treated me more like family than anyone ever had. The day they gave me my full rocker patch was the happiest day of my life. These brothers have my back, and I have theirs. It's simple as that. If they bust my balls sometimes and call me names, it's okay. It's kinda like having a bunch of big brothers watching out for me, and I'll die for my guys." Scab realized he was gripping the steering wheel too tightly, as evidenced by the white knuckles on his hands. Summer reached over, and tenderly laid her gloved hand on top of his, surprising him.

"Scab, you have no idea how special you are. Your loyalty is rare to find, and I don't think I ever thanked you for saving me back at the Ranch. You really did save my life, and I don't take that lightly." Summer gently rubbed his hand through the silky glove, and Scab felt as if he was on the verge of tears. Summer reached over with her other hand, and softly caressed the stubbled cheek, letting her fingers feel the bumps and sores on his face.

"So Ms. Summer, tell me your story. What's the story behind that beautiful necklace you wear? It's very pretty, and I can see that it's very expensive." Summer sat for a moment, looking at this sunburned, scraggly man sitting next to her, and felt a kinship with him despite their opposite appearances. Folding her hands in her lap, Summer looked back at Dave, snoring in the back, then turned her attention back to Scab.

"Well, let's see. My mother dumped me in a shelter when I was nine, and it kind of went from there. I was abused by several of the men who worked there, but all it did was make me stronger. I vowed to never let a man hurt me again, and when I was fostered out to a husband and wife, I knew what the man was before I ever stepped foot in their house. I used those years to not only expand my brain in school, but also to develop my talents, if you get my drift. I made more money than you could believe, but when the time came after my sixteenth birthday to get rid of them, I did just that. I killed three people that night, then burned the house to the ground. The authorities thought I was the third person in that house, but by that time I was in Europe, and that was where I honed my craft. When I met my husband Nikoli, we seemed to be a perfect match. He's the one who taught me the power of thirteen, and of his family's crest." Holding up the necklace, Summer showed it to Scab. "The two triangles are their symbols of masculinity and femininity, of having their power working for them at all times and all in all places. The thirteen, now that is the age of true, unbridled passion. It is also the number that cleans and purifies everything. The number 13 brings out the test, the suffering and the death. It symbolizes the death to the matter or to oneself and the birth to the spirit: the passage on a higher level of existence.

When Nikoli turned thirteen, his father bestowed on him his first girl, and taught him how to use her to make him money. By the time he was 17, Nikoli had over 100 women working for him all over Europe, and when his father died unexpectedly, Nikoli inherited his father's entire business empire, making him the largest purveyor of female flesh in that part of the world."

Summer's voice was soothing to Scab's nerves, which were a little on edge given the current job.

"When I met Nikoli, we fell for each other very quickly. We also realized that we both had the same passion, the same desire to be as wealthy as possible. During our time together I showed him many, many things that could improve his business, and I travelled with him extensively, to teach his girls how best to please the men they were with. We both had a fascination with my hands, and that single connection made us one more than anything. He presented me with this necklace the day he bought it for me and helped me to understand the power it gave me. On Nikoli's last day, he was meeting with some eastern European businessmen, and I walked in to hear them talking about my son Giorgio. I heard just enough to know what they were planning to do, and I immediately went after Nikoli, in front of his associates. Nikoli had never wanted children, but when I had become pregnant, he had conceded to allow me to have the child.

That fateful afternoon we had gotten into a huge argument, with him smashing a wine glass against the fireplace in frustration. After his visitors left the fight had rapidly escalated and moved upstairs, and when my intoxicated husband tried to slap me, it had been very easy to shove him and watch him tumble down the curving staircase, his head bouncing off the marble steps." Summer sat, talking but with her eyes shut, reliving that moment when she had saved her son from the flesh peddlers that her husband had invited into their home. "I can still see, in my mind's eye, the blood pooling around his skull as he lay on the marble floor dying. I could also feel the smooth texture of his finely groomed hair as I took his head in my hands, his dark eyes meeting mine, begging for mercy and seeing my true intentions. I leaned down, kissed his forehead, whispered *I love you* to him then twisted his neck, feeling the vertebrae snap. His eyes went blank immediately, and when Gorgio came running down the stairs I told him to call the police."

Scab sat, his gaze going back and forth between the road ahead and the woman next to him. Before he could respond to what Summer had revealed to him, there came a grumbling voice from the back seat.

"God, would you two bitches shut the fuck up? It's like a fucking hen party in here." Dave sat up as he spoke, his eyes bleary, the smell of the previous night's partying still wafting off him. "Where the fuck are we?" he asked, as Scab reached down and handed him a beer from the paper sack beside Summer. Taking the can, Dave swallowed half of it, then poured some of the cold liquid on his face to help him wake up. Some of the beer splashed onto Summer's dress, and she scowled at Dave, her eyes dark and brooding.

"We're about 2 hours from Tahoe," Scab told him, looking at the GPS unit on the dash. "We stopped for gas about 2 hours ago, and we decided to let you sleep. The boys are about 45 minutes ahead of us. I talked to them just before you woke up, and Spiderman said they would let us know when they hit city limits. It's about 20 minutes to that cabin outside of Tahoe, and when we stopped earlier I checked out the gear in back. Everything's ready, and I told them we would meet up with them when we get there, so just lay back and rest until we do." Dave stared at the man driving, shocked. This was the longest stretch of word Scab had ever strung together to anyone at one time, except Summer, and Dave thought he could see a difference in the dirty man's demeanor as well. He seemed to be sitting up straighter than before, his eyes more focused than Dave could ever recall. Dave felt Summer's eyes on him and turned to look at her. The woman had a smile on her face, a genuine look of pleasure, and Dave had to admit, it damn well scared him.

"See, you guys never took the time to talk to Scab here, and really get to know him. You have a true, died in the wool diamond in the rough in this man, and you're too blind to see it." Dave, still waking up, looked back at Scab and indeed did see a different person. Scab gave his brother a quick look before turning back to the road.

"Lay back and get some rest Dave," Scab said, the words sounding like more a command than a request. Dave did just that, taking a small vial from his vest pocket and snorting twice from it, then stretching out again and quickly dozing off. The pair in the front of the Jeep looked at one another, a small grin passing between them.

Thirty minutes later, as they passed a rundown diner, Summer spotted a black and white car coming in the opposite direction and recognized it at the same time Scab did. They kept their eyes straight ahead, hoping the car would just move past them, as Scab checked his speed. Watching in his rearview mirror, he saw the car go past them, then continue down the highway. Exhaling a sigh of relief, he and Summer looked down the road ahead, when suddenly the sound of a siren and the red and blue flashing lights lit up his mirror.

"Fuck," he said under his breath, as he slowly decreased his speed, trying to give himself time to think.

"Pull over Scab, it's okay," Summer whispered, touching his hand lightly. Scab, a look of fear on his face, could hear the officer behind him telling him to do the same thing. Easing to the side of the road, Scab felt his heart pounding in his chest as the lights behind him filled his vision. Summer handed him several piece of paper from the glovebox, then smiled reassuringly at him.

The highway patrol officer exited his car, adjusted his hat then began to walk towards the Jeep, hand on his gun. The tags were valid, they had not been speeding or breaking any traffic laws, but the man's face had caught his attention enough to warrant pulling them over, at least to his way of thinking. It would never stand up in court, but if the driver was who, or what he thought he was, then it wouldn't matter. The driver had the same look as the biker garbage he had passed about twenty miles north of where he now stood, and Bradley Allen White always listened to his gut feelings.

As he approached the vehicle, Brad, or Officer Brad Ass as he like to be referred to, saw the driver's window down and walked up carefully alongside the rig. "Driver, show me your hands now!" he yelled, Scab obliging with the papers in hand. Stepping closer, the officer unsnapped the restraining strap on his holster, looking at Scab through the window. "Keep your hands out the window, and passenger, put yours on the dashboard!" Taking several more steps, the officer saw the beautiful woman sitting on the opposite side of the vehicle, her glove covered hands on the dash. Looking at Scab, the officer took the papers still in his gnarled hand, stuffing them into his back pocket. "Where are you headed?" he asked, his eyes still locked on Summer in her dress.

We're just headed to Tahoe to do some gambling," Scab answered, making the barrel-chested man laugh out loud. Scab, confused by the man's laughter, felt his gut tightening as he heard Dave moving in the back. Suddenly the policeman saw him as well and pulled his pistol from his holster.

"You in the back, show me your fucking hands right now!" the officer commanded, as Dave sat forward between the seats.

"What's the problem?" Dave asked, as the officer pulled open the driver's door and ordered Scab out of the vehicle, keeping his gun trained on Dave and the still silent woman.

"You, open that back driver's door now and exit the vehicle!" the officer shouted, as Dave shook his head at being disturbed.

"Fuck, all right. I'm coming out deputy dog, don't shoot," Dave told him, the man keeping his gun trained on Dave. As the back door slid open the officer was momentarily distracted by Summer, who had pulled her skirt up to reveal her tanned thighs. As the man's eyes saw the smooth flesh, Dave rapid fired two rounds from the .40 caliber pistol he always kept tucked in the small of his back, for times such as these. The officer, stunned by the shots, dropped onto the dirt road, sending up clouds of dust, his gun falling out of reach.

The first bullet had struck him dead center in the chest, knocking the breath from him with the impact. The second had taken him in the just above the right eye, the bright red blood exploding and pooling quickly around him. Dave walked up and knelt next to the dying man.

"Sorry dude, but I got a lot on the line here, and I can't let some fat fuck highway patrolman screw that up, now can I. Oh, by the way, when I'm all done with this job, I'm planning on fucking this bitch until she screams, and I'll tell you what- I'll think about you while I'm doing that." Reaching down, Dave patted the man's cheek softly, then straightened up, seeing that Scab had already gone back to the patrol car, started the engine and drove it off the road, leaving it half sunk in sand in a nearby arroyo. "Great job Scab," Dave told the man, who had returned, covered in sweat. Scab, a smile on his face, climbed into the Jeep as Dave took his place in the back seat. Scab looked over at his passenger, his grin revealing the brown, rotted teeth.

"That was great, what you did to distract him. I thought we were screwed there for a minute, but when you pulled your dress up, man he just froze." Summer sat in her seat, her hands throbbing in pain, and smiled at her companion.

"Let's go Scab," she said quietly, as Dave stretched out again in the back.
"Jesus, are you too going to fucking go steady or what? Get the hell out of here," he yelled, as Scab put the Jeep in gear and headed towards their destination.

Chapter 16

Traffic was extremely heavy on the 101 as the trio sped towards their latest target. Cowboy was up front, Mikey and Terry right behind, the engines reverberating loudly in the morning air. Cars honked at them as they weaved in and out of traffic, each of them extending a middle finger and an evil glare at the cars. Spotting the exit for I-80 East, they cut across two full lanes of traffic, causing the morning commuters to have to slam on their brakes to avoid colliding with the motorcycles. The three men accelerated onto the desired road, a nondescript blue Dodge van trailing behind them. Passing the first cutoff, the bikers pulled alongside one another in formation, as a U-Haul in front of them began to slow, irritating the trio. Before they could react, a second van came from behind and pulled up directly next to the motorcycles, while the pursuing blue van boxed them in from behind and forced them onto the next exit. Their blood pumping, the trio quickly spied the concrete roadblock ahead of them, as the three chase vehicles converged on them, and men with semi-automatic rifles leaned out from inside the vans. The trio, without speaking a word, immediately screeched to a standstill and quickly climbed off, Cowboy reaching behind him and withdrawing a silver .357 revolver, opening fire at the officers. He was hit almost instantly by return fire, dropping the revolver and falling face down on the pavement on top of his bike. Mikey and Terry watched their brother die and were filled with instant rage. Mikey pulled the Mac-10 out from the leather pouch on the side of his bike, emptying the clip towards the policemen and sending them scurrying for cover. The two bikers took refuge behind the large barriers that had been placed to stop them, hunkering down, resembling Butch Cassidy and the Sundance Kid in the last scenes of the famous film by the same name.

"Fuck man, Cowboy's dead!" Mikey screamed over the noise of the authorities yelling for them to come out. Terry punched him in the arm, showing him the surprise he had. From the leather sack slung over his shoulder, he pulled several objects. In his hands he held two objects, one a fragmentation grenade that would devastate anything in its path, and the second an even bigger and nasty surprise. This one was a white phosphorus grenade, or Willy Pete as they had been called back in the day. It was even more deadly, in that when it exploded it covered its victims with white phosphorus, which would ignite and burn continually while exposed to oxygen. Mikey smiled when he saw the all too familiar devices, not a little surprised that Terry had brought the evil little gifts along for the ride.

"You loaded there, bud?" Terry yelled, as they heard the approaching vehicles and knowing their time was short.

"Fucking A," Mikey answered, catching sight of the officers dragging Cowboys body away. With a split second of silence, the two men paid homage to their fallen friend, then Terry grinned as he handed one of the explosives to Mikey.

"See you in hell brother," he said, clasping the other man's forearm. Their eyes met for a split second, then both men jumped to their feet, throwing the grenades as far as they could, and opening fire on the policemen and SWAT officers who had taken up position in preparation for a prolonged gunfight. They were both hit at almost the same time by multiple shots, Terry taking two to the chest and one to the forehead, dead before he hit the ground. Mikey managed to hang on a little bit longer, the first shots only angering the drug fueled man. He had enough left to slap another clip into the second Mac-10 and begin to fire, as a single shot from the SWAT sniper on top of the U-Haul van took him directly in the cheek. Mikey slumped lifelessly to the ground, as the officers who had escaped the first grenades impact swarmed the area, as the ones left behind were being treated for their injuries, a task made much more difficult by the white phosphorus grenade. Several men were screaming as the fiery substance burned through their clothes, as finally someone realized what they were dealing with and called for EMS.

Clifton Arabel, the SWAT commander on scene, stood looking over the chaos and shaking his head. "Are you fucking kidding me? White phosphorus grenades? Where the fuck did this white trash get hold of these, and why did we not know about this?" His second in command, Adam Lopez, shook his head as he tried to answer.

"Boss, we had great intel on these three, we knew what guns they had, hell we even know what they had for dinner last night, but these grenades, well that shit never showed up on any of our radar." He knew this was of little consolation to his boss, but the commander also knew what he said was true. Their surveillance had been perfect on the three dead men, who had a mile long string of felonies and had been wanted for way too long, which was why they had finally been targeted this morning. Clifton looked at his charge and knew what he said was true. Adam was an outstanding officer and tactician, and never missed anything, and he could hardly be blamed for this. That being said, he was the one who was going to have to call the wives of the three dead officers and explain to them what had happened. That hat, unfortunately, was his alone to wear, and he exhaled deeply as he watched his men being loaded up in the meat wagon.

Vince Bandini sat in the front of the Bell Ranger helicopter, his gaze on the pilot next to him.
"What's the problem?" Vince asked, his voice quiet but stern. The pilot looked at his gauges, then his air speed indicator. "You aren't going to want to hear this, but we're going to coast into Tahoe on fumes. When they did the last service on your chopper here, they put in a slightly larger, higher torque cam, which means more power, but we also burn fuel a little faster. It's about 468 miles from Vegas to Tahoe, and at our speed of 167 miles per hour, we burned a little faster than expected. We should be touching down in about 18 minutes. We'll

make it, I just want you to know what we're dealing with." Vince's eyes bored into the pilot, making the combat veteran squirm in his seat. Before Vince could say anything else, his headset was filled with the voice of one of his men in the back.

"Boss, we just got a call from our man in San Francisco, and it's no deal. The three blind mice got nailed by the cat on their way east, but the cat didn't get away unscathed."

At the news, Vince was both happy and disappointed. He never failed to feel good when the do-gooder police force took a hit, but the loss of his, as they were called in conversation, three blind mice was something he would have a hard time replacing. They had always been at the ready when Vince called and had never failed to perform their assigned task. Vince recalled the lawyer a few years back that had been giving him a lot of problems. He had called Cowboy, told him what he wanted done, and three days later mission accomplished.

"Boss, I'm getting some more news that might make you happy. Our eyes and ears called, and we won't have any problem being in place before the bitch arrives with her boys." This indeed did put a smile on the man's tired face. "Our people in Tahoe are waiting at the landing sight, and everything is in place for when we land. They say it should take about thirty minutes to get in place near the cabin." Vince took a deep breath, then exhaled, as he thought about what he had planned for Miss Summer, and those thoughts put an evil, wicked grin on his handsome face.

Chapter 17

"*Érchomai gio mou*". Ryder stood, listening to Micah mumbling the strangely familiar words in his sleep. In his right hand, Ryder held his phone, recording the boy's words so he could let Lacey hear them later.

Micah had been his usual self the majority of the day, playing with April and keeping her entertained. After dinner last night they had settled down and watched Finding Nemo on DVD, with both Ryder and Lacey finding the adventures of the lost fish and his friend Dory very soothing to their rattled nerves. Even Joker had settled in on the large rug and seemed to be watching the film, although Ryder did notice that the dog positioned himself in front of April the entire time. When the movie was done and the popcorn bowls rinsed and put away, Lacey had laid April in their room, while Ryder had taken Micah to his room to tuck him in. While Micah brushed his teeth, Ryder had pulled back the covers and fluffed the pillow for the boy, wanting, needing to make things as normal as possible. There had not been anymore of the angry outbursts that Micah had displayed earlier that week, for which Ryder and Lacey were both glad.

The only real difference had been Micah's reciting several phrases in what they had deemed to be in Greek. The phrases "*I'm coming for you, my son, I am the wolf, they are the sheep and be cautious, my son*" had each been spoken at least twice by the boy, usually when he was extremely tired or sleeping. Lacey and Ryder both grasped the severity of the terms being spoken in the foreign language and understood the inevitable meeting that would take place. He, at least, would be glad when he had the chance to kill the psychotic bitch who was terrorizing his family and making their lives a living nightmare. He also understood how badly Lacey wanted her shot at Summer as well and would have to keep her in check when the showdown finally came.

His revelry was broken by the hand on his arm, and he jerked slightly as Lacey lightly squeezed his arm. "Is he doing it again?" Lacey whispered, as Ryder nodded slightly and Joker took a seat at their feet, looking into the doorway where the boy lay. "I think we need to talk to him about this," she said softly, as Ryder slowly pulled the door partly shut.

"I hate to say this, but I think you're right. I hate to do that to him, after everything he's been through, but it may be our best shot at learning why this is happening. We need every advantage we can get when this finally, you know, comes to a head, and as hard as it is to accept, he is the key to all of this."

Ryder slid his arms around his wife to embrace her, when from their room April began to fuss. Exhaling deeply, Ryder patted his wife on the bottom and shooed her towards their room, as he and Joker walked in the direction of the front room. "Joker and I are going to do our nightly check, then we'll be back, and we can wake Micah up and have our talk." Lacey blew him a kiss across the room, then went to tend to her daughter, as Ryder and his partner opened and closed the front door, making sure it was locked behind them. Stepping out into the cool night air, Joker took the lead, as usual, being careful where he stepped, his highly sensitive nose detecting the surprises awaiting the coming enemies. Ryder inhaled deeply of the mountain air, wishing this was a family vacation instead of a trek for survival, comforted by the weight of the pistol under his shirt. He and Joker made their way down near the locked gate, checking the razor wire wrapped around the gate. They then turned to the left, making their way around to the back of the house, barely visible through the thick forestation of trees.

Carefully, they continued their walk, Ryder checking on several trip wires and flares he had set up to warn them if any unannounced visitors arrived. As they rounded the southern part of the property, suddenly Lacey's scream pierced the still of the night, and Ryder and Joker took off running for the house. As they ran, Ryder pulled the 9mm pistol from his waistband, chambering a round as they came around by the kitchen. Ryder carefully opened the kitchen door, as Joker slipped quietly inside. Seeing nothing, Ryder moved towards the bedroom, when his wife screamed again. Detecting the sound as coming from Micah's room, Ryder pushed the door open, seeing Lacey on the bed, Micah in her arms, his face bright red and a small amount of foamy spittle coming from the corners his mouth. Ryder laid the gun down on the nightstand and picked the boy up. "Micah, wake up son, wake up, wake up!" he yelled at the boy, whose eyes had rolled back in his head, showing just the whites of the conjunctiva. Lacey had jumped off of the bed and to her son's side, as Ryder shook the boy. "Micah, wake up son," he repeated, as Lacey ran into the washroom and returned with a wet cloth. Laying it on his face, Micha began to cough, sputtering out spittle as he slowly regained consciousness. Ryder held tightly to the boy, feeing the breathing resuming against his chest. Lacey continued to wipe off her son's face, whispering words of love to him, as his eyes slowly opened.

"Mom, why are you washing my face?" he squeaked out, while Ryder held him even tighter. Sitting up, Ryder moved to the bed and sat on the edge Micah still in his lap, Lacey beside them, and even Joker making an appearance, licking the boy's dangling hand, causing Micah to giggle softly.

"Micah, what happened son?" Ryder asked, his voice soft and low. The boy looked at him as if he had no idea what he was talking about. Lacey leaned over and kissed his flushed cheek.

"I don't know. I was sleeping, and all of sudden a voice was saying to me, Gorgio, be cautious and that she was coming for me. Who's coming for me? Is it that lady Summer?" At the mention of the dreaded woman's name, Ryder picked the boy up and went into the large living room, Lacey and Joker joining them as he sat the boy down on the leather sofa, then retrieved his cell phone from the breakfront near the large bay window. Lacey took a seat next to her son, as Ryder pulled up a chair and sat down, facing the boy.

Ryder thought for a moment before beginning. "Micah, do you remember The Ranch? Do you remember the room you were in?" The young boy looked at him, as a strange look crossed his face.

"Well sure, I remember our room. It was small, but nice. Why do you ask?" Lacey's eyes met Ryder's at the *our roo*m comment, but she could see he was telling her to stay silent.

"Well, your mom and I, we had a really hard time trying to find you when we got there, and we have never talked about this. Did you ever talk to Mrs. Collins back in Santa Barbara about your time in the room?" Micah stared at Ryder, who prayed he was headed down the right path.

"Well, we never talked about our room, just about me, what I did when I was there, what Summer said to me, that kind of stuff." The boy seemed a little perplexed at the man's questions but seemed willing to talk. Picking up on the second reference to *our room,* Ryder had a thought.

"Micah, when you say our room, did you stay with one of the girls there? Is that what you meant by our room?" Micah looked at him and laughed, a strange sound they hadn't heard lately.

"No, I would never sleep in a room with a girl. It was our room, Giorgio and mine. You know, Giorgio, my brother." Lacey's hand went to her mouth to stifle the cry that wanted to erupt, and Ryder had to force himself to stay calm.

"Micah, you know you don't have any brothers, just a little sister April, who loves you very much." Ryder knew he had to try and push the boy to find out what else had happened. Micah just shook his head at Ryder's denial.

"Don't be silly. Summer told me that we were brothers, just with different dads, and that when Giorgio, the older brother died I had to step up and fill his shoes. She showed me pictures of Giorgio, and boy, did we look alike. I wish I had known him, but Summer used to come down and talk to us every day, usually in Greek, but sometimes in English too. She told me his daddy died a long time ago, and that I was her son now." As the boy spoke, Lacey, silent and shaking on the end of the sofa, looked at her son and began to cry. "I really liked it when she told us stories about Greece, and about the history of it. She even taught me a few words in Greek, but I think I forgot them." Ryder was stunned at the boy's revelations.

"What happened to you the day you escaped from the Ranch?" Lacey asked, her voice eerie in the quiet in the room.

Micah looked at her, concerned by the distraught look on her face.

"My friend DeDe, who was next door, began using morse code to talk to me. When the doors popped open that day, there was smoke everywhere, people yelling, guns shooting, and I went next door to find DeDe. She found me, and I wanted to go back in and rescue my brother Giorgio from the room, but DeDe said no, it was too dangerous, so we escaped out the back of the building because of all the men with guns. When we got outside, we started around the back of the house, towards the east. I know it was east because the sun was just setting on the opposite side. We were trying to be real careful, because there were still a lot of men shouting, and when we got around the side of the house, we thought we were safe. Just as we were headed towards the front of the house, someone shot DeDe, making her fall. I tried to help her up, I wanted to, but she just laid there and told me to run, and not to look back. I was scared, and didn't want to leave her, but she yelled at me and told me to run fast and keep running. I waved goodbye to her and ran towards the front of the house, then hid in some bushes when I saw some really big men with guns. When they left, I ran to where the cars were, and there was a big explosion. It hurt my ears, and made my eyes sting, but I stayed put and waited. A few minutes later a man in a white outfit like Chef Boyardee's came running out of the house, looking scared and holding a gun. When he saw me he pointed the gun at me, then saw I was just a boy. He grabbed my hand and pulled me with him into the dark, where we finally found a blue truck. He shoved me inside and then got in and started the engine. I asked him where we were going, and he patted my hand and said it would be okay. He told me his name was Carlos, and he was a chef at The Ranch. He had really kind eyes and a nice smile and told me that everything was going to be okay. I sat back and watched as he drove, then must have dozed off because when I woke up we were at his house. It was small, and there were no other houses around, and he took me inside. He told me that I would be safe there, that the police would be looking for anyone who had been at the Ranch, and we could live together. He seemed nice, and I didn't have anywhere else to go, since my home at The Ranch was gone."

Ryder and Lacey sat, stunned at the events that had occurred. All the time they had thought he was dead, he had been alive and well and living in the Nevada desert.

"Didn't you ever wonder about your mom back In Santa Barbara, about your room, your things?" Ryder asked him, as Lacey sat unmoving. The boy, seemingly unaffected by the story, simply shrugged his shoulders. "I guess I kind of forgot about Santa Barbara for a while, until one day while I was watching TV at Carlo's house. A news story came on about an oil spill off the Santa Barbara coast, and when I heard those two words something happened. In my mind I could see a poster of Tom Brady in a room, some books on a shelf, and I heard a woman crying. Before I could do anything, Carlos got home and he had a friend with him, a truck driver named Andy. Andy had a long, long truck and trailer parked outside the house, with a bunch of pretty cars on it, and one of them I remember, looked like yours."

Looking at Lacey, he continued. "I remembered riding in that car with you, playing Slug Bug and listening to the radio. I heard Andy talking to Carlos, who was headed to a dealership in Santa Barbara with some of the cars, and I decided to catch a ride and find that Tom Brady poster. I went to my room and folded up a few clothes, then when they went outside I snuck into the kitchen and grabbed a jar of peanut butter, some crackers, a packet of string cheese, oh, and Carlos's watch by the sink where he always took it off to cook. I put the food in a plastic bag, slipped the watch on and went back to my room to get my clothes. I heard Andy saying goodbye to Carlos, and I slipped out the back window and next to the truck. I crept up onto the trailer, trying to be quiet while the truck warmed up, and when I found a car door that was unlocked I crawled inside. I felt real bad not saying goodbye to Carlos, cause he was real nice to me, but I knew I had to find that poster."

Lacey sat on the couch, her hands trembling both in anger and sadness at what the boy had been forced to do while away from his home. His precious childhood had been cruelly ripped away, and Lacey's rage at what that woman had done to her son was fueled even more, and a small part of her wanted the woman here right now, so she could finish what she had started in the desert. Her green eyes, misty with unshed tears, stared at her son as he continued. The therapist back home had told her and Ryder to let Micah come to them about what had happened, that if they tried to push him to open up prematurely, it might actually do more harm than good.

"Micah honey, I know what that woman told you at The Ranch made sense to you, since you and the other boy looked so much alike, but he was not your brother. She was lying to you the whole time, wanting you to replace her son, who died, but she was sick, just using you to make herself feel better. Do you know what blackmail is?" Micah looked at her as if she had taken leave of her senses.

"Sure I do. It's when someone forces you to do something by holding something over you that can hurt you." Lacey nodded slightly at the brief but concise definition.

"Well honey, that's what that woman was doing to your dad. She made him take you to The Ranch by holding something he had done as leverage over him." Micha just sat, trying to come to terms with everything, then a huge smile came over his face, as he suddenly looked much older than his twelve years.

"Oh, you know what else she told me. She said that when I turned thirteen that everything she had would be mine. She told me that at thirteen a young boy becomes a man, and that when I turned thirteen I would become a man and take over the business. She told me that at thirteen, a man achieves greatness and is set to fulfill his destiny of great riches and power." The adult appearance that had shown on his face just seconds earlier disappeared, and he looked like a boy again. "Do you think that means when I turn thirteen that I can buy that dirt bike I always wanted and have you show me how to ride it, Ryder?" The question, so innocent in its nature, shocked both the adults sitting on the sofa. This child, this precious gift, was obviously so badly scarred by his experiences at The Ranch at the hands of his father and that bitch, that he actually believed when he hit thirteen he was destined to achieve financial and personal greatness. Ryder just looked at the boy, reached over and touched his small arm.

"You know what son, why don't we talk about that when we get home?" Micah looked at the man's hand on his arm, then back up at Ryder, that earlier, ugly expression crossing his face once again.

"What did I say before? I'm not your son, and don't fucking touch me again." Lacey and Ryder sat, stunned by the boy's unprovoked, vicious attack. As Micah sat, staring at the two people in front of him, a deafening silence filled the room, then Joker stood up on all fours, placed himself between the boy and the adults, sat back down, his dark, black eyes staring at the boy staring back at him.

Chapter 18

Darius saw the sign up ahead which read CEDARS PASS, 9 MILES. Preacher was focused on the windy mountain road, as the American River flowed east to west on their left side. The sides of the mountain were covered with luscious green spruce pines, oaks in full color, and as he caught sight of the gently rolling river again, he wondered what the fishing would be like down there. Darius must have read his mind, pointing out several flat areas down below with easy access to fishermen. "I bet that suckers chock full of rainbows and steelhead," Darius told him, as Preacher smiled.

"I bet you're right," he answered, seeing the same road sign. "Nine miles. Guess I better touch base with Cindy before we get there, because once we do I know Ryder's going to want us to be on radio silence." Darius, with no military background, looked quizzically at his traveling partner. "That means no cell phones, no radio, nothing when we get there. Remember, this is Ryder's fight, and we are just there to support him and watch his back. I know it's your cabin, but this is Ryder's show, and what he says goes."

Darius nodded in agreement. "Hey, no worries here. I just want to get this over with and get back home to my wife, like you do." Before Preacher could respond, Darius's cell phone rang, and he slipped his earphone into place, to keep the conversation private. Preacher, on the other hand, had no such concerns about anyone hearing his chat with his wife.

Pressing the #1 button on his smart phone, Preacher heard the phone ringing back at home, stretching his neck and shoulders as he heard Cindy's voice. "Hey there handsome, where are you?" she asked across the miles.

"Well, we're about five miles from Cedars Pass, so it should be about 25 minutes to the cabin, give or take. What's new at the house?" Preacher asked, cherishing the sound of his wife's soft, gentle tone.

"Well, Terra's still asleep, the girls are having dinner and I'm just really missing my man. How long do you think you'll be gone?"

"Well, it's hard to know. We're here until this thing ends. How are you feeling?" Preacher asked, concern over his wife's recuperation filling his question.

"Well, Terra is a great nurse, and I actually feel really good. There is one thing though, that Terra can't do that makes me feel better." Preacher could almost feel his face flushing at his wife's barely masked comment.

"Well sweetie, as soon as I get home, I promise to do that very thing, if it helps you to heal faster." Preacher swore he could hear her breathing speed up slightly at his answer, and again he thanked God for this amazing woman. "Cindy, I need to go honey. We're almost there, and I need to focus on the road, so I promise to call as soon as I can. I love you Peaches," he told her, as Cindy laughed.

"I love you-" suddenly the line went dead, Preacher automatically assuming it was the mountain range, and praying deep down in his gut that it was not an ominous precursor of events to come. Shutting off his phone, Preacher looked at Darius, who was still on the phone, a look of concern on his face. Preacher looked straight ahead, not wanting to make the man uncomfortable. As they crossed over the twin suspension bridge with the American River running almost 200 feet below, he spotted the sign which read Entering Cedars Pass, gateway to the Tahoe basin, Preacher exhaled deeply, glad they were almost at their destination. He wanted to see his friend and hug him, and to let him know he was not alone in this fight.

Darius removed his earpiece from the phone and rolled it up, set the phone back on the dash and looked out the window.

"You okay?" Preacher asked him, while Darius just stared out the window for another moment.

"What? Oh yeah. Tish just got a call that an old friend of hers who passed away unexpectedly. They were pretty close, so it shook her up pretty good." Preacher felt bad for his friend's wife, but somewhere deep in his gut he had the feeling that Darius was not being totally honest with him either.

As they crossed into the city limits of Cedar Pass, population 2,176 people, Preacher looked around and could see why people who lived here did indeed live here. There was an old-style movie house, with the words **CLOSED FOR REPAIRS** across the marquee. There were several trucks parked in front of a coffee shop that looked as if they still made everything from scratch. Across the street from the diner was a mom-and-pop hardware store with a mannequin in the front window wearing a bright orange vest, an Elmer Fudd style hunting cap and holding a shotgun. Next door to the hardware store was a small, obviously freshly painted office with the words SHERIFFS OFFICE painted across the window.

As Preacher started to drive by, suddenly Darius sat forward. "Stop!" he shouted, startling Preacher. "Pull over. I need to go talk to Sam Raymie, the local sheriff for a minute." Preacher pulled into an empty slot about three doors down from the office, and Darius nearly jumped from the vehicle before it even came to a complete stop. Before Preacher could say anything, his passenger was out the door and nearly running to the office. Preacher shut down the engine of the Dodge, then a thought entered his mind. Opening the driver's door, he climbed out, and walked next door to the hardware store. A bell *dinged* over the door as he walked inside, and he was immediately aware of the welcoming smell of gun powder, fishing bait and cinnamon rolls.

"Can I help ya, big guy?" came the question from behind him, and when Preacher turned around he would have sworn he was looking at the reincarnation of Art Carney. The white hair, the warm eyes and the gentle smile caused Preacher to recall his one of his favorite movies, *Harry and Tonto*. He had watched that film innumerous times and had even gotten Cindy hooked on it.

"Hi there. I was wondering if you had seen this man come through in the last few days?" Preacher opened his wallet and displayed a photograph of him, Ryder and Joker, taken two summers ago down at the Santa Monica pier. The store owner peered at the picture over his bifocals, up at Preacher then back at the photo.

"Gorgeous dog there," the man said, his voice raspy, but smooth, like very fine sandpaper. "Mom, come look at this beautiful dog this man owns," the man yelled, as his wife came out from behind a curtain, her hands coated with flour. Clapping them together, she walked up to where the men stood, looked at the photo, then at her husband.

"Looks just like old Jasper," she whispered, her voice full of emotions at the memory. Preacher stood, a little confused, but not wanting to be rude.

"Actually, the dog isn't mine. He belongs to the other man in the picture with me," Preacher told the couple, who kept staring at the images.

"Damn it all Al, can't you see the other man in that picture is the same one who stopped by several days back? You know, the one who bought all that wire and those flares?" The elderly man stared at his wife, then snapped his fingers.

"Sorry mister- I'm sorry, I didn't get your name."

"I'm Preacher, just Preacher," he said, as the man stuck his hand out.

"Nice to meet you Preacher. This is my wife Ellie, and I'm Al. Yeah, he came by a few days back. Why you asking? He owe you money?" Preacher just laughed, then put this wallet away.

"No sir, he doesn't owe me any money. He's my best friend, and I think maybe he's in trouble, the kind he needs a friend to help him with." Al stared at the large man in front of him, as Ellie returned to her baking.

"Son, I don't what kind of trouble you might be talking about, but I damn sure know if I was in trouble I'd want you helping me. Now let's see. He bought up about five or six rolls of razor wire and some regular bailing wire, the kind you use to keep things inside or outside. He also bought a bunch of road flares, the kind with the strike top. Must have bought about 15 or 20 of those. Oh yeah, he also bought a bunch of metal tent spikes, but no tent." As Al finished the mental sales inventory, Preacher saw Darius exit the sheriff's office and head for the truck.

Preacher extended his large hand to the storekeeper, then shook it as he walked towards the front door. As he started to leave, he heard Al say, "Watch your back big fella. You never know who you can truly trust until the chips are down." Preacher turned and looked at the man, who gave him a warm smile, then waved.

Preacher got back to the truck, where Darius was sitting quiet and still. "Everything okay? What was so important in the Sheriff's office?" Darius looked over at Preacher before answering.

"I wanted to see of anything unusual had been reported in the last few days, especially at the cabin." Preacher started the truck's powerful engine, backed up then headed out of town.

"Well? Anything we need to know about?" Preacher asked, his eyes on the road. "Let me know when we get close to the cutoff," he told Darius, who was busy staring out the window at the beautiful mountain scenery.

"No, nothing. I just wanted to make sure everything was good," he finally answered, as he began to watch for the road which would take them to the cabin. Ten minutes later Darius spotted the massive, forked pine tree which marked the entrance to his road. "Turn here," he told Preacher, who turned the truck to the right, leaving the paved road and heading up the single lane road, the massive truck handling the road with precision and ease. About five minutes up the road Preacher spotted a large gate and pulled the truck to a stop. Darius got out to open it, using a key from his keyring. Suddenly Preacher heard a loud "Shit!" from the lawyer, who stood shaking his hand, droplets of blood flying in every direction. Preacher tried not to laugh as the black man came back to the truck, his hand wrapped in his handkerchief.

"There's fucking razor wire wrapped around the lock and the whole damn fence," he said, his voice revealing the pain he was in from his lacerated hand. Preacher got out and reached behind the seat, withdrawing a small canvas bag. Opening it, he withdrew a pair of small wire cutters, showing them to Darius.

"Looks like Ryder wanted to slow somebody down," he said, his voice loud in the quiet mountain air. Walking up to the fence, he carefully began to snip the treacherous wire, tossing the piece off of the road and into the brush. When he was done he went back and got the key from Darius. Opening the gate, he motioned for Darius to slide over and pull the truck through. When the Dodge was inside, Preacher closed the gate and locked it back up, noticing almost comically the bailing wire which ran from either side of the fence out along the property line. *"Brother, what are you hiding from?"*

Climbing back into the truck, he drove up the road, then spotted the large cabin, and was stunned by the sight of the gorgeous structure. Pictures definitely did not do it justice, and as he pulled around the side of the house he saw movement in the front, then the side windows.

"Look, when we get out you just stay put for a minute. Let him see who it is first, so he doesn't think we're whoever is coming for him." Slowly closing their doors, the two men stood silent, then Preacher walked around the back of the pickup, his hands raised. "Ryder, Lacey, it's me, Preacher. I'm here with Darius, and we're here to help you. We know what's going on, and we came to help." As he spoke, the kitchen door came open a crack, a rifle barrel making its appearance. Preacher could feel his heart racing, but he trusted Ryder. Preacher took two steps closer, then another, when suddenly the door burst open and Joker came running out, leaping at the large man. Right behind was Ryder, a rifle slung over his shoulder, Lacey and the kids standing in the doorway. As Joker greeted the two men, Ryder came out, a look on his face that was mixture of relief and anger.

"What the hell are you two doing here? I told you, and you promised me that you wouldn't tell anyone, even Preacher." As Ryder chastised Darius, Preacher walked up and engulfed the man in his arms, and Ryder breathed a sigh of relief. "All right, let's get your gear and get inside. These nights get really cold."

The people sitting around the dining table looked as happy as any normal family, completed by the two children and the dog at his master's feet. "Man Lacey, that was good. I had no idea you were such a great cook," Darius said, the compliment not falling on deaf ears.

"Well thank you Darius, it is much appreciated." Ryder and Preacher were whispering at the other end of the table, and April was growing fussy, so Lacey and Micah began to collect the dishes. When they took them into the kitchen, Lacey saw over her shoulder that Darius had joined the duo in deep conversation. Setting his stack of dishes on the counter, Micah let out a loud yawn, making Lacey laugh with his exaggerated facial expressions.

"Getting tired buddy?" she asked, taking his hand and heading back into the large living area, where the three men sat huddled. In her baby rocker, April was beginning to grow louder in her protestations at being ignored, and Joker had gone to his young charge and laid down at her feet, his dark eyes keeping tabs on everyone in the room.

"Okay gentlemen, I'm going to put these two down to sleep, then I want in on whatever you roosters are clucking about over there." Ryder looked up at her and smiled, blew a kiss to Micah, who was either too tired or not in the mood for such demonstrative acts. Lacey picked up April in her arms, then she and the children went into the room Micah was staying in, as Joker joined them. "Goodnight bug," she whispered to her son, who had slipped into his sleeping bag and doubled up his pillow. "I love you," she said softly, leaning down to kiss his cheek, April chortling quietly as if she too was wishing her big brother a peaceful night's rest.

Looking at his mom, Micah scratched his nose before speaking. "Do you think you'll always love me?" he asked her, making Lacey's heart nearly break. Leaning down she rubbed her nose on his, as they had done since he was a baby.

"Micah, I will always love you. There is absolutely nothing you could ever do that would make me stop loving you," she whispered, her green eyes beginning to water. Their noses touching, their foreheads together, the pair stayed like that for a moment, until April emitted a foul smell. Micah began to laugh, gently at first then harder, as Lacey joined in the rare moment of levity that struck them. Kissing her son again, she got to her feet and walked towards the bedroom door, then stopped and looked back at her son.

"Se agapó," the boy whispered, as Lacey stared at him, her heart beating faster.

Her voice shaking, Lacey asked "What does that mean?" Micah, already turned over on his bed, quietly whispered.

"It means I love you." Lacey fought to control her trembling hands as she opened and closed the door and walked across to where she, Ryder and April slept. Joker still sat outside the boy's room, his dark eyes locked on the door, then darting to where the woman and baby disappeared.

Ryder and the two men had been discussing what was about to happen, and when he saw his wife come out of Micah's room and slip into their room, he could tell something was definitely wrong. "Sorry guys, but I'll be right back," he said, standing up and covering the distance across the room probably faster than he needed. "Lacey, you okay?" he asked softly, opening the door slightly to avoid startling her. Sticking his head inside, he saw his wife changing their daughter, noticing that she was not looking at him as he spoke to her. "Lacey honey, you okay?" he repeated, entering the room and gently closing the door. Walking across the room, Ryder smiled at his baby girl laying on the king-sized bed, her chubby fists opening and closing. Putting his hand on his wife's shoulder, Ryder could feel the subtle vibrations under her skin, and realized she was quietly crying. Tenderly he pulled her to him, and as she turned, she suddenly grabbed onto her husband, as if he was a life preserver on the Titanic. She pulled him tight against her, and he felt the emotions coursing through her, and engulfed her in his arms. "Baby, what's wrong?" he asked, holding her tight.

Lacey couldn't speak for a moment, and she just held tight to Ryder. When she was finally able, all she could get out was "Micah." Ryder, now more confused, kissed her cheek and started to stand up to go check on his son, when Lacey grabbed his hands. "Don't leave me," she begged, confusing her husband even more.

"Honey, let me go check on Micah, and I'll be right back, I promise." Ryder stood up, as Lacey remained sitting on the edge of the bed, where April had begun to doze off, her right hand in her mouth, the drool running down onto the bed. Ryder held up one finger to his wife, then blew her a kiss before exiting the room. Outside of Micah's room, Joker still sat, as if on sentry duty, Ryder gently patting the dogs head as he went into the boy's room. Quietly he closed the door behind him, then stood for a moment in the semi-darkness, listening to the boy sleep. After about five minutes and with no signs of any unusual activity, Ryder departed the room, and when he did he noticed Joker had moved over next to the room where he and Lacey slept. The dog met his eyes, and for a moment they almost seemed to be communicating. Ryder crossed over to his room, knelt down and kissed his friend's furry head. "Thanks buddy," he said to the dog. Reopening the door, he peered inside, and saw that his wife was curled up next to their daughter on the large bed. Lacey's arms were wrapped around her baby, and her face was next to the babies, as if in silent communion. Ryder closed the door, then went back to where the other two were on the couch.

"Is everything okay?" Preacher asked, as Darius adjusted on the sofa. Ryder sat down, his elbows on his knees and shook his head.

"I don't know. I feel like we're just hanging on by a thread, and that thread seems weaker and weaker every day. I almost wish that bitch would just show up so we could end this nightmare." Preacher reached over to touch his friend's shoulder, as Darius watched.

"Listen Ryder, you guys are doing fine. We're settled in up here, where we can see them when they try to get here, we have weapons, food, water, and everyone is safe. I know you're getting frustrated and angry, but now's when you need to suck it up. You can't let that murderous woman get into your head like that. Remember what you learned over the years as a SEAL. If you can survive that hell hole you were in, then you can handle this." Preacher was squeezing his friend's shoulder, understanding that he needed to reinforce to his friend the absolute need to refocus and stay in control.

"Thanks, old buddy. Oh, and Darius, I hate to say this, but thank you for breaking that promise and you two coming up here. At first I was pissed, but now I see maybe I was wrong." Darius looked at Ryder, a sad smile on his face.

"No problem Ryder. If you two will excuse me, I'm going to get some fresh air for a minute. "Getting up, the black man walked to the kitchen door and opened it, stepping out into the night air. The two remaining men sat on the couch for a moment. "Is he okay?" Ryder asked, as Preacher got to his feet and went to the front window, staring out into the darkness.

"Yeah, I think he's okay, but he has been acting kind of squirrely since we left. I thought that was just because I sort of kidnapped him." The two men stayed quiet for a moment, listening to the night sounds.

"You want something to drink?" Ryder asked his friend, who nodded. Together they headed into the kitchen area, where Ryder opened the icebox and pulled out two bottles of cola. Handing one to Preacher, Ryder took the cap off his and set it on the counter. Preacher did the same, and that was when the side door came open, and Darius stepped inside. The two men in the kitchen stood for moment, stunned at what they were seeing.

Darius stood, a sad smile on his face, and holding a rifle in both hands. "Sorry guys, but this has to be how it goes down."

Chapter 19

The chopper hit several small pockets of clear air, and the men inside, all except the pilot, were getting a little green around the gills, as they say. They were almost at the landing area, and Vince had decided he was going to sell this fucking chopper for something safer, like a skateboard or a unicycle.
"Can we put this fucking thing down please? I'm about ready to puke, so unless you want to clean a really nasty mess, I suggest you land this thing!" The pilot, a clean-shaven man in in his early 30, just looked at his passenger and grinned.

"Sorry for the bumpy ride boss, but you know how the weather is. It does what it want's when it want's, like a woman." Laughing aloud, the pilot spotted what he had been looking for. "Vegas 279, we see you and are heading down." Replacing the handset, the pilot maneuvered the expensive craft carefully down to the forested area where the trucks sat waiting. When the chopper was down and shut off, one of the men in the back smacked the pilot on the back of the head. "Thanks for nothing, dipshit," he whispered, as the pilot simply nodded and smiled. Once the four men had exited the chopper and began to walk towards the two waiting trucks, suddenly and without warning six vehicles came bursting from the nearby forest, alarms and lights blazing.

"Motherfucker," Vince whispered under his breath, as he began to run back to where the chopper still sat.

"All of you, get your hands up in the air right now!!" came a booming voice over the loudspeaker, as Vince continued running towards the aircraft. As he neared it, the pilot slid out, a 9mm pistol in his hand.

"Freeze Vince, and I mean now!" he yelled, pointing the gun at the crime boss. Vince stopped for a moment, in total shock. He could tolerate almost anything, but betrayal was on the top of his "Not Tolerated" list. The pilot approached him slowly, watching his every move as he drew near. "Put them up Vince, now!" he repeated, drawing within several feet of the man, who was glaring at him with snake like eyes.

"You know you're dead, right asshole?" he whispered, as he saw his other three men being handcuffed and taken down in the grassy meadow. The pilot just looked at him and smiled.

"Vince, my name is Charlie King, and I'm a federal officer with the ATF. You are under arrest for transporting illegal weapons across a state line." Vince just stared at him, then began to laugh.

"What fucking state line? We just landed in Nevada, you ass wipe, and Nevada is my home state." Charlie just looked at him, shook his head, then reached into his pocket and tossed a map at Vince.

"See for yourself Vince. You're standing on California property right now. While you and your boys were trying to hold down breakfast, we carefully crossed the border into the Golden state. Oh, and by the way, we have several of your people back in Vegas who are singing like songbirds right now to my people." Vince stood, his hands shaking, as two of the rigs departed, his men in tow. Charlie spotted one of the other men approaching, and when he diverted his eyes for a split second, Vince suddenly lunged, his right hand coming out from behind his back, a silver knife in hand. As the blade struck the officer in the shoulder, two shots rang out, and Vince fell face down in the dirt. A final thought went through his mind before he died, that thought being *Summer you lucky bitch, you better be glad I didn't get to your psycho ass first.*

Charlie followed suit, his knees buckling and dragging him down, as the blood began to flow from the puncture wound. The approaching officer who had fired quickly screamed for help, then pulled a bandana from his pocket and applied pressure to the gaping wound.

"Hang on Charlie, helps coming," he whispered to the man, whose face was rapidly draining of color. His hand and rag both soaked in blood, the young pilot looked up at his partner.

"Well, at least we got the fucker," he croaked out, the other man holding him tightly, as Charlie's went to his friend and co-worker. "Man, that shit hurts," he whispered to his friend, who nodded.

"That's what you get for getting stabbed dumbass," he replied, the laughter from the injured man causing him to wince in pain.

Chapter 20

Summer spotted the sign which read CEDARS PASS, 5 MILES, and a feeling of exhilaration washed over her. Scab was peering intently at the road as Summer leaned back in her seat, the thought of the task nearly completed in her mind, and Dingo Dave was on the phone in the back, talking to Spiderman. The bikers had passed through the tiny, quiet town about twenty minutes earlier, the raucous noise of their motorcycles shattering the quiet serenity of the peaceful mountain community. Several of them had wanted to stop at the small grocery store to load up on beer, but Spiderman had waved them on with a nasty look, and the delay suddenly seemed like a bad idea. They had pulled over about 10 minutes out of town, several of them urinating alongside the road, while others stretched and smoked after the long ride.

"Yeah, I got it. We're at that turnoff the blonde told us about," the lanky man said into the phone, trying to be heard over the noise being generated by his brothers, three of whom had decided it was time to partake of some chemical refreshments.

"Hey, put that shit away!" Spiderman yelled, the trio looking at him as if he might be joking. By the tension in his face and the way the namesake tattoo around the right side of his face was drawn up taut, they knew he was dead serious. Slipping the leather pouch back into his jacket pocket, Mongo looked as if he had just been caught stealing from the cookie jar. With a frown on his face, the heavily built man went back to his bike and leaned against it, his eyes downcast, as Spiderman walked over, while the other two began laughing. "Hey, come on Mongo, don't look like that. You know we have work to do, that's all." Slipping his arm around the man's broad shoulders, he looked at the remaining bikers watching him.

The extremely large man had been brought into the club by Dingo Dave several years ago, and had become a very useful asset, with his massive strength and tolerance for pain. Spiderman had taken him under his wing after Mongo had patched in, believing that the man could become a very useful tool.

When they had killed that deputy in San Diego several years earlier, Mongo had been the one who had held him while they beat, then murdered him. The deputy had been well built and in excellent shape but had been no match for Mongo's freakish power and strength. As a reward, he had been allowed to go along on the attack on the tiny black-haired girl in the condo last year as well, when he and Dingo had paid her that fateful late-night visit. Dave had told the other brothers, when they returned, that Mongo had actually been very gentle with the girl, despite the violence of the attack.

"Hey man, let's get this shit going," one of the brothers yelled, breaking Spiderman's daydreaming about the slow witted but loyal man next to him. Spiderman raised his middle finger, as his cell phone began to ring. Holding it up to his ear, the tattooed man let a smile cross his face, revealing his yellow, jagged teeth.

"Okay, we'll meet you up the dirt road, and the bikes will be on the left side of the road where there's a flat spot in the brush. All right, we'll see you in a few." Walking back to his bike and mounting it, he made a circular motion in the air with his index finger. "Follow me and keep your pie holes shut. From here on out its all business, and that rat bastard Ryder Raynes is ours for the taking." At the man's name, the other bikers tensed up as they headed up the road. There wasn't a man among them who hadn't felt the pain of losing at least one brother at the man's hands, and each and every one of them wanted a piece of his skin, as well as that of that fucking vicious dog partner of his.

Pulling off the road, the men pushed their bikes into the flat, low-lying area that was hidden by the shrubs, manzanita and pine trees. When they had all secured their bikes, they walked back onto the dirt road, as Spiderman noticed the sun beginning to descend in the west, over the mountains. Before he could say anything, a blue Jeep Grand Cherokee came turning onto the dirt road, kicking up dust as the men stood back. When the Jeep stopped, Dave came popping out of the back seat, a look on his face that instantly stopped any thoughts of screwing around. They all knew how badly the club wanted Raynes, and even more so how intent the blonde woman was on getting her hands on his wife.

As Dave walked up to his brothers, Summer came out of the rig, her hands obviously hurting, as she held them close to her body and shut the door with her hip. Scab came scurrying around from his side, taking up position between Dave and Summer, as she slid her gloves off.

"Okay, let's talk. Now, we know from our friend that they're all up there in the cabin. We also know from the same friend that they have weapons inside, but that shouldn't surprise anybody. My brother knows how to use guns, and he isn't afraid to do just that. Now, I know how badly you guys want him, and despite his being my brother, I say have at him. Do whatever you feel is necessary with him to make you feel better about what he's done to you, but the woman and children are mine. No exceptions."

Holding up her mottled, disfigured hands, the men all took a long look, and mentally agreed with her. They knew what she was capable of, and although they weren't afraid of her, they were also in no hurry to push her too far.

"I also just got a call from another "friend' that our pesky little Italian buddy Mr. Vince Bandini has been permanently removed from the equation. Seems his pilot was actually an undercover ATF agent, and they had arranged a little greeting party when they landed. So, good riddance to bad rubbish, as they say. Now, there's a cache of weapons in the back of the Jeep, so here's what we're going to do. Dave, you send two of your men up through that thick growth to the east of here, which will bring them up behind the cabin. You guys, keep your eyes peeled for any little tricks my brother might have waiting. Get up as close as you can but try to hurry. You need to be in place when the fun starts. Scab, I'd like you and Dave to stay with me when we approach the house. I trust you, and I'm going to need your help. Our little rat in the house should have everything wrapped up by the time we get there, but I'm not leaving anything to chance. The rest of you, spread out around the house from the northwest side. For those of you who don't know directions, that's that way over there." Pointing in the direction she had indicated, Summer knew she was going to piss off the bikers standing around her, but she also knew that, as of right now, she didn't give a damn who she offended. She could almost smell the raven-haired bitch's fear, and it smelled wonderful.

Summer carefully slipped the gloves back onto her hands, and Dave walked around the back of the Jeep, raised the hatch, pulled off the tarp and lifted the wheel well area where the guns had been stashed. Two of the men, a pair known as Mutt and Jeff came around to where Dave stood, holding two M-14's. Handing one to each of the men, they reached in and took three clips each, just in case. Without a word they moved off to the east, through the low-lying scrub and tree line, moving surprisingly quiet for two such hefty men. Dave watched them disappear through some manzanita brush, then turned back. Mongo, Spiderman and the other two remained, each taking a weapon from the Jeep, and enough ammunition to end this feud once and for all. Dave slung an old-style AK-47 over his shoulder, tucked two additional clips into his belt, then shut the lid. "All right assholes, this is our night. This motherfucker up there in that cabin has killed three of our brothers, and I'm calling his fucking marker due. He's ours, like the lady said, but no one kills him. This dude has been a thorn in our side for way too fucking long, and tonight we get to take our time with him. As for the dog, well, I don't give a crap if you shoot and skin that snarling bastard, but the man is mine. Now, also remember, we get the lady her prizes first, then we get to have some fun, and the nice thing is, way up here in the middle of fucking nowhere, nobody is going to hear him scream, and brothers, I want him to really, truly scream. I want him to know what happens when you fuck with the Devils Disciples." Dave could almost feel the men's blood pumping, the testosterone flowing through their veins, and could see their need for revenge in their bloodshot eyes, and he had never been more proud to call himself a Disciple. He truly hoped that

Jake was looking down smiling, well wherever Jake was, smoking some fine ass shit, sucking a Jack Daniels bottle bone dry, and getting some serious head. "This is for you Jake," he said, as the others passed around a silver flask.

Summer stood, watching the macho, bullshit bonding ritual, but kept her attitude one of deference to the men. Now that she was this close, nothing was going to stop her from what she wanted, so when the flask was passed to her she gingerly took it and raised it to her lips, the bitter liquid burning her throat. She passed it to Scab, who took a long swallow before returning it to Mongo. The four remaining men took off through the brush, off the road and could be heard in the distance stumbling though the brush. Summer looked at Dave, a soft smile on her face.

"You ready?" she asked, Scab tucking his pistol into his waistband as he sidled up next to Summer.

"Lady, I've been waiting for this for a long, long time. We're about to each get what we want, kind of like Christmas." Scab's eyes went to Dave, a puzzled look on his face.

"What do you mean like Christmas? All I ever got for Christmas was an ass beating, and maybe a cigarette flicked at my head or stuck in my chest." Dave looked at the tiny man, and for a split moment something almost like pity came over him.

"Don't you worry little buddy, Ole Dingo Dave is gonna show you how to really celebrate." Dave punched the man in the arm, and Scab just smiled. Summer came up right next to Scab, and gently pressed into him.

"Don't you worry Scab. I'm going to make sure that whatever your heart wants, it gets." Leaning down, she softly kissed the man's stubbly cheek. As Scab began to blush, Dave chambered a round in the rifle he was holding.

"Okay, that's enough kissy kissy bullshit. Let's go." Heading up to the gate, Scab and Summer fell in behind Dave, the blonde woman staying close to Scab.

Chapter 21

Ryder stood, stunned and not believing what he was seeing. Darius was in the doorway, his face tense, his eyes darting around the room to watch each of the adults. Ryder's initial thought was *I'm glad the kids are in the other rooms.* His second thought was for Lacey's safety, as he heard her coming out of the bedroom and towards the kitchen. Before he could shout out a warning, Darius kicked the door shut and pointed the rifle at Ryder, as Preacher stood off to the side, a stunned look on his face.

"Call her," Darius whispered, moving closer to the men, but maintaining a safe distance as well. Ryder's eyes darted toward the entryway, and as they did, Lacey stepped into the kitchen, a strange look on her face.

"Ryder, what"- Lacey stopped when she saw the gun in Darius's hands, and she took a step in his direction, as Ryder grabbed her arm and pulled her to him.

"What the hell are you doing?" she asked Darius in disbelief, who stood his ground while keeping the trio covered. "Are you fucking kidding me?" she yelled, her voice growing higher in pitch out of anger and fear.

"Do I look like I'm joking?" the black man asked, reaching back and locking the door. The two men waited, hoping for a mistake by the man so they could overpower him and get the rifle back. Out of the corner of his eye, Ryder spotted the breadbox where he had stashed one of the guns when they first arrived and started to speak to cover his seemingly innocuous movements.

"Darius, what are you doing? How can you hold us at gunpoint when you know what's coming down the road towards us? What the hell are you thinking?" Continuing to move slowly down the counters edge, he had also positioned himself between Lacey and their captor, as she noticed Preacher's furtive movements in the other direction. Darius turned towards Preacher, as Ryder reached into the wooden container, and felt nothing.

"Sorry old buddy, it's already been removed. Wouldn't want the little guy to get hurt now, would you?" Ryder's stomach tightened as he met Darius's gaze, and Preacher stood as still as a statue. Ryder was already thinking about the two in the living room, and knew he had to stay calm in order to survive. Pulling his hand back, Ryder stared at the black man, his mind going a mile a minute at the betrayal, while he kept his demeanor cool and calm.

"Listen Darius, whatever this is about, we can help you. Man, we've been friends for how many years now? What the hell has gotten into you, pulling this crap on us?" Darius swallowed deeply, then with the rifle barrel he motioned Preacher and the others towards the living room.

"Preach, please don't make me shoot you. I really don't' want to, but I will if you force me to." Preacher would have sworn he saw sincerity in the man's eyes, and decided to go along, at least for now. Ryder carefully took hold of Lacey's elbow and guided her into the front room, as Preacher slowly walked over to the large sofa. Suddenly the still of the air was broken by the ringing of a cell phone, and Darius deftly held the phone up to his ear while keeping the three people covered.

"Yeah, it's all taken care of." Hanging up the phone, Darius went to a bag sitting next to the sofa where they had recently been sitting. Reaching in, he retrieved two bundles of rope, and tossed them on the couch. Preacher looked at them, then at Ryder and Lacey, and began to laugh.

"Really? Rope? Couldn't you be more imaginative than that?" As Preacher began to laugh, Ryder began to, almost imperceptibly, move towards the end table where the 9mm was stored.

"Preach, laugh once more and I swear I'll shoot you, and Ryder, you can forget about that piece in the end table as well. It's mine also. You see guys, I've got it all covered. Now Preacher, I need you to tie Lacey and Ryder to the sofa, and I'm not asking." Preacher looked at the rope, then the man again. With a look on his bearded face that spoke volumes, Preacher stood still, as Darius spoke again. "Preacher, I don't have time to play games with you. Pick up that goddamn rope, tie Ryder, then Lacey to the couch, or I swear to God I'll shoot you, then the children."

At the mention of her children, Lacey looked over her shoulder at the nearby rooms where they both lay sleeping and totally unaware of what was taking place. "Darius, I beg you, leave my children alone. I know you have two daughters of your own, so I know you can relate as a father. I don't care what you do to me, but for God's sake please don't hurt my babies. They haven't done anything to you, and as far as that goes neither have we." Lacey was begging for the safety of her children, but she also knew that if she was tied to the sofa they would be at his mercy.

Darius just smiled, a sad, weak look on his usually strong face, and looked at Preacher again.

"Preach, tie them up, both of them. We're going to have visitors in a few minutes, and I can't have you guys ruining the party. I'll do this, though, I will tell you the why of this whole situation while you tie them up." Preacher reached down and picked up one of the bundles, his eyes boring into Darius's, fire burning behind them.

Ryder sat down, slowly and carefully, as his large friend approached. "I don't want to do this Ryder," he whispered, as Ryders eyes locked on his.

"It's okay Preach. We'll be just fine," Ryder spoke, as Preacher began to slowly wind the rope around his wrists, then his ankles, binding them to the heavy frame.

"Come on Preacher, hurry it up," Darius said from his vantage point, his voice revealing the emotions building up inside him. "Okay, a promise is a promise. About three years ago, I went to Reno on a trip with an old college friend of mine. While we were there, we decided to do a little gambling, and I had no idea how much fun it was. All those years I worked, I always fought to hang on to every penny, but when I saw the people on that casino floor, it was unreal. The machines, the poker tables, the craps tables, and of course that damned roulette wheel. We spent about four hours at that one table, and when we walked away I was up almost four thousand dollars. It was a total, complete rush, even more so than the feeling I got when I practiced law, and after we got a bite of dinner we headed back down to the tables. I tried craps, but it didn't do the same thing as that spinning, lovely wheel and those beautiful black and red squares. I lost almost everything I had won earlier, in a very short piece of time, and I felt deflated. My friend wanted to go catch a show, but I waved him off, and headed for the sports lounge. That was where the real problem began. I lost another nine hundred dollars that night, betting on everything from the horse races, and when my friend came back later, I was waiting on the final game of the college world series. I had placed a six hundred dollar bet on the underdog to win, and when they lost on a controversial call at the plate I went ballistic. I threw my glass down, knocked over my chair, and but for the grace of my good friend, probably would have been arrested. He took me back to my room and put me to bed, but my head was spinning." Darius paused for a moment to collect his thoughts, and saw that Preacher was in the process of tying up Lacey, who was shooting daggers at the black man. "Tie her tight," he said to the large man, who gave him a deadly look as he continued tying up the woman. "Hey, Ryder, where's Joker? "Darius had forgotten the dog in all his efforts to subdue the people. Ryder just shrugged as he said "I don't know. Maybe you should go look for him." Darius moved closer to the captive man, letting him see his eyes.

"Tell me where he is, or I swear I'll shoot Lacey, and I'll make sure it hurts too." Their eyes locked, Ryder looked at his wife, then tilted his head to the right.

"He's in with April. He sleeps by her all the time," he said quietly, as Preacher finished tying up the woman.

Moving to his left, Darius kept the rifle trained on the three people, as he neared the door to the bedroom. "Preacher, get over here and open this door. Be ready to grab him when he comes out and understand this- I will shoot him if I have to." Preacher could see the man's eyes and the dangerous look in them and wanted at all costs to avoid any shooting. As Preacher took the door handle, he whispered softly, to avoid disturbing the baby or the young boy in the other room.

"Joker, come here boy, here boy, come," as he slowly turned the handle. Darius could hear the dog breathing on the other side, and kept his gun trained on the door.

"Hurry up," Darius whispered, his voice growing more anxious as the door came open, and Joker walked out, looking around. Seeing Preacher, he went instantly to him, as he reached down to pet the sleek dog. "Good boy," he whispered, as Jokers head suddenly came up, staring at Darius holding the strange object. Preacher tightened his grip on the dog's collar to keep him in check, when without warning the dog growled, broke free of Preacher's grip and lunged at the dark-skinned man, Darius swinging the rifle butt around, catching the dog fully on the side of his head, knocking him to the floor, unconscious.

Ryder couldn't see what was going on behind him, but when he heard his friend growl, then the sickening crack of wood against bone, his stomach dropped, while next to him Lacey began to cry, as April began to whimper from the far bedroom.

Preacher stood, his heart pounding loudly in his chest as the dog lay on the floor, unmoving except for the shallow rise of his chest. Looking at Darius, Preacher stepped towards him, and was stopped by the ratcheting of the bolt. "Preacher, I want you to pick him up and carry him down to the basement where he won't hurt anyone." Preacher stared at the man in front of him, as Ryder began to talk from the couch, his voice packed with emotion.

"Preacher, is he okay? Is Joker alive?" he asked, his voice shaking. In the distance April continued to cry from her room, and Ryder felt his soul being ripped apart.

"He's breathing Ryder, he's okay," Preacher told him, as he slowly stepped to where the dog lay, a small stain of blood on the floor. Kneeling down, he carefully slid his arms under the furry body, gently lifting it, as if handling a newborn child. Darius stood, motioning towards the basement door off the living area. As he and Preacher walked across the space, suddenly a door opened, and Micah came out, rubbing his eyes as if still half asleep.

"What's going on out here? How come nobody's getting April?" As he asked the question, Lacey, her voice fighting to stay steady, spoke to her son.

"Honey, it's okay. We're just getting up to go check on her," Lacey told him, as the boy came around the couch, Darius and Preacher standing at the head of the stairs.

"Mom, why are you and Ryder all tied up? Is it some kind of a game?" Lacey fought back the tears at the absurdity, but honest assessment of the situation.

"Kind of. Now here's what I need you to do. I need you to"- before Lacey could finish her sentence, she heard Darius telling Preacher to get the dog downstairs. She heard Preacher say something, as did Ryder by his body movement, and tried to turn to see what was going on.

Standing by the door to the basement with Joker in his arms, Preacher had hoped for a momentary distraction to try and attack Darius, but the man kept the gun trained on him at all times. When he saw Micah walk over to where the couple sat on the sofa, he felt a renewed hope that maybe, just maybe the boy would give him the edge he would need. Instead, as Micah was speaking, Darius poked at Preacher with the rifle barrel. "Get the dog downstairs-NOW!" came the man's angry voice, and Lacey could hear the large man's big feet on the steps, then a sudden slamming of a door and the sound of a deadbolt locking. Within seconds, Darius was back in front of the pair, Micah staring at the gun as if amused. In the distance, April was renewing her displeasure at being ignored, and Lacey struggled against her tethers.

"Darius, please, let me get my baby. She's been sick and I'm afraid she might be spiking a fever again." Lacey's eyes met

Darius's pleading with him to let her go to her daughter's aid. Instead, he looked at Micah.

"Micah, go get your little sister and bring her in here so we can check on her," he told the boy, who looked at his mother.

"Go ahead," she whispered, as Ryder met her gaze. Micah walked across the room and into the bedroom, returning a few moments later with the baby in his slender arms.

"Boy, she smells bad. Mom, can I untie you so you can change her, cause it makes me want to gag?" Lacey fought back laughter at the innocence of his comment, and despite the odor emanating from her daughter's diaper, neither Lacey nor Ryder had ever seen or smelled such a beautiful sight as their son and daughter safe, at least for the moment.

Preacher stood on the top step of the heavy wooden staircase, his ham sized fists pounding on the solid oak door. Below him, Joker lay on the hardwood floor, his breathing shallow, but beginning to move slowly, his doggy head swimming from the hard knock he had taken. He laid there for a moment, slowly regaining his senses, then saw his friend at the top of the stairs making a loud noise. Getting carefully to his feet, Joker stood for a moment, getting his legs under him and steadying himself. Preacher saw the motion below, and saw his old friend standing, wobbly, but upright. Pausing his pounding on the door for a moment, he walked down the stairs and knelt beside Joker, his arms embracing the dog, who laid his still aching head against the large man's shoulder, smelling the good smell he always associated with the man.

"It's okay boy, we're getting out of here." As he spoke these words and petted the dog, Preacher looked around at the area, looking for anything that could be of help. There was a wooden worktable, a medium sized leather sofa, a table mounted skill saw, and several free-standing cabinets.

"Hang on Ryder, I'm coming."

Chapter 22

The two bikers, affectionately known as Mutt and Jeff cautiously made their way back towards the large house, doing their best to stay low, stay quiet and keep an eye out for any little surprises the man in the cabin may have left. Neither one had military experience, but both had grown up in the outdoors of the northern Idaho mountains, where they had been best friends since grade school.

Holding up his right hand, Mutt stopped, his eyes catching sight of something just ahead. Jeff immediately stopped, trusting his friend's instincts without fail. His eyes tried to pick up whatever had caught Mutt's attention but was unable to from his vantage point behind the slightly larger man.

"Hang on, I'm gonna creep up and see what the hell that is at the top of that small hill." In the distance, even through the trees, Mutt could see the back of the cabin, and wanted to be sure he got there first. Lowering himself to the ground, the man belly crawled through the leaves and brush, making surprisingly little noise for someone of his stature. Jeff watched, his gun at the ready, then moved up to the spot his friend had vacated, watching him make his way forward.

Mutt laid still for a second, his eyes focused on the metal object laying almost totally covered in the leaves ahead. Smiling to himself, he pulled himself forward a little more, keeping his eyes peeled for, well whatever. Raising up on his elbows, the stocky man carefully reached out to brush away the small pile of leaves, then saw the foil wrapper. Lowering his head, he tried not to laugh, then turned back to look at Jeff, who had crawled closer to his brother.

"It's a fucking candy wrapper," Mutt told his friend, who reached up and smacked his friend on the calf.

"All right then, let's get past this badass Milky Way wrapper you found and get down to business." Both men got to their feet, brushing off their clothes, then resumed their trek towards the house. Mutt looked back at Jeff, waved him forward then took another step, when suddenly he was violently whipped by the legs into a completely vertical position, dropping his gun.

"WHAT THE F-!"- the shocked man screamed, his words cut off as the snare device slammed him against the base of a huge pine tree. Jeff stood, stunned and suddenly unsure of what to do. Mutt was hanging upside down, screaming and with blood flowing down his legs from the razor wire device, which was increasingly cutting into the man's flesh with his downward weight pulling against gravity. Mutt was screaming as he reached up to grab the wire in an effort to save himself, the razor-sharp line slicing easily through his hands and causing him to fall backwards again. Jeff could see the crimson color soaking through his brother's tattered jeans, and went to his aid, but when he got to him, he realized he had no idea how to help him. The device was looped around a branch about eight feet off the ground, and even by jumping he fell short. Mutt continued screaming, the pain becoming almost more than he could bear, as the wire chewed into his flesh.

"Help me damn it!" he croaked, his voice growing weaker with the sudden blood loss, as Jeff looked on helpless. Pulling a hunting knife from behind his back, he began to frantically cut at the wire to free his brother, succeeding only in lacerating his own hands in the attempt. Without warning, as Mutt continued writhing around, a sudden burst of blood flooded the dying man's pants and the ground at Jeff's feet, as the wire chewed through the ragged jeans, into the flesh and into his femoral arteries. Jeff watched in horror as his friend's face went ashen, and his screams tapered off almost instantly. Jeff stood there for a moment, a state of shock washing over him. *"Don't worry brother, that fucker has killed the last of my guys,"* he thought to himself, as he stepped back. Tears filled his eyes as rage and hatred filled his soul. Picking up his rifle, as well as Mutt's, he walked about six feet ahead, looked back at his dead friend then stopped when he felt a tugging sensation on his ankle. Before he could react, a loud shotgun blast burst from the brush, hitting the man in the back and throwing him forwards. His face hit the dirt pile, and kicked up rocks into his face, blinding his vision as the fiery pain set in. Laying in the leaves, he tried to turn to see how bad he had been shot, then saw the massive, gaping hole which had blown out his entire right side, from front to back. Gagging, he reached down blindly to feel the wound, and felt what was left of his rib cage poking through the ripped flesh while his entrails lay strewn on the ground. As he began to vomit, he looked up at Mutt, and a sad smile came over his face, as the darkness washed over him.

The two pairs of men who had been dispatched to the western side, and were to approach from there heard the screaming, followed by the booming blast of what sounded like a shotgun. The two teams were about forty yards apart, and each one knew what the ominous sound meant.

   Spiderman stopped at the gun's blast, as did the smaller man behind him. He also noticed that the noisy pair off to their left had stopped, and even the birds had ceased chirping. "Shit," he muttered, more to himself than anything. The man behind him closed the gap, coming up right behind Spiderman.

   "Do you think?"- he started to say, as the taller man turned around and smacked him in the face, knocking the smaller man off his feet and into the scrub brush. "What the fuck was that for?" he asked, his mouth bleeding, as he regained his footing.

   "Do I think what? That maybe that was some of our brothers getting bagged? What the fuck do you think, ass wipe?" Wiping his mouth, the bearded man picked up his gun and took off towards the sound. Before he had gone ten feet, the ground beneath him opened up, and he dropped instantly out of sight into the pit. Spiderman ran up to aid the fallen man, stopping just short of the gaping hole. Five feet down Mongo lay dead, impaled on multiple metal and wooden stakes, his vacant eyes cast to the heavens.

Spiderman paused for a split second, whispered goodbye to the man, then began his slow, methodical trek through the forest.

Shaggy and Rat heard the ruckus to their right, then heard their leader cussing.

"Shit man, we best be really careful, cause there's no telling what other surprises that fucker has waiting for us." Looking at one another, the two slender men carefully resumed their march towards the house.

Entering the next clearing, the two men paused for a moment, catching their breaths and taking a quick sniff from the small leather pouch that Rat had pulled out. Each man took a snort from the bag, then headed out in the direction of the house. Shaggy reached up to push a low-lying branch out of his way that the shorter Rat had ducked underneath, and as he did, a loud *whooshing* sound filled his ears. The large log and spike device came swinging down at breakneck speed, having been hoisted to a high enough level to avoid detection. Before Shaggy had a chance to shout out a warning, the improvised booby trap hit Rat full force, the metal spikes piercing his torso and neck, his finger instinctively squeezing the trigger of his weapon. A long blast from the automatic rifle ripped straight up Shaggy's back and flanks, the bullets killing him instantly. The only sound that could be heard, after the gunshots, was the sound of the rope creaking as it slowed it's swinging, the man's body impaled on the wooden stakes.

Spiderman heard the echo of the gunshots, and realizing they were already down one and probably more brothers, he carefully made his way towards the sound. When he pushed through the oak and scrub, he saw Shaggy lying face down, covered in blood then spied Rat's corpse hanging lifeless, blood from his mouth dripping onto the bed of leaves beneath him. Looking in the direction he was headed, he had a single thought -*No more blood, motherfucker, at least not ours.*

   Picking up the dropped weapons and slinging them over his shoulders, Spiderman began the slow trek towards the house where the brother killing man was, an evil smile crossing his pock marked face.

Three minutes later he spotted a red truck parked out front, the cabin looming large behind it. Quietly he crept up behind the truck, checking the weapon in his hands to make sure it was ready.

Summer stopped as the sound of a scream, followed closely by several gunshots hit her ears. Dingo Dave had taken several more steps, as did Scab, then the two stopped, Summer in the rear. "Did you hear that? That sounded like a guy screaming," Scab asked, as Dave looked curiously in the general direction of the sounds. "Are you fucking kidding me? Of course we heard it, dipshit. It sounded like it came from that way," Dave said, pointing to the path the single pair had taken. Exhaling deeply, he started to speak, then was stopped by the booming sound of what seemed to be a shotgun. "Shit," he whispered, as Summer came closer to the two men.

"Sounds like my brother was waiting for you," she told the biker, who gave her a deadly stare. "I told your guys to be careful, and from the sound of things I"- as she tried to finish her thought, the sound of rapid gunfire erupted in the other direction. Dave and Scab both knelt down, looking for the sound, as a deadly silence filled the mountain air.

Dave maintained his position for a moment, as he and Scab whispered back and forth, then both men got to their feet. Scab took off in the lead, as Dave pointed his index finger at Summer. "Not one more goddamn word about my brothers, you get it? If you think I'm joking, then fucking say something, please. I swear to God I'll shoot you and leave you out here in these nasty ass woods to rot. Not one more word lady, I mean it." Summer had no fear of the rank biker or his empty threats, but she also understood that she still needed his help to get to Lacey and those precious children.

Giving him her best *I'm sorry* look, Summer held up her hands. "No problems, I mean it. I just want to get to the woman, and I know how much you want my brother, so I promise." Dave turned and walked after Scab, without a word, and Summer began walking again, staring daggers at the lanky man behind his back. Ten minutes later she saw Scab stop and drop down, Dave joining him as they peered around a bend in the road. Summer slowly crept closer, wanting, praying that they had arrived at their destination. When she was directly behind the two men, she saw the pickup truck sitting, and there, like the fabled city of Oz, stood the cabin. Closing her eyes, Summer let her mental channels open as she spoke, at least in her mind. *"Na eiste prosektikoi o gious mou,ego erchomai gia sas"* (*be cautious my son, I am coming for you)* As she knelt on the road, Summer could almost feel the boy receiving her message, and a warm smile crossed her face, when suddenly a small rock hit her arm, causing her to cry out in pain. When her eyes opened, she saw Dave staring back at her, a sly grin on his face.

"Pay attention," he told her, his voice low to avoid detection, as Summer stood up straight. Walking up to where the lanky man stood, Summer laid her hand on his shoulder, causing him to turn back around, their eyes locking momentarily. When he saw the look in those beautiful blue eyes, Dave realized the size of the error he had made. As he swallowed deeply, Summer's eyes never left his, as she slowly lowered, then opened her mouth to gently let her tongue kiss the rapidly bruising area. Dave watched, knowing he should have been aroused by the sight of the woman, but suddenly aware of how much he actually feared her.

"You should be afraid Dave," she whispered, as the man turned back around.

"Okay Scab, here's what I need you to do. Head over there, just past the deck, and sneak up on it to see if there are any more surprises waiting for us." Pointing to his right, Dave nudged Scab in the direction he had mentioned, as the tiny man looked back at Summer, then scurried away. Summer watched him as he made his way up to, then to the side of the massive deck in the front of the house. She and Dave watched as he slowly, meticulously checked around the steps for any signs of danger, then around the rails and finally up onto the deck, squatting beneath one of the large bay windows.

Chapter 23

Ryder slowly wiggled his fingers around the knotted rope, hoping for just a small amount of slippage. Lacey, sitting beside him, looked frantic, as April continued to cry.

"Micah honey, why don't you get the diaper bag and change your sister for me?" she asked, as Micah, sitting between the two tied up adults, looked at her funny.

"You want me to change her?" he asked, looking to Darius for help with the untoward task of changing the dirty diaper.

"Go ahead Micah, go get the diaper bag and bring it back here," Darius told him, the young boy slipping off the sofa and making his way towards the bedroom. Lacey was leaning over, cooing to her daughter, as Ryder stared at the captor, who resumed his story.

"When I got back from Vegas, I was in such a state of euphoria about the thrill of gambling, I never even realized how much I had lost until I got home. Tish found out when she called the bank, and she about lost her mind. I had lost almost eight thousand dollars that weekend, and I never seemed to even realize it. We sat down, and I told her that I would never gamble again, and I swear on my mother's grave I meant it at the time, but something had changed in me. I began to frequent an Indian casino not far from Santa Barbara, and I was always, always careful not to lose more than I had on me, but one afternoon when Tish thought I was out on the boat, I lost my ass at the craps table. I couldn't hit a roll or a number to save my soul, and I lost nearly six grand in less than an hour. I covered my losses by selling a couple of my prized collectible pistols, and that gave me the extra pocket money I needed. That was when I met T.J. I was playing at the craps table, and this guy walked up and smacked down a five-hundred-dollar chip. Five hundred dollars. He gave me a look like he knew I was going to hit, and when it came up sevens, he smacked me on the back as his stack and mine grew larger. He introduced himself, and when we walked out that afternoon I was up nearly three grand and feeling great.

   We went to have a drink and celebrate our winnings, and that was when he introduced me to the dogs. In the back of this bar there was a small area with a number of closed-circuit TV's. They were showing dog races, horse races, even a cricket match from India, and that was when I met my downfall. I lost all of my winnings that same afternoon, but T.J.

reassured me it was not a problem. He showed me a list of NFL playoff games coming up and told me that my credit was good with him." Darius paused for a moment, licking his lips as if his mouth had suddenly gone desert dry, then continued. "By the time the playoffs were over, and the Super Bowl was set, I was into T.J. for almost one hundred thousand dollars. I was betting on everything, from the races to Pop Warner football to ices skating to just about anything I could find, and my luck was shit. I went to him to talk about how to settle things, but suddenly he wasn't my friend T.J. anymore, he was this no bullshit loan shark, so I made him a business proposition. I put the cabin and my boat as collateral, and then he sprung it on me. He was going to give me one chance to settle it up. He told me that if the Chiefs, a 7 ½ point underdog, beat the Vikings in the upcoming Super Bowl, we would be dead even. I gave him the deed to the cabin and the beloved boat as my marker, then prayed like I had never prayed before. The day of the game we had some folks over, Tish's family mostly, and I sat on the edge of my seat the whole time, hoping for a miracle. When that final whistle blew and those fuckers didn't even win the game, let alone cover the spread, I knew I was screwed. I begged off, saying I was bummed about the game, and drove down the coast, trying to think what to do. T.J. called me about five minutes after I left, and said we needed to talk. Man, I had just lost this cabin and my boat, my wife was going to leave me when she found out, and I felt like driving my car off into the ocean. I ended up at T.J.'s place, and he had a drink waiting for me when I went inside. For someone who had just cleaned me out, he actually didn't look all that happy."

"Tell you what," he said to me, as I had sipped my drink, the whiskey as sour as my belly. He then went on to inform me that he had actually sold my paper to a man down in San Diego. I asked him what that meant by *sold my paper*, and he leaned in and smiled. "I couldn't handle the amount of your debt anymore, so I called an associate in San Diego, who understood and had the perfect solution for everyone involved." As he told me the news, I felt a coldness inside me that went through all the way to my bones. T.J. had motioned for the bartender to bring another round, and as he set the glasses down, I felt a huge hand on my shoulder. In no mood to be played with, I turned around, and there stood two of the nastiest and evil looking men I had ever seen. The one in front smiled at me, his teeth brown and rotting, and when he spoke I wished I was dead.

The massive biker was the handler for a motorcycle club in San Diego called the Devils Disciples, and my marrow froze at the name. He went on to explain, in great detail, exactly how I could fix this current situation. When T.J. had given my name to the man in San Diego, certain bells had gone off. He had made a couple of phone calls, and inside of thirty minutes they knew who I was, and even more so, who I knew. He mentioned the name Ryder Raynes, and he went on to tell me exactly what I needed to do to get out of this mess."

Darius paused for a moment and looked at his previous friend, tied and sitting on the sofa, the man's eyes glaring at Darius. "I swear Ryder, I never meant to go through with it. I just wanted to stall until I found another solution. They kept me in their sights all the time, waiting for the right moment, and when you came to my house that day, they knew they had us both. I swear Ryder, I never meant for this to happen. Everything just spun out of control, and before I knew it you and I were buying the new Jeep, and so help me God, they made me put the bug in it. They told me all along that if I helped them find you, they would wipe out my debt, but I swear if I could go back I would have driven my car off that cliff that evening." Darius was standing about four feet from Ryder and Lacey and would have sworn he could feel the hatred and anger coming off of them. The look in Ryder's eyes actually scared Darius, so he kept the rifle at the ready just in case. Next to him, Lacey sat still, her attention torn between the baby on her right, her son between her and Ryder. April, after Micah had changed her diaper, had dozed off, as if bored by the people in the room. Lacey could hear the faint sound of pounding from Preacher in the basement, the noise somewhat comforting her, as beside her Micah suddenly sat upright, his eyes wide and locked on the window in front of them.

"What's wrong Micah?" Lacey asked, her voice almost a hush as she prepared for what she was afraid was coming. She saw Ryder's jawline tighten up as he saw the boy's reaction. Micah sat, staring at the window as words came from his mouth which startled both adults on the sofa, and even causing Darius to stare at the boy sitting motionless on the couch.

"Na eíste ypomonetikoí o gios mou . O chrónos mas érchetai grígora. Empisteftheíte kanénan , allá eména."

(Be patient my son. Our time is coming fast. Trust no one but me.") were the words that emanated from the young boy's mouth, the unusual phrase sounding familiar to both Lacey and Ryder.

"Micah, what are you saying son? What does that mean?" Ryder asked the boy, who turned to stare at the man sitting next to him.

"Don't call me son. I'm not your son, I'm hers." Ryder was in a state of near shock at the boy's response and saw Lacey looking at Micah.

"Honey, you're my son, my Micah. Please tell us what those words mean." Micah turned slowly and met Lacey's gaze, his dark eyes boring into hers, which had begun to shine with unshed tears, her voice nearing panic level.

"Don't you call me son either, bitch. I'm not your son, I'm hers.' Ryder, when the boy had said he was *hers,* had assumed he was talking about Lacey, but when he repeated it to his mother, the stark reality of his words hit both he and his wife about the same moment.

Darius walked across the room to where the doorway to the basement was and yelled to Preacher. "Be quiet big man, because the end is almost here for you." The noise stopped for a second, then resumed, and Darius just shrugged as he returned to the living area, facing the people on the sofa. With the rifle cradled in his arm, he reached into his pocket and withdrew his cell phone, depressing a button and placing a silent call. "Hey, it's me. Yeah, come on in. It's all clear." Slipping the phone back into his pocket, Darius looked up as kitchen door opened. Ryder heard the noise also, and made sure Darius saw his eyes.

"You better kill me now asshole, because if you don't' I swear Joker and I are going to tear you to pieces, and I mean slowly." Ryder could feel his heart rate beating faster, and he fought to slow it down. Shifting slightly on the couch, he felt a small lump under his right hand, and carefully closed his fingers on it. He looked at Lacey, who was peering to her right, as a large man entered the room, a look on his face that not only alarmed her but made her gasp.

"Ryder," she whispered, not wanting to look away, as if to do so would bring the monster closer. Ryder turned as much as he could, and saw the disheveled, angry looking man standing there, an evil grin on his face.

"Well, well if it ain't Ryder Raynes, in the flesh. And this must be the lovely Mrs.

Raynes. Damn sweetie, you are a fine-looking woman. What the hell you doing with this scar faced prick?" Spiderman stepped around the front of the couch, his eyes undressing Lacey, as suddenly April began to fuss again. Spiderman looked at the infant, his eyes growing darker. "Shut it up right now, or I will," he said under his breath, as Micah slid off the sofa and placed himself between the hulking man and his sister.

"Get away from her," he said, the tone of his voice deeper and more mature than it should have been. Spiderman stared at the tiny young man and withdrew his knife from behind him. Micah appeared to be unfazed by the object, a fact not unnoticed by the biker. "Get away from her before I hurt you, motherfucker," Micah told the man, in a quiet but forceful way, standing his ground. As Spiderman stepped towards the boy, without warning the front door burst open, and a small, scraggly looking man entered, followed by a much larger and more ominous presence.

Put the knife away, and now!" Dave told the man, making it clear that he was in no mood to play games. At least not yet. As Dave walked into the room, his friend slipped the knife back into his waistband, then high fived Scab, who appeared distraught over the crying baby. Micah had his sister in his lap and was rocking her, and Scab sidestepped closer to the boy and infant.

"Well, hello little brother. So nice to see you again," came the soft, almost gentle voice from across the room. Summer stepped across the threshold into the house, a smile on her face and a look in her eyes that scared everyone, even the bikers. "Hello dear Lacey. How have you been?" she asked, the room suddenly as silent as a tomb, as Summer slid the gloves off her hands.

Preacher stopped his relentless pounding on the door, as Joker's ears perked up, and the dog's demeanor abruptly changed. He was standing right next to Preacher on the landing, but his entire focus was on something beyond the door. When the man reached down to touch the dog, Joker was as taut as a live electric wire, his black fur and hackles raised, a low growl coming from his throat. "It's okay boy, we're going to get out of here." Preacher turned and quickly descended back into the basement, making his way over to the free-standing cabinets on the far side. Opening one of them, he looked inside, not seeing anything that could be helpful. Pulling the doors open on the other, he looked first high, then low, and a smile crossed his bearded face. Picking up the item, he went back to where Joker sat, still locked on the basement door. "Okay old friend, I need you to move back down the stairs," he directed the dog, who looked at him, as if in understanding. Moving down the staircase, Joker sat at the bottom, watching the man and the thing in his hands.

Joker sat, his head still aching from being hit, but also as alert as he could ever recall. The bad smell had hit him like a bolt out of the blue, and he suddenly remembered where he had smelled the bad thing before. It burned his nose and eyes, but despite the pain he stayed focused. Suddenly, before the big man could do anything, Joker heard the sound of his girl crying, and he stared at the man at the top of the stairs, silently pleading with him to hurry.

Chapter 24

Lacey's heart was pounding in her chest, her wrists burning from the ropes, as the blonde woman smiled at her. Next to her on the sofa, April was still fussing, having been laid down by her brother, who had reclaimed his seat between Lacey and Ryder. Lacey could feel the palpable tension in the room and could see it in Ryder's jawline and the way his fingers were jiggling behind his back. Lacey felt the eyes of the biker trash boring into her, stripping her with their gaze, and fought to keep the gorge down in her throat.

"Summer, please, do whatever you want to me, but for God's sake don't hurt my children. They're innocent in this whole fucking mess, and you can make me pay any way you want, but I beg you, please don't hurt them." She knew that her words were falling on deaf ears and seeing the scars and the discolored tissue on the woman's forearms that she herself had inflicted, Lacey knew she was in for the fight of her life. She was also acutely aware that the pounding on the basement door had ceased, and she could tell that Ryder had noticed as well. While Lacey was begging Summer not to harm her children, the blonde had slowly, almost sensually, moved herself into position in front of Lacey, relishing in the dark-haired woman's misery and pain.

"Oh sweetheart, if you only knew what I had planned for you, you would beg me for the sweet mercy of death." Summer took great pleasure in seeing the color drain from the captive woman's face, and carefully knelt down in front of the sofa, directly facing April, as Lacey struggled against her restraints. Gently touching the baby's face, Summer inhaled deeply of the sweet innocence of the baby, as Dingo Dave stepped up next to her, directly in line with Ryder.

"Well Mr. Ryder Raynes, how you doing today? Looks like you're a little tied up right now, but not to worry. We'll cut you free from those ropes in just a bit, but first we need to talk. You've been a really, really bad boy now, haven't you? Remember that man you killed last year in San Diego? That was my baby brother Mickey. You left him in a fucking toilet to die, and that just won't do." Dave paused for a moment, wanting Ryder to look deep into the recesses of his soul and see what awaited him. Across the room, Darius stood, watching the scenes being played out, and hating himself for being the one responsible for this whole horrible mess. Suddenly a loud, raucous barking began behind the basement door, followed by yelling, and Darius turned in that direction, as Dave motioned Spiderman towards the noise. The two men stood in front of the door, as Darius pleaded with Preacher.

"Man, make him stop that, please," he begged through the door, knowing that the dog would never stop until he was dead. The biker pushed Darius aside, spreading his feet shoulder width apart and raising the rifle he carried.

"Dude, if that fucking dog barks one more time, or I hear one more yell from you, I'm gonna open up with this rifle, and anybody in front of the door is gonna get filled with holes." The noise stopped again, and Spiderman looked over at Dave. "See, you just gotta reason with em"- Laughing, Spiderman made his way back behind where Ryder sat, the two bikers enjoying the little game they were going to play before they got serious with Ryder.

Preacher had stepped back from the door when the man had shouted to him, but he had no intentions of stopping. He and Joker were on the stairs, waiting for the distraction that would allow them to make their move. Preacher had located a punch and die set in one of the cabinets, and one of the punches was almost an inch thick. He could see the hinges on the solid wood door were heavy duty, built to support a door of its weight and size, but had been unable to find anything he could use, until he found the punch. Holding a roofing hammer in his right hand, he held the punch in place, motioning to Joker to take his place in front of the door. The two beings locked eyes, as if in silent communion, then Joker began barking at the top of his lungs, while Preacher started yelling, praying they were making enough noise to cover the pounding as he attempted to dislodge the hinges from the door. The bottom hinge came loose easily, the pin dropping heavily to the landing, and he had started on the top bracket when the man's voice had told him to stop. Preacher could see that the door was loose, loose enough for him to burst through, once the time was right. Reaching over, he petted Joker with his left hand, his right hand still holding the hammer. Joker sat still, as if knowing the time was coming to act, and he gently nuzzled the man's hand when it stroked his fur, as the bad smell filled his nostrils.

Ryder could feel his wife shivering next to him on the couch as he cautiously, slowly manipulated the rope around his wrists, feeling the cool metal object in the cushion. That stopped him momentarily, as the two bikers came face to face with him. Dave held a large hunting knife in his right hand, slowly turning and spinning it, the blade shimmering in the brightly lit room. Spiderman was simply looking into Ryder's eyes, first one way, then the other, then turned and looked at Micah. "Hey boy, how you doing? You like having a pussy for a daddy?" Before the boy could respond to the vulgar question, or the biker could ask any more, Summer side stepped, staring down at Spiderman.

"I told you to the children are mine. You do whatever you want with my brother but leave the children alone." The man looked up at her, then got to his feet, towering over the blonde woman.

"You know what, I've had just about all the shit I'm taken from you, bitch. Yeah, I know Dave, she's paying us a shitload of money to do this job, and yeah, I know we finally get our hands on this prick, but I'm about done taking orders from you." Staring at Summer, the lanky man seemed to be daring her to say anything, when suddenly

Dave was taking the man's arm, pulling him aside.

"Listen, don't fuck this up asshole. Ten million dollars is gonna set the club for life, and not you or anybody else is gonna bitch this up. I'm in charge of this club, and I say what we will or won't do. I ain't crazy about taking orders from her either, but we're almost done here brother. She gets to have some wicked fun with this pretty little thing, we get some payback from this son of a bitch, then we all split up and go our merry fucking ways. You got it?" Dave was holding the other man's vest, their eyes glued together.

"All right, fine, but that fucking money better be there or I'm gonna off this bitch myself." Their foreheads touching, the two men's meeting was done, and Ryder watched as they returned to him, Darius by the front door, Scab next to Summer, in front of Lacey and the children.

Summer looked at Micah, and for a brief second seemed to almost be saddened by the sight of him between the two on the couch. "Se agapó (I love you)" she whispered to him, his eyes boring into hers, as if they were the only two people in the world.

Lacey could feel herself wanting to fall apart as that murderous bitch stood in front of her, talking to her son and touching her daughter, who had (Thank God) finally settled down, oblivious to all of the insanity around her. Lacey suddenly found herself face to face with Summer, the woman's blue eyes boring into her like a laser. Lacey was unable to break her gaze, until Summer slapped her hard, then spoke. "You know, I've had a lot of time to think about you and those gorgeous green eyes of yours and what I would like to do to them. You took my precious hands from me, left them torn and scarred, and now I am going to leave you in the same condition you left me in back in Las Vegas." As she spoke, Summer slowly stood up, reached into her pocket and withdrew a silver object, which she slowly turned over in her hands, making sure Lacey saw it.

    Lacey, her face still stinging form the slap, swallowed deeply when she saw what Summer was holding, and felt Ryder's reaction to it as well, as the two bikers resumed their verbal assault on him.

"Man, do you have any idea how fucked you are? You're so far removed from not being fucked that, well I guess that means- YOU'RE FUCKED!" As he spit out the words, Dingo Dave slammed his fist into

Ryder's mouth, tearing his lip and setting the blood to flowing, while Spiderman held the close-cut hair to keep Ryders head from moving. Ryder sat and refused to show any fear, until he saw Summer click open the box cutter in her right hand and lean in towards Lacey. Just then Micah jumped up from the sofa, putting his hands on Summer's arm to stop her.

"No, you can't do this. I won't let you hurt her in front of my little sister. I can't let you scare her like that." His voice was that of a pre-teen boy, but the tone and inflection was that of someone much older and forceful. Summer paused, but before she could speak a loud pounding sound came from behind them, near the basement door. Darius ran over to the door, and was quickly rejoined by Spiderman, as Darius began to plead with Preacher.

"Preacher, please stop, right now. If you stop now, we can make this all right for everybody, but if you keep up that noise, my friend here is going to hurt not just you, but everyone out there."

Inside the basement, standing on the landing, Preacher could hear the black man talking to him, begging him to stop, and he leaned in closer to the door. Next to him, Joker began to sniff at the door, his hackles raised at what was happening on the other side. Preacher reached down without looking and touched the dog, feeling the tension in the strong body. "Hang on boy, just a few more seconds," he whispered, the dog leaning into the touch as if understanding the man's words. Preacher braced himself as he heard the biker's raspy voice from the other side, telling Darius to get the hell out of the way. Preacher readied himself as he heard the man on the other side, and prayed this would work. Looking down at Joker, Preacher whispered "Now," as the dog began to bark violently, spittle flying from his black lips. When Preacher heard the man on the other side start to speak, he stood up to his full height, stepped back a single step, and threw himself against the unhinged door, hoping against all hope that this would work. When his massive frame hit the door, he felt it give, and he forced himself through, pushing against the solid wood, then felt it hit the unseen man behind it, and he used all of his strength to reinforce the doors plunge, then began to fall forward, the door landing on the biker, with almost 500 pounds of combined weight landing on him, knocking the breath from him.

Preacher rolled off of the fallen door and quickly lifted it off of the downed biker before he could recover, then slammed his fist into the man's face several times, stopping when he heard the ratcheting of a rifle lever.

Darius stood by and almost yelled out when the large basement door came flying open and into the biker holding the rifle. He was too stunned to move at first, and when Preacher shoved the heavy door away and began to smash the stunned biker's face, he failed to react as quickly as he should have, and just as he started to move he heard the sound of a rifle lever being pulled back. With the gun in his hands, he turned to his right, as Preacher, facing him, got up and looked to his left, both men seeing Dave, grinning, his gun trained on them, a look of pure of evil on his face. "Damn, you are one big dude," Dave said to Preacher, who stood, glaring daggers at the man. Looking at Summer, Dave said "Okay, it's about time to wrap this shit"- before he could finish his statement, Spiderman began to stir on the floor, and before Darius realized what he was doing, he pointed the gun at the fallen man and pulled the trigger, the bullets slamming into the man's torso and neck, the blood instantly beginning to flow from the wounds. Everything seemed to go into slow motion, as Darius dropped the rifle. Preacher immediately moved towards the weapon, and as he did several shots rang out, knocking the big man sideways and onto the floor.

Joker had leapt through the door right behind Preacher, growling and snapping at Darius as the black man had killed the downed biker. The dog stopped when he heard the sound of Ryder's voice. "Joker, Voraus. Voraus!! (HEEL NOW!)" Ryder had yelled, the dog immediately heeding the command, running into the kitchen area and out of the line of fire. Preacher lay on the hardwood floor, the bullet wounds in his leg bleeding freely, and spotted the rifle laying too far away to reach. The gunfire had awakened the baby, who began to cry at the noise. Micah instantly moved towards her to soothe her, taking her into his arms and gently rocking her.

"ALL RIGHT GOD DAMN IT. THIS BULLSHIT ENDS NOW!" Dave's face was flushed bright red, as he tried to figure out how to settle things down around him. Looking across the room at Darius, Dave fired two quick shots, hitting the man and knocking him through the shattered door frame. He then stared at Preacher, who was attempting to slow the blood flow from his wounds. "Scab, go tie that fucker up, and be quick about it!" Tossing the shorter man a set of leather ties, Dave looked at Ryder, whose eyes were wide, though whether with fear or anger, or both, was anyone's guess.

"Looks like another of my brothers are dead because of you, asshole. Guess maybe it's time to wrap this party up, collect my money and get the fuck out of Dodge." As the man was speaking, Ryder's mind was going a million miles a minute. He had maneuvered the small metal object from the couch into his hand and fought back a smile when he realized it was the pocketknife from his bedroom, which Micah must have picked up when he retrieved April. He had it partially open when Summer spoke to Lacey, her voice surprisingly soft.

"Lacey, I am so sorry that this didn't go quite as planned, but rest assured before I leave, I'm going to make sure you never forget my name." Smiling at the dark-haired woman, Summer lashed out with the razor-sharp box cutter, cutting Lacey's left cheek, leaving a four-inch-long gash. It happened so fast that Lacey never had time to react, but when the pain set in she began to cry out, then realized it might scare her children even more if they saw her crying. Biting her lip against the burning sensation, she steeled her nerves for what she was about to say, but before she could say anything, Dave began, without warning, to beat Ryder again, his gloved fists slamming into his face, his chest, beating the defenseless man without mercy. Ryder took the beating silently, even when the blood began to flow from his shattered mouth and nose. Dave paused for a moment, the sweat running down his face and dripping onto the floor. Even in severe pain, Ryder was still working the hidden knife over his restraints and felt them loosen enough to slip his right hand out.

Summer looked at Lacey, then down at her tied hands on the sofa. "My, but you have beautiful hands. Hard to believe they could inflict upon me what they did, and now I guess it's my turn." Looking over at Dave, Summer held her hand out to him, as he reached to his right side and withdrew a long-handled object. Summer took the hammer, turning it over in her hands, as Lacey's eyes grew wide, as did Micah's and Ryder's.

"DON'T!" Micah laid his sister down on the sofa, then turned towards Summer. "Don't," he said, quieter and less forceful, his eyes meeting with hers in silent conversation. "I'll go with you, but don't hurt her anymore. If you do, then I'm not going. I'll kill myself first." Summer smiled at the young man, a look of something like maternal love crossing her face. Lacey was struggling against the ropes, staring at her son to stop what he was saying.

"You know my son, you are a true man, displaying that type of courage and love for this person. I won't use this on her, as you asked, but both you and your sister are coming with me. That's the deal, take it or leave it." While the woman and boy negotiated their terms, Lacey's pulse rate was climbing faster with every minute.

"Micah, no, you don't have to do this," she told him, the panic in her voice climbing quickly as she thought of losing not only her son, for the second time, but her precious daughter as well. Beside her Ryder had half turned, keeping his right hand concealed for the moment.

"Micah, listen to me. I know you don't want to do this, and you don't have to. You're our son, and a big brother to"- Dave stepped closer and punched him in the side of the face again, bringing stars to Ryder's vision. Meanwhile, Scab was standing quietly by, silent but present, and Summer looked at him with pleading.

"Scab, go get their Jeep from out back and pull it up front. I think our business here is just about finished." Scab hesitated for a moment, then ran out through the kitchen door. "Finish with him, because it's time to go, Dave," Summer told the man, who glared at her.

"I'm not done with this prick yet. You get that brat and his sister loaded up, then I'll come out and get in." About that time, Scab skidded to a stop in front of the house, leaving the Jeep running as he ran back into the house. Micah had picked April back up again, holding her tightly, and Lacey and Ryder were going mad at the unbelievable events that were unfolding. Micah walked past them, both of them struggling against the rope, their minds reeling, their eyes bulging in panic.

"Bye mom, I love you, but I have to do this," he said quietly to Lacey, whose face was flushed, and panic stricken.

"Micah, no honey, don't go, and don't take April, please son, don't go!" she begged, the tears running down her face and mixing with the blood on her cheek. Micah gave her a sad smile, as he turned and looked at Ryder. Before he could say anything, Dave grabbed him and shoved him towards Scab, who was standing by the door.

"I warned you not to touch the boy again," Summer said, under her breath but loud enough for everyone present to hear. Dave just waved her off, and Summer began to walk to where Scab and the children were waiting. "Let's go," she told them, Scab helping them down the steps and into the idling Jeep, while inside Ryder and Lacey were going crazy. Hearing the slamming of the doors outside, then the rig crunching gravel as it left, Lacey began to wail, causing Dave to step up in front of her.

"Well, well, sweet pants, look like I might get a crack at you after all," he said, the tone in his voice causing her to cringe. Reaching down with his right hand, Dave began to rub his crotch, moving in front of Lacey. Without a word, Joker came barreling through the front door, leaping across the empty space and latching his mouth on to the side of Dave's face and neck, his canine incisors finding purchase in the tattooed flesh, and biting deep. Ryder reached down and quickly sliced through the ropes on his ankles, then cut Lacey's feet and hands free, while Joker crunched down on the dying biker's neck, blood pulsating from the damaged arteries his teeth had punctured. Ryder picked up the dropped rifle and fired a single shot into

Dave's forehead, ending a lifetime of suffering.

"Ryder, we have to go after them now!" Lacey yelled at him, as he fought to clear the cobwebs. He saw Preacher laying on the floor, a pool of blood beneath him.

"Oh God NO!" Ryder yelled, going to his friend's aid. Preacher was quiet, but Ryder could feel a pulse, and it seemed fairly strong. "Preach, come on big man, don't check out on me yet," he begged the man, whose blue eyes slowly opened.

"Go get your kids. I'll be fine," he whispered, as Ryder wrapped his shirt around the leg wound, then his belt around the large thigh. A single gunshot rang out, and he dropped to the floor instinctively. Preacher motioned for Ryder to look in the doorway of the basement, and that was where he saw Darius, leaned up against a wall, blood on his shirt and on the wall behind him, a single shot to the temple, a pistol in one hand and his phone in the other.

"Ryder, we need to go," Lacey yelled across the room, as her husband got to his feet, somewhat unsteady. Lacey ran to him and slid her arm around his waist, as they and Joker moved to the front door. Ryder looked back at his friend, waved to him, then they went outside, spying the red Dodge truck.

"Keys are in the ignition," Preacher croaked from across the room. Lacey helped Ryder down the stairs, then they made their way to the pickup, Ryder opening the passenger's door and letting Joker jump up inside.

"I'm driving," he told Lacey, eliminating any argument. Rabbit quick she jumped into the truck beside Joker, who climbed over her to get to the window. Ryder came around and got in, starting the powerful engine. Putting it in drive, he spun around the driveway, kicking up rocks and dust as they proceeded down the long road from the property. He knew he was driving too fast, but he also understood that Summer had a big enough lead that they might not be able to track her and the children. Hitting a rough spot on the road, Lacey looked at her husband.

"How do we know which way to go when we hit the highway? They could go either way, and if we choose wrong we may never see our children again." The sorrow and frustration in her voice was heart wrenching to him, but he had a plan for when they left the dirt road. His next thought was the gate, but when they rounded the bend before the fence, he was grateful to see they had finally drawn some luck. In their haste to escape, the fugitives had left the gate wide open, saving them precious time in their pursuit.

Four minutes later Ryder saw the end of the dirt road and the highway beyond, and when he got to the roads end, he stopped the truck, causing Lacey to lurch forward against the dash.

"Why are we stopping?" she screamed at him, the tension in her voice mounting. Ryder just looked at her, jumped out and came around to the passenger side. Opening the door, Joker leapt out, Lacey looking at Ryder as if he had lost his mind. The dog ran around for a few seconds, looking this way, then that way, then back again. He sniffed the road, several sets of tire tracks, then froze, his mane growing stiff in the cool of the day. Ryder walked up and knelt beside the dog, as Lacey saw precious seconds ticking away. The pair returned as fast as they had left, Joker taking up his vacated spot by the window, and Ryder climbing back into the cab.

"They're headed west," Ryder told his wife, who looked at him as if he had lost control of his senses. He could see the look of doubt on her face, and he gave her the best smile he could muster, wincing at the pain in his battered face. "Trust me, and more importantly trust Joker," he whispered, looking at his partner, whose gaze was locked on the road headed west. Lacey shut her eyes for a split second, said a silent prayer then looked at her husband.

"Let's go get our kids," she told him, gently touching Ryder's rapidly bruising face.

Chapter 25

Scab kept his eyes peeled on the windy road ahead of him, while beside him Summer stared straight ahead. To their left, the American River wound its way through the canyons they were now navigating to escape the cabin. Inside, Summer felt cheated, but when she looked over her shoulder and saw her boy and the baby in her car seat, both looking as if this was an everyday occasion, being kidnapped and taken for a ride, she knew she had caused the woman more pain than any physical torture could cause. With every ticking minute, Summer felt her confidence growing that this was indeed, going to be a happy ending tale. She looked at the man beside her, and carefully reached over to touch his forearm.

"Thank you my dear one," she said to him, and would have sworn that she saw him blush. From behind, Micah spoke up for the first time since leaving the cabin with his little sister.

"Where are we going?" he asked, no note of fear or urgency in his voice, only boyish curiosity. Summer turned around as best she could to answer him directly.

"Well, we're heading to our new home, someplace warm, someplace very sunny and very, very nice," she told him, seeing the look on his face that he was in need of a more specific answer. She had seen the same look on his face a number of times back at The Ranch and tried to think of a way to tell him. "We're heading to Mexico," she told him, as he mulled over the answer.

"Mexico, huh? I guess that sounds nice. I've never been there before." Summer was not surprised by his reaction and turned back around in her seat.

Scab was playing with the GPS unit on the dashboard, trying to get a bearing on where they were, and even more importantly where they were headed. According to the unit, they were about 70 miles from Sacramento, which this road would take them directly to, but he had a feeling that they might need an alternate route to avoid the authorities, especially with two children. He knew that the first time a police car saw him driving the rig and spotted the beautiful woman next to him, they would find a reason to pull him over, and he couldn't let that happen. Utilizing the GPS, he was able to locate a secondary road about ten miles up the highway and just past the Twin Bridges, which then split off of I-50 and went southeast through the mountains. It was a longer trip by about a hundred miles, but in his gut he knew this was their best bet. "Yes Scab, I agree with you. We should find a less travelled route, especially with the kids. By the way, I've meant to ask you this since we first met down in Nogales. What's your real name?" Scab swallowed, more nervous than he could ever remember being. Keeping his eyes peeled on the road ahead, Scab spoke, his voice so quiet that Summer almost had to ask him again.

"Theodore. My name is Theodore." He had not heard himself use that name in almost forty years, and even saying it seemed abnormal to him. He had been Scab for so long that that was the only name he recognized, and he silently prayed that the woman beside him wouldn't laugh. Instead, when he dared to look at her, she had a single tear rolling down her smooth cheek.

"Theodore. I love it. May I call you Teddy, as in teddy bear?" she asked him, smiling at him. Scab seemed to be seeking any sign of betrayal or deception in her face. Seeing nothing but sincerity in her beautiful face, Scab nodded, afraid to speak.

Summer patted his hand gently with hers, as Micah spoke up from behind.

"I think April pooped again. Can we change her, cause the smell is pretty gross?" Summer, at that moment, realized that she, in all of her planning, had not thought to bring supplies suitable for caring for an infant.

Ryder held tight to the wheel, his stomach churning, as was his wife's by the look on her face while she spoke on the cell phone. Joker was peering intently out the window, as if to look away would make him lose the trail of his girl and boy.

"Yes sir, we're heading west on I-50, and I just saw a sign saying something about a suspension bridge. No, they're in a blue Jeep Grand Cherokee, no, no plates as it's new. The man driving is a ratty looking little biker, and the woman with him is a tall, blonde, and they have our children with them. They tried to kill us back at our cabin but took off with our kids instead. Please, get someone headed this way to stop them. I see by my map that I-50 splits just past that bridge, and if they get there we may never get our kids back. What do you mean you got a call just a little bit ago? From what number?" Opening her husband's cell phone, she scrolled down and checked a contact number. "Yes sir, 805-555-2745." Looking at the number on Ryder's phone,

Lacey choked back the tears. "Yes sir, he was at the cabin with us, but he's dead now." The very matter of fact way Lacey used the words caught Ryder off guard. "Yes sir, thank you very much. We're about ten minutes behind them, in a red Dodge Ram 1500 truck." Disconnecting the call, Lacey met Ryders stare head on.

"Why did you say he's dead? We don't know that and believe me it's going to take more than gunshot to the leg to kill Preacher. Besides"- Lacey silenced him with a quiet look.

"It wasn't Preacher that called, it was Darius. They said the call came in that we were being held hostage, and they traced it to Darius's phone." Ryder's stomach went cold when he thought about Darius and his betrayal and all that it had cost Ryder and Lacey, not to mention Micah and April. He decided right then and there that that forgiveness for the sin was not within him, and Lacey obviously caught his feeling, when she slipped her hand into his.

Scab spied a turnout in the road about fifty yards ahead and began to slow the Jeep as he prepared to pull over. Summer looked at him, wondering what he was thinking, but the smell in the back brought her back to reality. "Okay Micah, I need you to help your little sister out of those nasty clothes before we stop." Micah looked at her as if she had horns, his nose wrinkled up at the stench.

"Oh gross, she pooped all the way through her outfit. It's all soggy now," the boy exclaimed, as Summer looked at him over her shoulder, and the Jeep came to a stop. Micah was undoing the snaps on the outfit April had soiled and had it off of her top half when Scab opened the passenger door, Summer standing there. Scab looked confused as he looked at the baby.

"I never changed a baby before. Maybe you ought to do it," he told Summer, who stepped up and saw the now naked child, cleaned up as best he could by her brother. Reaching in she readjusted the baby's legs, which seemed to be pinched in the car seat. Micah was slipping his t-shirt off, and Summer met his gaze.

"Well, she has to wear something, and nobody brought any diapers," he explained, slipping the blue t-shirt over his little sister. Suddenly Summer's eyes went wide, as she saw the fecal matter on her otherwise pristine glove. She began shaking it, trying to get rid of the offensive material, when Scab appeared, a bottle of water in hand, and began to pour it over her glove and wiping it gently with his bandana. Summer stood for a moment, staring at her once gorgeous material, now smeared with baby shit. Taking a deep breath, Summer thanked Scab as he held her door open for her. Closing both passenger's doors, he went back and got into the driver's seat, then pulled back onto the road. Up ahead stood a sign saying TWIN BRIDGES 1 MILE, EXIT STATE ROUTE 171, 2 MILES.

Ryder was fighting back the nausea from the pain in his shattered face, his right eye weeping non-stop, the loose teeth painfully keeping him alert and on the road. Beside him Lacey sat quiet, except her lips which moved silently as if in prayer. Joker's eyes were locked straight ahead on the road, his nose seeming to point the way for Ryder.

"Are they too far ahead? Did we lose them?" Lacey asked, breaking her silence and making Ryder think about the questions.

"No, I don't think we've lost them, or Joker would be acting strange." As he spoke to his wife, his stomach in knots, he spotted something just off the road ahead about thirty yards. Slowing the truck, he pulled over into the gravel, the tires crunching underneath the loose soil. Before Lacey could say anything, Ryder jumped from the pickup and ran ahead several yards, picking up a dirty, discarded item. When he got back to the truck, he showed Lacey what he had found, and she began to cry, as Joker began to whimper loudly. The dirty, smelly items were the discarded clothes Micah had tossed out of the Jeep when they had stopped, and to Ryder they were the most beautiful things he had ever seen, despite the odor. Tossing them in the bed of the truck, he climbed back in, pulled back out onto the road and hit the gas, as they spotted the TWIN BRIDGES, 1 MILE, EXIT STATE ROUTE 171, 2 MILES.

Scab saw the structure for the first time when they rounded the bend that would drop them down onto the bridge, then across to freedom. "There it is," he said to Summer, who looked at the bridge and smiled, then back down at her hands, wrapped in the red bandana. "Just over that bridge is 171, and that's our road to freedom," he told her, trying to elicit a smile from his passenger. Ever since she had seen the baby's poop on her hand, she had been much quieter, and Scab hoped she was okay.

God knows he had had much, much worse than a little shit on his hands before, and as they began the descent onto the bridge, he felt a sense of relief he had never known. As the Jeeps tires hit the metal bridge and they began the drive across, his heart sank, and he felt like throwing up. Beside him, Summer saw the look on his face, and when she saw what was waiting, her anger flared up like a gas fueled fire.

"Keep driving," she told him, her teeth clenched, as Scab pressed the gas pedal down, the powerful engine accelerating them across the bridge, just in time to see the three Ford Bronco's, red and blue lights flashing, parked in a staggered pattern to prevent anyone from getting through.

"Honey, I can feel it. We're going to catch up to them," Ryder told his wife, who was holding onto the dash with one hand and Joker with the other, as Ryder powered the truck's engine for all it was worth. Rounding the last bend before the bridge, he spotted the metal structure, then another sight to behold. "Look, they have them stopped on the bridge! All we have to do is come in behind them and close them off." Lacey saw the flashing lights, and for the first time since this nightmare had begun felt a ray of hope. As they approached the bridge, Ryder saw the blue Jeep heading forward, towards the parked vehicles, as if on a collision course and hell bent on getting through.

Summer saw the three large blue and white SUV"s parked, so as to prevent them from getting through, and when they were about 100 feet from the cars, Scab suddenly slammed on the brakes, startling all three of the other occupants and causing April to begin crying. Micah slid up and peered between the seats, spotting the police vehicles.

"Cool. Are those for us?" he asked, his boyish eyes bright with excitement at this new piece of the adventure they were on. Reaching over, he placed his hand on April to help calm her, as she put her tiny hand on his. "It's going to be okay April. I'm going to take care of you." Leaning over, he gently kissed her cheek, then was jostled back into his seat as Scab threw the Jeep into reverse and began to back up across the bridge. Halfway across he looked in the rearview mirror and spotted the red truck speeding towards them from the other side. Summer looked back over her shoulder and saw the oncoming truck as well, not slowing down, as Scab hit the brakes and spun the Jeep halfway around, its nose pointing at the waist high railing of the bridge. The red Dodge screeched loudly to a stop, twenty feet behind them. Looking directly forward at the mountains in the distance, Summer reached over and touched Scab's hand, as he softly caressed hers. In her side mirror, Summer saw the truck doors opening, then the occupants getting out.

Summer sat for a moment, looking at Scab. "I think it's time for the gloves to come off," she told him, doubting the man would catch the metaphor in her cryptic statement." Scab watched as she slowly, painfully began to remove the silky, stained items, wincing when he saw the pain on her face when her left thumb, so badly mangled by Lacey, snagged momentarily on the material. Summer let out a small whimper when it did, then held the gloves for a moment, as if recalling a pleasant memory. Several seconds passed, then she looked at Scab as she laid the gloves on the dashboard, as gently as if they were made of glass.

"Okay my friend, it's time," she told him, leaning over to place a soft kiss on his chapped, dried lips, as they opened their doors, then stepped onto the asphalt and looked at the man and woman staring back at them. When Scab saw Summer opening the rear door on her side, he did the same, Micah joining him next to the Jeep, then turning as he heard his sister's crying.

Joker hit the ground running when he jumped from the truck, and started towards the Jeep, when Ryder yelled at him. "FUSS! BLEIB!" (Heel! Stay!) he commanded, the dog instantly stopping and sitting, despite his burning desire to get to his baby, and even more to attack the bad smell coming from across the way. Looking at the vehicle, Joker was as tense as an electric wire, the trembling of his body nearly visible as he spotted movement up ahead.

Ryder saw the driver's door opening and the scraggly man getting out, who looked over at Ryder and almost seemed to be grinning. Lacey, standing right next to her husband, inhaled sharply as the passenger door opened and the tall blonde woman got out and opened the back door on her side, as Scab did the same on his side. Lacey felt the tears starting as she heard her daughter crying, then allowed her fury to dry them as quickly as they had started. Next to her, she felt Ryder stiffen as he too heard the baby crying and saw Micah exit the Jeep.

"Ryder, Lacey, listen to me, and listen good. I know you want Micah and April back, but it seems as if we are at a standstill here, because I want them as well. I am going to make you both a deal for your precious daughter, because I want to see just exactly what you are willing to do to save her." Before Summer could continue, a man's voice pierced the still air and echoed through the canyons.

"This is Sheriff Rudy Webb of the El Dorado County Sheriff's Department, and we need you all to step back and place your hands on the hood of your vehicles. Do it now!"

Even through his swollen eyes and face, Ryder could see the man at the far end of the bridge who was speaking, and he leaned in and whispered something to Lacey. Stepping forward one step, Lacey looked at the officer across the expanse of space.

"Listen, we have this under control. It's all just a misunderstanding, and we are all fine. Please, just leave us be!" she yelled, begging the man to listen to her pleas. Before he could respond, Summer, who had ignored the commands, spoke again.

"Ryder, Lacey, listen to me. If you want your daughter back, you need to do exactly as I say. Lacey, step back to the driver's side of the truck so I can see you better. Ryder, follow her, but slowly." As Summer was directing them to move, Lacey was whispering to Ryder, "What's she doing? She can see us just fine from up front." Ryder shrugged, never taking his eyes off the blonde, as the man with Summer came around to the passenger side of the Jeep, Micah by his side and April in his tattooed arms, the baby quiet, at least for the moment.

"Just move slowly to my side," Ryder told his wife, as they stood next to the driver's door. Ryder turned for a moment and felt sick at the pain and anguish on Lacey's face. Her eyes were glazed over with a combination of unshed tears and unreleased anger. Turning back to face Summer, Ryder exhaled deeply, utilizing every ounce of focus and energy to keep his cool and not go rushing forward to save his children, as Summer continued speaking.

"Okay Lacey, now open the driver's door, slowly and all the way." Ryder barely heard his wife whisper "What the fuck?" under her breath, as she grabbed the handle and carefully pulled the heavy door open, as Ryder finally grasped what the sick bitch had planned.

"Now, step in front of the door, and Ryder, you move to the side and take the handle." Summer was breathing heavy as she moved the bastards into place, a sadistic smile on her face, and Scab moved up next to her, the restless baby beginning to squirm again in his unfamiliar arms.

"What are you doing?" he asked her, keeping his voice down, as behind them the law officer began to speak again, which Summer continued to ignore, and judging by Ryder and Lacey's faces, they were as well.

"I'm finally going to get my payback for what that bitch did to me back at my ranch," she told him, her voice soft and gentle but with a tone of hatred, confusing the man. April continued to squirm, as Micah spoke up.

"Yeah, what are you doing? Can't we just go now?" he asked. Summer looked at him for a split second and smiled at him.

"We'll be leaving very soon my son, but first I have to do this," she told him, as he moved closer to her.

Joker was still sitting, unmoving but whining softly under his breath. He could see his baby by the other car, and the boy as well, but the bad smell was filling his nostrils, and he wanted in the worst way to attack the terrible scent.

The tension in the air was nearly palpable, as Summer resumed her instructions. "Now

Lacey, here's what I want you to do. Slide your hands into the gap between the door and the truck frame, and do it now, if you ever want to see you baby daughter again." Lacey knew exactly what was coming, and by the pasty look on Ryder's face, so did he. Their faces were covered in sheets of sweat, in spite of the cool air temperature.

"Ryder, when her hands are in place, I want you to grab the handle." Ryder refused to move, even as Lacey put her hand in position.

"What the hell are you doing?" he asked her, as she slid her delicate hands into the narrow gap, her face sheet white and sweating, her heart beating so hard in her chest she thought her ribs might break..

"I'm doing whatever I have to to get my daughter back, and I need you to do what she says," Lacey implored of him, their eyes locking as he slowly moved to the side of the door, touching the cool metal.

"I can't do this," he told her, staring directly into those beautiful green eyes, his rapid heartbeat visible to Lacey in the artery pounding in his neck. Lacey gave him a small, sad smile.

"My love, you can do anything. This is to save our children, and I know you can do whatever it takes, even something as sick as this. I love you, and I forgive you."

Summer watched the couple move into position and felt a small sense of victory at what was going to happen. Micah was looking at the people by the truck, and suddenly his heart and mind were filled with a mix of emotions that a boy should never experience. He was excited about going to Mexico, but a small voice inside was saying *what are you doing? You need to protect your little sister now, like a big brother is supposed to, and you can't let this woman do this to your mother.* As he had these thoughts, Summer reached down and, grimacing in pain, took his hand in hers and held it tightly.

"Come with me, and let's look at the beautiful water," she said to Micah, who was unable to rid himself of her grip despite her weakened hand, as he looked back over his shoulder again at the people standing by the truck. Dragging him to the metal walkway, she had him look over the railing at the fast-flowing American River almost 150 feet below. "See how mighty it is, flowing along uninhibited and free. That's how we'll be once we get to Mexico." Micah looked at the water so far below, then his attention was drawn back to April, where the baby had started to cry and wiggle around in Scab's arms.

Micah pulled free of Summer and went to where Scab was attempting to quiet the baby. "Here, let me have her," Micah told the man, who looked at the boy, then at Summer, who was continuing to stare across the bridge at Ryder and Lacey. "Ryder, grab that handle now, and I want you, with all your might little brother, to slam the door shut. I want your wife, your bitch to feel every ounce of pain that I feel every fucking day. DO IT NOW!" she screamed at him, as Ryder turned to look at his wife.

Ryder held the door handle in both hands, the feeling of wanting to vomit at the back of his throat and wanting to explode. His wife, his beautiful, amazing, talented wife was staring at him, no fear in her eyes, practically begging him to do what the woman was telling him to do. With tears streaming down his bloody, swollen face, he whispered, "I'm sorry," then slammed the door closed, Lacey's piercing scream filling his ears and shattering his heart.

Summer saw the door bang closed, then heard the shrieks of pain from across the way. "Leave the door closed on her precious little hands and get over here now little brother. If you don't, then my friend here is going to give your little girl her first and only swimming lesson. NOW DAMN IT!" she screamed at Ryder, staring at Scab then realizing that Micah, not Scab had the baby.

Ryder could never recall feeling this helpless, not as a boy in foster care, not during his SEAL training or deployments, never, but when he saw his baby girl being held by her brother, he prayed that everything was going to be okay. "I love you Lacey DeVane-Raynes. I'm going to get our children back," he whispered to his wife, leaning in to kiss her as she stayed trapped by the metal vise like grip, fighting to hang onto consciousness, despite the stars she was seeing and nausea filling her belly. Ryder took a deep breath, then began the short walk to rescue his children.

Summer watched her brother approaching, and a feeling of elation washed over her despite the dire circumstances. As he neared, Micah came up beside Summer, slipping his right hand back into hers, April cradled in his left arm, and causing Summer to wince in pain. Ryder stopped four feet away from her, his eyes going first to Micah, then his daughter.

"We did what you said, now give me my children," he told Summer, his voice taut with tension, his eyes revealing the rage and fury he was fighting to keep at bay. Summer tilted her head slightly, then taunted him with her smile.

"Little brother, did you really think I would let you have these children, especially my boy?" she asked, her voice quivering with excitement. "When you did what I told you to, I knew I had won. On my orders you slammed your own wife's hands in a truck door and left her standing there trapped like an animal. You cannot defeat me, and these children are my prize, so just leave now, before I cause you any more pain." As Summer was speaking, suddenly the police officer's voice came booming through the speaker again, startling her and causing her to turn slightly. As she did, Ryder quickly moved towards Micah and the baby, when out from behind the Jeep Joker leapt at Scab, sinking his teeth into the man's arm and bowling him over onto the walkway. Ryder pulled the .357 revolver Lacey had picked up on their way out of the cabin from his waistband, and as he tried to grab hold of Micah, Summer moved and roughly pulled the children next to her. Taking April from Micah's arms, Summer held her against her body, stopping Ryder from shooting, as Summer cried out in pain, gripping the boy and his sister, then tugging at them and pulling them onto the walkway of the bridge. Joker had Scab pinned on the ground, and when the man punched the snarling dog directly on the nose, Joker released with a yelp, and Ryder fired a single shot into the dirty man's chest, killing him instantly. Joker turned and stood over the dead biker's body, as Micah fought to save his baby sister. The boy grabbed hold of Summer's hands, squeezing them tightly and causing her to cry out in agony.

Micah held tight to the t-shirt April was wearing, as he fought to keep her safe. His eyes met Summer's as he spoke. "Mom, no. Giorgio says you can't hurt my little sister. She didn't do anything to you." The boy could hear his mother's screams of pain near the truck, and something in him clicked. Joker jumped over the dead biker's body and bit into the woman's calf, causing her to stumble. Ryder was momentarily distracted by Lacey screams, and when he looked back, he saw Micah, his hands still wrapped around Summer's, pulling at his little sister to keep her from being dropped, and Joker with his teeth deeply embedded in the woman's leg. Summer faltered on the slippery grating, and fought to keep her balance, and as she started to regain her footing, Micah pulled hard on his sister, causing April to fall to the ground, where she began wailing. With Lacey's screams resonating in his ears, Ryder saw the blonde woman grab for the railing, her hand too weak to hang on, the dog still locked onto her leg, and as a single shot rang out and a burning pain set in on his shoulder, Ryder watched as Micah looked at him, mouthed, "I love you," then watched in horror and disbelief. Micah wrapped his arms firmly around Summer, smiled at her, then whispered.

"Enough mom, enough," then braced his feet and shoved forward, tumbling the three of them over the three-foot-high railing of the walkway and toward the unforgiving river nearly fifteen stories below. Ryder picked up his daughter, screaming , "MICAH!" as he peered over the rail at the rolling water below, the three bodies already gone from sight, as the rescuers below began yelling unintelligible words to one another. Ryder, on the verge of collapse, held April tightly as he made his way back to the truck, opening the door and freeing Lacey, before collapsing on the asphalt, April still in his arms, the sight of Micah and Joker falling and Lacey's pained voice being the last things he could recall before he blacked out.

EPILOGUE

Lacey and Ryder were silent as they pulled into the memorial park just north of Santa Barbara, overlooking the Pacific Ocean. In the back of the car April was talking to herself, keeping herself amused, something both Ryder and Lacey were extremely grateful for, especially at this moment. Behind them, in the blue Dodge Ram truck, Preacher and Cindy rode, Terra following in her Dodge Charger, the powerful engine audible even through closed windows and distance.

It had been almost a year since the events on the bridge, and Ryder still felt the physical pain of the beating he had endured at the hands of the two bikers. He had to have his fractured cheekbone surgically repaired, leaving him with, ironically, an almost matching scar on the opposite side of his face. The gunshot wound to his shoulder, fired by the police sniper when they had spotted the pistol, had healed fine, joining the multitude of other scars on his torso. His broken nose had healed as well, but he did have some loss of vision in his right eye, causing him now to have to wear glasses. Lacey's facial wound had been treated by a top-notch plastic surgeon, and unless you knew she had been cut you would have been hard pressed to see any mark. Her severely fractured hands had been tended to and set, only the right one requiring surgery, and spent six weeks in external fixators and three more months in casts. A thin scar ran horizontally across the dorsum of her right hand, and when she looked at the scar it always reminded her of Micah.

Preacher had been evacuated by chopper from the cabin, and almost comically one of the paramedics had been forced to stay behind in order to accommodate the extremely large man in the helicopter. He had spent several weeks in the hospital recuperating from the near fatal injury, but except for a slight limp had recovered completely. Darius's body had been recovered at the cabin as well and returned to southern California and his family.

Micah and Summer's bodies disappeared in the rapidly flowing water of the river, and to this day neither one had ever been recovered. The rescuers had found Joker washed up about a hundred yards downstream, and when they got there he was laying still on the rocks, his back legs splayed apart and not moving, his spine having been broken in the fall, his whimpers so faint they could barely be heard over the rushing water. They had carefully loaded him onto the river boat and returned him to shore, his breathing faint and shallow.

Ryder pulled up in the circular driveway and stopped the Escalade, with the people behind him following suit. Reaching over, he laid his hand on Lacey's, as tears filled her lovely green eyes. "I know sweetheart, I miss him every single day too," he said to her softly, her other hand laying on his. They sat for a moment, no words being spoken, then turned as April began jabbering behind them from her car seat. As they reached to open their car doors, the child smacked her hand on the front of her car seat, as if demanding their attention.

"Micah," she said, causing both of her parents to stop and stare. She had begun forming single words about six months earlier, but this was the first definite word she had spoken, and it stunned both Ryder and Lacey. Ryder got out and opened the back door to retrieve his daughter, while Lacey leaned against the GMC and began crying. With his daughter in his arms, Ryder came around to where Lacey stood, her body shaking in grief over her lost son.

They stood together for a moment, lost in each other, then the others slowly walked up and joined them. Preacher, limping slightly, slipped his arm around Ryder's shoulders, as Cindy came up beside Lacey and laid her head on the woman's shoulder. Terra stood, holding Ryder's hand and smiling at the baby. Silently Ryder handed April to Lacey and walked around behind the SUV. Lifting the tailgate, he reached in and carefully slid his arms under the dog's body, who was laying on the large tan padded cushion and blanket. As he lifted Joker out of the back, Preacher joined them, reaching in and removing the custom-made cart that the dog now used for mobility.

One of the rescue members in the boat that day was a professor at the Veterinary School of Medicine in Davis, near Sacramento. When they had loaded the severely injured canine into the boat, the man had instantly gotten on the phone to the waiting sheriff's vehicles, barking instructions. When the boat docked near the launch ramp, a truck had been waiting, and both the dog and his new benefactor had been hustled into, then promptly escorted, lights and sirens flashing, back to the animal facility almost 50 miles away.

There the doctor had taken Joker straight into surgery to try and save his life, his own German shepherd Alexa watching as he worked diligently on the dog. Besides the spinal injury, Joker had internal bleeding from the fall, a fractured hip, dislocated front shoulder and a severe concussion. Several of the doctor's students had assisted in the surgery and the post-operative period, even taking turns sleeping on blankets the first several nights until he was out of danger. The young veterinarian was upset that he was not able to do anything to treat the paralysis, but when Ryder and Lacey had arrived two days later, the joy on their faces was worth every drop of sweat the man had put out.

Ryder delicately lifted Joker's back half up as Preacher slid the cart underneath him, settling the injured dog into the cart and fastening the straps around his waist. The custom-made cart had been a gift from an engineering student at UC Davis, and Ryder would never be able to repay the kindness and generosity they had shown to him and his family. They had brought Joker home about three weeks after the incident, with his cart, and in time they had all made the necessary adjustments to their lives.

"Well boy, let's go see Micah," Ryder said to the dog, who looked at him as if understanding. Slowly the dog made his way around the SUV, keeping pace with Ryder, and with Preacher right next to him. They slowly walked across the well-manicured grass, joining Lacey and the other women. Ryder slipped his hand into Lacey's, while with her other arm she held their daughter. Preacher and Cindy also held hands, with Terra holding onto Cindy's arm. As they approached the large headstone, Lacey began to cry again, silent tears running down her face, as she, Ryder and Joker stood in front of the marble marker, their loved ones keeping one step back. Lacey handed April to her husband, knelt down to remove a single dandelion that was growing in front of the stone, then decided to let it grow.

"Micah, my love, my son, I will never forget you or how much you loved all of us, and especially what you did for your sister. You were a bright ray of sunshine to each of us, and we will never forget you. I love you so much." Leaning forward, Lacey touched her nose to the stone, then placed a soft kiss on the face of the marker, which had two carved angels, one on either side, hovering over the stone from the top.

MICAH KENNETH DEVANE
BELOVED SON, BROTHER AND FRIEND
SEPT 14TH, 2004- AUGUST 21ST, 2016
"Sleep gentle, ye little lamb of God."

Lacey brushed off some grass clippings from the front and the top, then got to her feet. Ryder, holding his daughter, knelt as well, holding April so she could see the stone. He bowed his head for a moment, praying that the young boy had finally found some peace.

"I love you son," he whispered, kissing his daughter as he spoke. Lowering his forehead he touched the smooth stone, his eyes shut. After a few seconds, he stood up, his friends and family behind him, and looked at his wife. Reaching up, he gently wiped away a tear on her cheek, as the others stepped up, Cindy laying a colorful bouquet on the ground in front of the marker, Terra setting an embossed football card with a picture of Tom Brady on it against the marker. They all stood for a moment, silent and reverent, even Joker keeping still in his wagon. The group began to move away from the spot, Joker leading the way, as if in a procession, when suddenly a voice rang out.

"Micah," said April, causing everyone to stop and look at her. Lacey kissed the baby's cheek, and let a soft smile cross her face, as Ryder looked at his wife.

"She knows her big brothers name," he said, the words comforting him, as Joker suddenly stopped and turned, staring at the tombstone. Ryder walked up beside him, letting his free hand reach down and touch the dog's coat.

"What is it boy?" he asked, as the others in the group stopped and watched. In her daddy's arms, April began to squirm around, as if trying to get down onto the grass.

"Micah," she repeated, as she too stared at the grave marker. The air around them suddenly seemed heavier, thicker, almost as if a presence was among them, and Joker continued to stare at the headstone. Ryder set April down on her feet, as Lacey joined them.

"What the hell is going on?" she asked her husband, who was standing ramrod straight and still, as Joker continued staring and whining. April reached up and took her mother's hand, her delicate little fingers soft on her mothers. Lacey looked down at her daughter, who was staring back up at her.

"S'agapó manoúla," (I love you mommy) the little girl whispered, her voice at that moment sounding just like Micah's, as Ryder gasped, Lacey stared in shock and

Joker turned and looked at the child. The rest of the group stood watching the scene, as April looked at the grave marker, a smile on her face, as her chubby little hands both went up and began to wave at a silent figure only she could see. "Bye bye," she cooed, making her parents stop and stare at the child. A feeling of cold rushed through Ryder, and, with Joker and the rest in tow, quickly returned to where the SUV stood waiting. Picking up his daughter, and with his best friend and partner by his side, he waited as Lacey went to open the driver's side rear door to put April in her seat. Ryder reached down to pet Joker, who was showing signs of just how tired he was, the others returning to their cars for the trip back home, when suddenly Lacey let out an earth-shattering scream, slumping to the ground. Ryder nearly dropped the baby when he saw his wife half faint, as Cindy and Terra got there first, Preacher bringing up the rear. Ryder handed the baby to Cindy and knelt on the grass beside Lacey, here face ashen, her eyes wide in terror.

"Honey, what is it?" he asked, feeling the tremors coursing through her body. Her gaze was locked on the back of the vehicle, the door standing wide open, as a single word came out.

"Gloves," she uttered almost imperceptibly, as Ryder's heart began to pound in his chest. Standing up, he went to the open door, looking inside the back seat.

There, in the back seat of the GMC, was April's car seat, attached as always, several small stuffed animals she liked when traveling, and nothing else. Ryder exhaled slowly, then turned back to Lacey, who was still sitting on the ground, Cindy and Terra beside her.

"Honey, there's nothing there," Ryder told her, kneeling next to her, their eyes connecting. Lacey, a look of disbelief on her face, grabbed Ryder and pulled herself up to her feet. Peering into the back of the SUV, she saw the car seat holding only the toys. Lowering her head she turned into her husband's warm embrace, still shaking.

"I'm so sorry. I swear they were right there," she explained, feeling ashamed and embarrassed by her overreaction. Ryder held Lacey as Terra got April fastened into the baby seat, then he guided her around to the passenger side and helped her into the rig.

Joker had stood patiently, his back half still fastened into the cart, which he had grown to love. He liked the feel and the smell of the leather when it was around his waist, and he felt young again at being able to keep up with his people. At first, the cart had been a sort of irritant to the dog, but when he finally learned how to make it work for him, he felt like the king of the world. When they went for walks, he liked how people would come up and pet him, talking to him about how brave he was. In his canine way, he knew what he had done had been very brave, but sometimes it was nice to hear from people too. Sometimes at night his hips hurt really bad, and then his man would lay down with him on the floor, give him one of the bitter tasting pills in a piece of cheese or ham, and talk to him until the pain went away and he drifted back to sleep. As he waited for the men to take his cart off him and get him back in the truck, his nose caught something on the wind, and he paused for a moment. It smelled different, but a good different, and when he saw his man coming towards him, he let the smell go.

Ryder went back around to the rear, where Preacher was unhooking the cart from Joker. When the straps were undone, Ryder carefully lifted his friend back onto the pillows in back, and Preacher set the device inside.

"She'll be fine buddy, it's just going to take a long time for all of us to deal with this," Preacher told him, as they embraced.

Releasing his friend, Ryder climbed into the driver's seat and started the engine, as behind him his friends flipped their vehicles around to leave the cemetery. As he turned the GMC around, Ryder looked at Lacey, who was sitting quiet and still in her seat. In the rearview mirror he saw his daughter, smiling and looking at her hands, a stuffed pink pig next to her on the seat as she caressed the soft fur of the toy.
Lifting her eyes, April looked to her right and smiled at Micah, sitting next to her in the opposite seat, a smile on his young face.

Behind her Joker looked at the young boy in the seat, then back to his baby. Satisfied that all was finally right in their world, the dog laid his head on the overstuffed pillow, let his eyes close and allowed the hum of the road to lull him to sleep.

R.L. Seago resides in Redding, Ca in the foothills where he was raised. He lives with his wife of 32 years Anna, and their two Pembroke Welsh Corgis, Bella Rose and Sophie Marie. (Yes, the Corgi's in the book are named after ours)He looks forward to the thrill of sitting down and facing the challenge of his next project, There Are None So Blind. **The Rebirth of Innocence is** the hair-raising sequel to *Tears of the Innocent.* He is also the author of *Voices of the Passed*, the 5-star reviewed mystery suspense novel as well as *The Chains That Bind,* the combined work of his first two novellas.

Made in the USA
Monee, IL
14 October 2023